VIRAGO
MODERN CLASSICS

THE TORTOISE AND THE HARE

Imogen, the beautiful wife of barrister Evelyn Gresham, is facing the greatest challenge of her married life. Their neighbour Blanche Silcox, competent, tweedy, middle-aged and ungainly – the very opposite of Imogen – seems to be vying for Evelyn's attention. And to Imogen's increasing disbelief, she may be succeeding – for in affairs of the heart the race is not necessarily won by the swift or the fair.

'A subtle and beautiful book . . . Very few authors combine her acute psychological insight with her grace and style. There is plenty of life in the modern novel, plenty of authors who will shock, amuse, amaze you – but who will put on the page a beautiful sentence, a sentence you will want to read twice?'
Hilary Mantel, *Sunday Times*

'Wonderfully sinister, so enchantingly written and so sad. Everyone should read it'
Jilly Cooper

'One of my favourite classics . . . elegant and ironic'
Carmen Callil

THE WRITER

Elizabeth Jenkins (1905–2010) was educated at St Christopher School, Letchworth, and Newnham College, Cambridge. She spent a decade as a senior English teacher at King Alfred's School, Hampstead, and also worked in the wartime civil service. Jenkins was a founder member of the Jane Austen Society, and became a leading authority on the author and her times. In her seventy-year writing career she published over twenty books, including biographies of Jane Austen and Elizabeth I, and many novels, the most acclaimed being *The Tortoise and the Hare*. In 1934 Elizabeth Jenkins was awarded the Femina Vie Heureuse Prize for her novel *Harriet*, and she received the OBE in 1981.

THE DESIGNER

Florence Broadhurst (1899–1977) was born in Queensland, Australia. She led a colourful life and was a master at self-reinvention. Broadhurst was a singer, dancer and entertainer, and by the early 1920s was touring in India, South East Asia and China, where she set up her own performing arts academy in Shanghai. By 1933 she had renamed herself 'Madame Pellier' and was living in London where set up a dress salon on Bond Street under the same name. Broadhurst stayed in England until 1949, when she moved back to Australia. Although untrained as an artist, she began to paint enthusiastically and prolifically. At the age of sixty, she started a wallpaper business, creating hundreds of opulent, luxurious designs with rich, vibrant colours. By the mid 1960s, her company had monopolised the Australian market and her work was in demand internationally. She continued to work until her death in 1977.

THE TORTOISE
AND THE HARE

ELIZABETH JENKINS

INTRODUCED BY
HILARY MANTEL

VIRAGO

This hardback edition published in Great Britain in 2011 by Virago Press

First published in Great Britain in 1954 by Victor Gollancz Ltd and
The Book Society
Published by Virago Press in 1983

3 5 7 9 10 8 6 4 2

A CIP catalogue record for this book
is available from the British Library.

ISBN 978-1-84408-747-1

Typeset in Goudy by M Rules
Printed and bound in Great Britain by Clays Ltd, Elcograf S.p.A.

Papers used by Virago are from well-managed forests
and other responsible sources.

MIX
Paper from
responsible sources
FSC
www.fsc.org   FSC® C104740

Virago Press
An imprint of
Little, Brown Book Group
Carmelite House
50 Victoria Embankment
London EC4Y 0DZ

An Hachette UK Company
www.hachette.co.uk

www.virago.co.uk

Emilia: O, who hath done this deed?
Desdemona: Nobody; I myself. Farewell.

Othello, ACT V, SC. II

INTRODUCTION

Apart from a war, what could be more interesting than a marriage? A love affair, though it is one of the central concerns of fiction, is a self-limiting tactical skirmish, but a marriage is a long campaign, a grand game of strategy involving setbacks, bluffs and regroupings – a campaign pursued, sometimes, until the parties have forgotten the value of the territory they are fighting over, or have abandoned their first objectives in favour of secret ones. I have admired this exquisitely written novel for many years, partly for its focus on a fascinating and lost social milieu, but also because through her close attention to the negotiations between men and women, and women and women, Elizabeth Jenkins has provided a thoughtful and astringent guide to the imperatives of sexual politics – and one which is of more than historical interest.

In 2004, in her hundredth year, Elizabeth Jenkins wrote a memoir called *The View from Downshire Hill*.* It offers graceful and startlingly fresh pictures from a long writing life, concentrating on her earlier years; educated at Cambridge, condescended to by Virginia Woolf, befriended by Elizabeth Bowen, she lived at the

---

* Michael Russell, 2004

heart of English cultural life, and published twenty-three books. She wrote biographies of Elizabeth I, of Lady Caroline Lamb, and of Jane Austen. She was a founder member of the Jane Austen Society, one of those practical enthusiasts who bought and restored Jane's house at Chawton, saved it from dereliction, furnished it with impeccable attention to the period, and opened it to the public. Jenkins's hypersensitivity to atmosphere may remind readers of Rebecca West. Her eye for colour and texture, her precise descriptions of the civilised surfaces of life, recall Sybille Bedford. Like both these near contemporaries, she wrote reportage as well as fiction. All three of them were interested in spies and poisoners, in hidden acts and the murky undergrowth of human intention. But more than she is like them, she is like Austen: formal, nuanced, acid. She surveys a room as if she were perched on the mantelpiece: an unruffled owl of Minerva, a recording angel.

The Tortoise and the Hare was the sixth of her twelve novels, first published in 1954. Its characters are recovering some ease in their lives after wartime dislocation; they now have the leisure for emotional discovery. Evelyn Gresham is a distinguished barrister, fifty-two years old, with all the trappings of success – a gracious house in the Berkshire countryside, a London *pied-à-terre*, a son about to go to public school, a younger wife who is pretty, gentle and artistic. Evelyn is critical and exacting; Imogen is a natural mollifier. In one elegant opening paragraph, Jenkins charts the course their lives will take. In an antique shop, the pair examine a mug, 'decorated with a pattern of raised wheat ears, of the kind known in country districts as a "harvester"'. Imogen's eye takes in the purity of the colour, her fingers learn the details of the moulding. Evelyn sees the chip at its base, from which cracks meander up the inside. Already we grasp the essentials of their story. We know what they have sown and what they will reap.

Imogen lives in an uneasy peace with her husband, one which depends on daily accommodation and adaptation on her part, on constant shifts and abnegation, a retreat from the frontiers of personhood. Evelyn is a conventional man with a flinty intellect. His cerebral self-satisfaction makes few concessions to those more self-doubting or imaginative. Imogen's soft girlish qualities, which originally attracted him, have melted into an ineffectuality that could be cloying. He receives deference from his courtroom juniors, and expects it from his wife – his expectations may not be reasonable, but we see why he has them. He wants his domestic life to run on oiled wheels, like his professional life, where his clerk waits to tend him when he comes out of court with a cup of hot milk laced with brandy. Driven and self-disciplined, he longs in one area of his life to be dependent, cosseted – to have someone plan his comforts for him.

In this world of half a century ago, men and women are required to play roles that make them more unalike than they actually are. Imogen has been asked to play the ingénue, and has missed the point where her husband changed, and required her to change: 'He was romantic and emotional once, but of course he isn't now. How should he be?' Perhaps the marriage has to end, because there is no role for her to step into; what does a tender-hearted ex-beauty do with her time? Part of Imogen's wistfulness comes from her preoccupation with her approaching uselessness. Gavin – an imperceptive, unlikeable child, who already treats her with the practised masculine contempt he has learned from his father – will go to school. Then what will be the use of her? She has a shrewdness in human relationships, though it offers her no protection. She has anticipated that, a few years into their marriage, Evelyn will want a mistress. She has imagined it would be a younger version of herself. She sees no threat from their country neighbour, Blanche Silcox, with her gloves like gauntlets, her quilled hats, her gruff masculine voice. Modern readers will be dismayed to find Blanche, a woman in her fifties, described as 'elderly', but that is how she seems to Imogen.

Miss Silcox, Evelyn says with admiration, 'practically runs the neighbourhood . . . Blanche is on the Board of Management of the Home for Incurables at Silverpath, and she's the Treasurer of the New Turning Club that takes in girls who are having an illegitimate baby – she's done any amount of voluntary work.' The reader has seen and heard enough of Blanche to imagine her tipping the incurables out of their bath-chairs, and making the 'girls' wish that they, as well as their babies, had never been born. Blanche believes the newly founded NHS is a charter for malingerers. Money-minded, severely practical, she is a 'countrywoman', in the sense that she enjoys shooting animals. These days, she would be a leading light in the Countryside Alliance. She can, on occasion, be considerate, even show vulnerability; but it is only when Evelyn is around that her voice adopts a low note, a note of intensity which Imogen hears but cannot account for. In Blanche's dogmatic opinions we hear the sour abrasive tone, the vicious generalisations, of what Jung called the 'animus-ridden' woman. The times have allowed no outlet for Blanche's abilities or for her assertive character. Her dowdiness makes her a figure of fun, until Evelyn – whose feminine aspect is on the loose, looking for a counterpart – discerns her strong, suppressed sexuality, and realises that here is a woman, rich, generous and omnicompetent, who will give him a rest from domestic pressures and emotional demands. Imogen's friend Paul asks her, 'Are you sure you know what men fall in love with?' She doesn't.

Elizabeth Jenkins describes her characters with remarkable even-handedness. She is remorseless with their pretensions, pointing out that one thing that prevents Imogen from expressing her needs is her own touchy pride, the pride of a fading beauty. Dismayed, the reader watches the erosion of Imogen's self-esteem, till she is 'run ragged', and unable to defend her position. It is the older woman who reads the emotional logic of the situation. The tortoise overtakes the hare. Exiled in defeat, Imogen has become a pensive woman who eats alone in the corner of a hotel dining room. Evelyn is the battered prize. Blanche is the sated winner, 'feet up on the sofa, eating a *marron glacé* with a meditative air'. How exactly is it done? Where is the psychological tipping point? Trying to locate it draws the reader back and back to the narrative, with a mixture of fellow-feeling and fascination and dread. Most women readers today will feel they are like neither of the rivals, but if they are honest they will see a bit of both in themselves. The author has separated the two types, drawn a clean line between them, so that the drama has free play. But neither woman is a stereotype; they are warm, human, contingent. Like all the most convincing characters in fiction, they seem to have free will.

The minor characters are expertly, swiftly drawn – the melancholy London doctor with whom Imogen has an old romantic friendship; his cold, shallow, beautiful wife; and Evelyn's professional colleagues. There is a superbly malicious glimpse of a successful authoress *en fête*, and satirical sideswipes at the local property developer and his pretentious wife, too 'busy with her ballet-work' to keep her children clean and fed. Their son Tim is a sad little scrap, the only being who truly admires Imogen, even in defeat. Elizabeth Jenkins never married – no doubt she had seen how the odds were stacked – and had no children, but she writes about them with tenderness and is keenly observant of them, showing even the obnoxious Gavin to be damaged by his parents' break-up, though the effects may take years to show. Just as she is grounded in people – their physicality easily evoked, their dress, their manner – so she is grounded in place; her descriptions of the countryside are both luminous and exact. The surfaces of the story, as well as its depth, give the reader pleasure. When we close the book we are left with the rustle of Imogen's muslin dress, the chink of fine china, the scent of white geraniums.

Elizabeth Jenkins describes in her memoir how when the book came out there was some 'severe, personal criticism from readers who felt that the interest of the book was too much confined to one class, not to say to one income bracket. I was told by a young man, a student in a university society . . . that what was wrong with the book was that it wasn't about anything that really mattered. As I felt that the suffering caused by the break-up of a marriage was something that did matter, I asked him, in surprise, what were some of the things that really mattered? After a pause, he said, "Well, trade unions."'

You wonder what the undergraduate knew about trade unions. He knew, or thought he knew, that the private sphere is inferior to the public sphere, and that emotions are for girls. Closer attention to the book might have spared him some uncomprehending misery in later life; no doubt he learned the hard way that the personal is political. The way we run our lives has changed vastly since Elizabeth Jenkins wrote, but this does not make her insights obsolete. People are 'run ragged' in relationships all the time, though they are just as likely to be men. What she offers us does not date: descriptive grace and narrative pulse, dry humour and moral discrimination, tempered elegance and emotional force.

Hilary Mantel, 2007

ONE

The sunlight of late September filled the pale, formal streets between Portland Place and Manchester Square. The sky was a burning blue yet the still air was chill. A gold chestnut fan sailed down from some unseen tree and tinkled on the pavement. In the small antique-dealer's a strong shaft of sunlight, cloudy with whirling gold dust, penetrated the collection of red lacquer and tortoiseshell, ormolu and morocco. Imogen Gresham held a mug in her bare hands; it was a pure sky blue, decorated with a pattern of raised wheat ears, and of the kind known in country districts as a 'harvester.' Her eye absorbed the colour and her fingers the moulding of the wheat. Her husband however saw that there was a chip at the base of the mug, from which cracks meandered up the inside like rivers on a map.

'You don't want that, surely,' he exclaimed. 'It would come apart in no time.' He turned abruptly to the window through which he could see his car standing at the kerb. Imogen with bent head silently put down the mug. She could hardly raise her face. There was nothing else in the shop which was within reasonable means as a casual purchase. She had come here because someone who had a concern for the proprietor had asked her to, and had hoped that

I

her husband might see something to buy; but the day was unlucky. Evelyn Gresham was not in a leisured or a buying mood, and though he would pay for anything she chose, she did not feel able to take something expensive which she did not want, or a cheaper thing which he had said he disliked. She could not buy anything herself for she was in the middle of a period of enforced economy. As her husband stood with his back to her, looking fixedly into the street, his influence was so strong that it overbore her anxiety to help the shopman who, well dressed but old and worn, showed in his fixed, propitiatory, despairing smile his consciousness of the ruin that was creeping towards him like a shadow. The painfulness of the moment was intense and brought a deep blush into her face. Paul Nugent who stood beside her knew that it was so, and that he could do nothing for her. He knew Evelyn Gresham's character intimately for they had been friends since schooldays.

Imogen looked once more at her husband's back. 'Very well,' she said softly. He turned at once with an air of relief and picked up his hat and gloves. 'I'm afraid we don't see anything suitable to-day,' he said. The shopman was too well-bred to urge anything else. He escorted them to the door and opened it with a slight bow. Imogen, never lifting her eyes from the ground, followed her husband to the car.

'Can we drop you anywhere?' he asked Paul Nugent.

'No, thank you.' Evelyn went round to the farther door while the chauffeur opened the nearer one for Imogen. As she paused to say goodbye to Paul, an imperious voice called out:

'Daddy! I want *you* to sit next to *me*.'

'All right, my boy. Let me get in.'

'Gavin?' said Paul Nugent. He would have put his head into the car after Imogen had settled herself, but Evelyn Gresham showed his impatience by saying to the chauffeur: 'Think we shall do it in an hour and a half?'

'I think so, sir, barring accidents.'

Imogen smiled at Paul Nugent through the glass. The unusual brightness in her cheeks made her grey eyes look bright, or were they smarting with tears? Without warning, the car shot forwards. When it was out of the street, Paul re-entered the shop and asked again to look at the blue harvester. He turned it about in a careful manner, and as he paid for it, he told himself in parenthesis that Evelyn Gresham was right in thinking it not worth the money.

Since nothing awaited the Greshams in Berkshire except afternoon tea there seemed no need for such promptitude in their setting off, but Evelyn Gresham's faultless sense of time made punctuality natural to him, and the overdriven life of a successful K.C. made it necessary, not only in his profession, but so that his very scanty leisure should be absolutely his own. He grudged savagely the loss of half an hour's relaxation after lunch because the meal was late, or the curtailing of a country walk when some workman did not arrive for orders at the time arranged.

Imogen leaned back in her corner and looked at her husband over the top of their son's head. At the first opportunity she had of buying a wedding or birthday present, she would return to the shop. As she could do nothing to improve the situation at present, she tried to put it out of her mind.

Gavin, after a good deal of floundering about and kicking of his parents' shins had brought to the surface a small travelling chessboard, whose tiny white and crimson figures were pegged into holes to prevent their sliding off the squares. His father had taught him the moves and he now wanted to play on every occasion. For a boy not yet eleven, he had, his mother thought, learned the game very quickly, but when she had said this in Gavin's hearing he had said, 'You only think that because *you* can't do it at all.' This rapidity and brusqueness gave a disagreeable impression, but it was not easy to find fault, first because what he said was almost always true, and secondly because he himself did not seem, or but rarely, to have any disagreeable intention.

3

The truth was that much of Gavin's quality and manner was a direct inheritance from his father: and that what she accepted, and even admired in Evelyn, who was fifty-two and fifteen years older than herself, she was not readily inclined to submit to in Gavin.

Gavin's dark head, bowed over the board on his father's knee, was almost pushed into Evelyn's waistcoat in his ecstasy of concentration. His father looked down on him. Solid, pale, black-haired, grey-eyed, Evelyn's features were too masculine to be called beautiful, yet beautiful they were: the shortness of the slightly aquiline nose being their only irregularity. The face was a full oval, yet the impression of the features was of something cut with extreme sharpness. There is a life in stone, and such life was what his lips in repose appeared to have.

He was everything Imogen admired; not only had he all the qualities she instinctively looked for in a man who was to take the direction of her life, but he had them in an unusual degree. When at twenty-seven, she had met him at forty-one, even handsomer if less interesting than he was now, she had been fascinated by his appearance, then riveted by the attraction of his personality and then filled with delight at his passion for herself, but she had never entirely lost her head about him: held back, perhaps, by the fact that he never wished it. Sympathy he wanted, usefulness, complete devotion, but not infatuation. Always she had felt herself on the smouldering verge of a conflagration which had never burst out. Occasionally the feeling would haunt her with a sense of loss, but on the whole she was extremely happy. Those characteristics of her husband which made some people think him difficult or even disagreeable, impatient criticism, uncompromising opinions, an unconscious severity, affected her no more painfully than a voluptuous pressure on a bruise.

They drove in to the Berkshire village as quarter past four struck on a stable clock in a turret overlooking a high, chestnut-bowered brick wall. The air was still unnaturally bright, but where

4

the light was reflected on window panes or ponds it was now transparent red-gold. Their house stood at right angles to the river, a small oblong where high, narrow windows, their upper panes pointed in Regency Gothic, looked down on a shallow lead roof, under which three french windows of similar design opened upon a verandah.

Gavin had been in London with his parents to go to the dentist; therefore he had not been able to visit his rabbits at lunchtime as he always did when he came in from morning school. While his father gave various directions to the chauffeur, he scrambled out and made off towards the hutches. Imogen, alighting, began to walk in the same direction.

'You don't need to come!' cried Gavin, stopping short and gazing at her darkly.

'I'm not coming. I'm only going to walk round the lawn.' She came slowly towards the verandah. Inside in the gloom of the drawing-room, the little chandelier, crowned and garlanded, gleamed like drops of rain. To her right the river lay as if unmoving on its silent bed, reflecting the hanging woods on the opposite shore. Behind them rose the chalk downs, bare on their rounded summits except, here and there, for groves of beech. The movement of the river was betrayed by the sound, coming clearly through the still afternoon, that it made on flowing round the bend, where the bed was spread with chalk-coated flints.

Imogen went into the house. From the end window of her bedroom she looked out on the drive, a yellow gravelled circus surrounded with glossy evergreens. The gate was pushed back against a box hedge, and standing with one hand on it, Evelyn was talking to Blanche Silcox, a neighbour who lived behind the hanger. She was on the way to post in the village, it seemed, for she held several envelopes in her leather-gauntleted hand. The tweed suit, expensive but of singular cut, increased the breadth of her middle-aged figure. She appeared kind and unassuming, which made it the more strange that her hats should be so very intimidating. For ordinary wear like the present they were stiff felts with unusually large-domed crowns; on dressy occasions they mounted quills that were absolutely formidable.

Imogen sat down at the dressing table and combed her hair. It had been fair in childhood and was now a pale brown. There was no pronounced colouring in her appearance. Her eyes were large and round, but though they were a true grey her lack of complexion, providing them with no heightening contrast, left their colour sometimes uncertain. The charm of her looks, so far as it depended on purely visual effect, was that of shape and contour. Her head was poised very gracefully on her neck, her upper lip had the true outline of the cupid's bow, her bosom was round and her waist small. The fault in her appearance came from temperament: she looked too often harassed or wistful, or to have withdrawn behind a cloud. Her step was naturally light and she was apt to walk with a slight, pensive bend of the head; at times these characteristics became so marked that their effect was as irritating to a highly strung man as would have been the presence of some Amazonian hockey player tramping through the house. Not, however, to a man who saw her infrequently and for whom her ways and mannerisms had the enchanting quality of some favourite work of art.

Looking at her reflection with keen, practical attention, Imogen thought again, as she had often done in the past two hours, of Paul Nugent. She divined the nature of his feeling for her and though he was not a man on whom her affections would have settled of their own accord, she was a little agitated by it. If he had ever shown the slightest sign of giving way to his fondness, even of speaking of it, she would have become greatly moved by it; as it remained unspoken, it was no more than slightly troubling, a little painful, rather pleasurable, melancholy and interesting. She sat, her eyes withdrawn from her reflection and fixed sightlessly on the hands clasped in her lap. When she raised them again, she saw by the travelling clock beside her that nearly half an hour must have gone by since their arrival. The housekeeper would be waiting to hear that they were ready for tea. She rose quickly and, turning towards the right-hand window, saw to her surprise that Evelyn and Miss Silcox were still in conversation. Evelyn still stood with one hand on the gate, the other tucked behind his back. He must be speaking, she supposed, for Blanche was standing silent, looking a little down over the bulk of her jacket. 'We must ask her to tea,' thought Imogen, and it passed through her mind that it was fortunate that Blanche's walk to the village had brought her to their gate almost to the minute of their arrival. The end window was not usually opened, and while Imogen unlocked the sashes before raising the lower one, she had the scene below full in her eye. She noticed again their unmoving position, and that the light while still limpid gold above the trees had died away from the undergrowth which now pressed dense and dark around the gate. The grind of the sash made them both look up, and before Imogen could call out her greeting and invitation, Blanche had given her a brisk nod and set off down the road followed by three Yorkshire terriers veiled in waterfalls of hair like spun glass. A rough-looking Airedale plunged out of the bushes and followed their retreating forms. Evelyn's face raised to the window bore its frequent look of repressed irritation. 'But it cannot be meant for me this time,' Imogen thought. 'I was doing the right thing.' It was an idea of Evelyn's which she tried hard to disprove, that she did not care for any friends of his.

'She had to get home,' he called up. 'Her sister and the children are here for the week-end.'

In the drawing-room Miss Malpas had lighted a wood fire whose light was already leaping in the shivering crystal drops overhead and on the tea equipage spread beneath. Gavin came in with an expression that dared anyone to ask whether he had washed his hands.

'What are you going to do on Saturday?' asked Evelyn, taking one of the butter-soaked scones.

'I don't know.'

'Well, would you like to go and see the badger's earth in Miss Silcox's spinney? You and Tim can go over there and spend the day if you like. Her man will be lopping trees. You could make a fire and roast potatoes – apples – chestnuts if you can get any.'

'Did Blanche say so?' asked Imogen.

'Of course she said so. I shouldn't be giving them permission to picnic on her land if she hadn't said so.'

Imogen leaned back and laughed delightedly at his sharp yet humorous tone. The firelight glowed on her jaw and throat. Evelyn looked mollified, then smiled himself and leaned forward with his hands clasped between his knees. Gavin felt the rapprochement between his parents and it annoyed him.

'We have been there without permission anyway,' he said, taking a large slice of cake on to his plate.

'Indeed. What were you doing?'

'Damming the stream that comes down by the hedge.'

'Really, Gavin, you'd no business to do that. How do you know what damage you did? You may have flooded the towing path and the whole part under the gate. Have you been there since?'

'No.'

'So you don't know what sort of mess you may have been responsible for. Did *you* know they had been doing this, and going there without leave?'

'No, but—'

'But what? Well – what?'

'Of course they shouldn't have been there at all, but I was only going to say I think those little dams they make don't do very much harm – we used to make them as children—'

'On other people's land?'

'I hardly remember; I expect it was, in the summer holidays.'

'I see. Well, however that may be, I want you to understand, Gavin, that you are not to trespass on Miss Silcox's land. You're not to go there unless she gives you leave. There are pheasants in those woods, and apart from the damage you may do, you may get a charge of shot in your leg when they're rabbit-shooting – traipesing about when nobody knows you're there. I'm not making any rules for your friend Tim: if he insists on trespassing and doing several pounds' worth of damage, and his parents choose to let him, that's between them and Miss Silcox.' (The unlikelihood, impossibility even, of the faint-hearted and pathetic Tim, left to himself, carrying out this stubborn and criminal course, could not but rise to the minds of Evelyn's hearers.) 'But you at least won't do it, please.'

Gavin scowled; he would have liked to remain silent but practical foresight obliged him to ask: 'Are we to go tomorrow?'

'We'll leave that for the moment. I shall ask how much damage you did first.'

When Gavin had gone out to his playroom, an outhouse beyond the kitchen, Evelyn said:

'I do hope, my dear, you won't encourage him in this sort of thing.'

'Of course not, dearest.'

'You don't seem to realize how serious that sort of thing is on a neighbour's land – pheasants, timber, it's all valuable. If a boy's brought up in the country he must learn to respect the country, and realize that idiotic games like that may do serious damage – particularly on a neighbour's property.'

'Oh, yes! I know. I was only trying to suggest, as you were really anxious about the damage, that those dams he and Tim make could hardly hold the stream: the ones they make down here are washed away overnight. But of course he mustn't trespass.'

'However you meant it, you did your usual thing, of going against my authority instead of backing it up.'

'Oh, Evelyn! I am so sorry! Is that really how I seem?'

'Never mind, never mind.' There was no unkindness in his tone, but when she came and stood at his elbow he did not linger. 'Shall you want to ring up anybody between half-past five and six?' he asked.

'No, certainly I shan't.'

'Then I shall be glad to have the telephone to myself.'

He usually had telephone conversations of a professional kind, at some time between tea and dinner if he were at home. There were telephone extensions in the drawing-room, Evelyn's study and their bedroom. Though the slight but carrying sound of the receiver's being lifted was nearly always heard in other rooms, Imogen had occasionally lifted it herself to find that he was in the middle of a conversation with a solicitor, or his clerk, or a colleague in his chambers. The strict training she had eagerly put herself under ever since her marriage, in regard to the attitude necessary towards her husband's profession, made her feel that such intrusions, even though involuntary, were almost shocking. She would be conscious, too, of a second's alarm on her own account as she replaced the receiver and knew that Evelyn would hear the click. Nothing, she was sure, would irritate him more, or more justly, than any idea that his professional privacy was not respected.

Evelyn now went into his library and shut the door and Imogen carried out the tea-tray to the kitchen. Here Miss Malpas, in a clinical-looking white overall but with bunches of glass red currants in her ears, was beating up eggs. She was a small, elderly woman whose face would have suggested a gipsy's but that it was too cool and rational. She received Imogen and her burden kindly but with an air that suggested that the kitchen was hers and Imogen her anxious, scurrying servitor. Miss Malpas was sometimes taken, by visitors who noticed her assurance and authority, to be a new development of the domestic scene, a forerunner of the classless society of the future. She was, in fact, one of those few but indestructible relics of a remote English past; her conception of her own importance in the family she worked for had been formed centuries ago, when the whole household ate together at different stations in one great hall, before the custom had developed of putting servants as far away as possible, in attics and underground.

Imogen piled the crockery on the draining board and Miss Malpas said: 'That Tim's been 'ere most of the afternoon.'

'Oh, has he? Poor child, hoping Gavin would be back before tea, I suppose.'

'Ah. I dare say. I give 'im 'is tea, early on. Boiled eggs as usual and sandwiches full of everything I could lay me hand on. Never 'as a square meal except in this house if you ask me.'

'No, I'm afraid not.' Imogen sighed.

'If 'e and Gavin are takin' the day out to-morrow, we must pack up plenty of food for them. Goin' over to Blanche Silcox's, I hear.'

'I hope so. But Mr. Gresham was rather disturbed to hear they'd been damming up the stream. He thinks they may have done some harm, and if so, they oughtn't to be allowed—'

Miss Malpas clicked her teeth. 'They won't have done no harm,' she said. 'Anyhow, Evelyn can put it right with her when he has a word with her this evening.'

'This evening—?' repeated Imogen, halted at the kitchen door. 'Why, is she—'

'Telephone, telephone, on the telephone,' said Miss Malpas impatiently, opening the oven and stooping down to test the heat against her face. 'Nice and cool that is. I'll pop in me meringue before it gets beyond us.'

TWO

Paul Nugent owned a house in Welbeck Street. He lived with his wife on the first floor and used one of the ground-floor rooms as a consulting-room. The rest were let to other specialists. Before the war, the two top floors had been occupied by the Greshams. These were now let to a doctor's family except for two small rooms, a bedroom and a dressing-room with a bath in it, that opened into each other. Evelyn Gresham retained these for the nights in the middle of each week which, during the legal terms, he usually spent in London.

Like Evelyn Gresham, Paul had married a woman much younger than himself but in his case the discrepancy in age was much greater and his choice had been made with a complete and fatal lack of judgment. His wife at the time of their marriage had been twenty-two. She was slim, lightly moving, an excellent dancer and tennis-player, with straight, silky brown hair. Paul had been fond of repeating to himself:

Her hair was long, her foot was light and her eyes were wild,

though indeed they were nothing of the sort, but small, bright hazel and of very strong sight. Paul, mature, reserved, melancholy and ardent, was not one likely to find much happiness. His life till nearly forty had been sombre with loneliness and disappointment. When he saw Primrose he was immediately dazzled by freshness, delicacy and youth. He gave her credit not only for qualities which she did not possess but for ones which could scarcely have been found in anybody. Her parents were a postmaster and a retired primary schoolteacher, well-educated, kindly, honest, of the salt of the earth. Their outlook was one of mild socialism; culture was represented in their home by a reproduction of Van Gogh's sunflowers, and the plays of Bernard Shaw. Mr. and Mrs. Waddy would never have influenced their child towards a distasteful marriage, but they could not but be gratified by Paul's professional standing and touched by the adoration of such a man for their little girl. Primrose had a certain degree of girlish reluctance to overcome in making up her mind to accept him; he had no physical attraction for her, and besides he was slight, sallow, dark, and liable, in her view, to talk in a peculiar way; and when she had vaguely pictured a husband to herself it had been a fair man in a blazer with a tennis racquet under each arm. Her rich but alien prospects as Paul's wife had almost as much of the uneasy in them as the attractive, yet once they had been accepted she could not give them up. She could not tell herself that she wanted to be married to him, but after a short experience of him as a lover, tender, protective, adoring, however uncongenial, she could not have returned to her state of unengaged girl, with nothing more important to look forward to than the next dance at the tennis club, and the prospect of a post as games mistress at a girls' school forming a cheerless close to the summer.

Paul's money was a very pleasant attribute but it would not by itself have influenced her any more than it influenced her parents; it was his devotion, making her feel that she had been suddenly floated into air by a magic carpet, that carried his cause for him. Yet this devotion she soon came to take for granted, and since she could not return his passion she became before long a little bored and irritated by it. Her slight tartness of manner enchanted Paul, as it enchanted him to see his presents of Redouté's rose prints and Battersea enamels ranged among but not displacing her photographs of school hockey groups and her green pottery rabbits. Her refusal to alter or modify her opinions or tastes under his influence seemed a charming instance of integrity. It wore a different air somewhat later, when he found himself bound down beside a being narrow and stubborn, with the strongest disinclination to compromise or learn.

For the ruin of his hopes and the blight upon his future he had no one to thank but himself. He had committed this blunder not as a dotard or a boy but at a time of life when it was inexcusable. He had only one aim left in connection with his marriage – that Primrose should find some happiness in it. Her coldness towards him had caused him very soon to cease any demands on her. He knew that in this he was not being true to her own interests, for he realized more accurately than she that if Primrose had had children she would have been fond of them, but he could not bring himself to overbear such unwillingness and dislike. Primrose none the less enjoyed a considerable degree of satisfaction. She made many friends among doctors' wives, women older than herself who liked her simplicity, youthfulness and self-possession. She had a strong sense of duty in some directions, and ran the house well enough for a man who felt it an obligation to be indulgent to failures and appreciative of every success. She could now play squash and tennis and skate at expensive clubs, and as she had always wanted to ride but never had the means, Paul was glad to arrange for her to do so. She learned quickly and used to drive down to a stables in Surrey two or three times a week, in the little car Paul had given her. He suffered almost the last of his severe pangs of heart, from the sight of a photograph taken of Primrose at these stables, erect and graceful in a bowler hat and habit on a very nice iron-grey mare.

The possessive instinct even in unfeeling women is often as sensitive to a hint of danger as the morbid quickness of passion. While the Greshams were living in Welbeck Street, Primrose was so recently married herself that Imogen was an object of little interest to her. It was later that, on Imogen's visits to Welbeck Street, on their own week-ends spent with the Greshams, that Primrose detected the situation, guarded, controlled, repressed as it was between Paul and Imogen. But she had no sooner felt alarm than she felt reassurance. She knew that Paul would never injure her. She once brought up the matter, saying:

'You are very fond of her, aren't you?'

'Very.'

'Do you mean you're in love with her?'

'I mean what I say. You know me well enough to know that.'

'Yes. But I thought you might be unhappy about her.'

'My only unhappiness has been, not being able to make you happier.' He laid his hand on her arm. She withdrew swiftly. She did not want what she described to herself as 'all that' to come up again. But she was now satisfied. From that time onwards she regarded Imogen resentfully as a woman who, she suspected, would have injured her if she could, and with a certain degree of contempt as one who had failed to do so.

When Paul returned from seeing the Greshams set off for Berkshire, he went to his study and stood his purchase on one of the lower shelves of the glass-fronted cupboard above his escritoire. The shelves were lined and backed with their original red moreen, darkened to the colour of wine lees. Against it the sky blue colour of the mug was intensified as it stood, separated from the room by a gleaming pane.

Paul had a consultation at three; it was now twenty-five minutes to. He telephoned downstairs for his secretary, and when she came up he gave her the file containing the patient's X-ray photographs, his case history and the letters of the doctor who had asked for the consultation. When the door closed behind her he sat quite still with his hands resting on the desk before him.

The room was dark, even in the brightness of early afternoon. Opposite the window, answering the light with a barely perceptible sheen, stood a collection of Chinese porcelain: plates of famille verte and the strange famille noir, jars in clair-de-lune and blanc-de-Chine, grey-green bowls and one, whose steeply sloping sides looked like the wings of a butterfly, of a pale but brilliant yellow. Below these were books on Hinduism, Buddhism, mysticism and travels in the East.

Paul Nugent pressed his hands firmly on the desk as he sat looking at the pale blue mug. He would never think of Imogen as occupying, in this life, the place of the woman whom he loved. He never permitted himself to see her alone. His admiration for Evelyn Gresham's powers, his unquestioning acceptance of Gresham as a man infinitely superior in personal attractions to himself, the knowledge, too, that Imogen loved her husband dearly, all together could not impair his acute perception. He knew that Imogen was intensely responsive to the charm of love, and that had he chosen to indulge his passion he could have so disturbed and agitated her that untold harm would have been done to the happiness of her marriage, and that its ruin, even, might have been the result. The horrible vision of himself as the murderer of Evelyn Gresham's peace, the wronger of Gavin's childhood, was a stark deterrent, but even this spectre had occasionally paled away before some moments of his suffering. What never failed him was the protective tenderness for Imogen that would have made him able to endure anything if it kept harm away from her. By now, though not happy, he was secure of himself.

'One dreadful error,' he thought, 'selfish obsession, wilful blindness. Please God, no more harm.'

The telephone on his desk rang sharply, and his secretary's voice said, 'Dr. Galt is here with Mr. Fairburn, Dr. Nugent.'

He left the room and walked down the long, shallow, gracefully turned staircase. Outside the tall Venetian window that lighted the stairs, dust had already steeped the afternoon sunlight with a faint milky haze. He thought of Ruskin's description of Turner's paintings, 'Space, mist and light', and the memory of painting brought with it those masterpieces depicting the Holy Family.

Born that Man no more may die.

The tremendous antithesis filled his head as he descended the last flight. He walked across the black-and-white marble floor to the door behind which, with lowered head, a desperately sick creature was waiting: opened it and went in.

THREE

Gavin's friend Tim Leeper was the son of an architect who was engaged, under the Ministry of Town and Country Planning, in developing the neighbourhood. The form this development might take had been a matter of some misgiving to the rural inhabitants, who were not reassured by Mr. Leeper's method of developing his own property. He had acquired two elegant little semi-detached Regency cottages, in sound condition, that stood at the end of the village street. These he tore down, and erected on their site a concrete dwelling with windows the size and shape of those in a railway dining-car, through which could be seen a spiral staircase with copper finish ascending from the ground-floor living-room to the upper storey. Some of the local dismay found a voice but Mr. Leeper ignored this with stately contempt. People who complained of what he had done he regarded as out of tune with progress and a drag on the future. Walking up the principal street of Chalk, lined with small eighteenth- and early nineteenth-century houses and little bow-windowed shops, he had been heard to say that all these buildings were due to come down anyhow. Mr. Leeper was tall, with a long, fat neck and of a weighty, not to say scowling, aspect. His wife was a brilliantly pretty woman with a head of curls like gold coins and an avid if not a well-informed approach to all topics of fashionable interest. It was she who was the origin of the Greshams' acquaintance with the Leeper family, for it so happened that her sister Zenobia had been married for a short while to Hunter Crankshaw, a young friend of Evelyn Gresham's.

Zenobia wrote verse which, though it made no concessions to popular understanding, yet sold at a small profit rather than a dead loss. This was very extraordinary, and it gave Zenobia the importance of a celebrity and of a serious artist. She had another claim to fame; she was a beautiful woman, so beautiful that her beauty was admitted everywhere as a matter of fact rather than opinion. Its character was intensity. Her skin had the warm whiteness of marble in sunlight, her eyes were so dark the irids were indistinguishable from the pupils; the whites were a pale blue. The huge, amazing ovals, like black and white onyx, drew the gaze into themselves as vertigo makes the victim long to throw himself down a well. The intensity of her beauty was equalled by the intensity of her self-absorption. Her passionate nature and her extreme sensibility to anything which concerned herself, laid her open to unmitigated sufferings and gave her entire existence a colouring of high tragedy. Indeed, she emerged from one emotional crisis and entered the next so rapidly, it was said that people who returned from America or got up from long illnesses found themselves enquiring about the progress of what was by then the last crisis, and receiving answers about the current one. It was also declared that beneath this proneness to anguish, Zenobia was, in plain language, as tough as an old boot. These remarks came as a rule from women who were jealous of her success, for by now she drew after her, like the gemmed train of a peacock, a galaxy of admirers, all of whom were publicly distinguished in some way or other: as racing motorists, masters of colleges, authors of smash-hit reviews, or financiers of international renown. It was Zenobia's way, though collecting admirers who could give her the most coveted of worldly advantages, to accept these tributes with an air of one touchingly grateful for kindness, but distraught by the hollow mockeries of pleasure. Invitations to Buckingham Palace, to villas in Capri, to first nights and private showings of famous dressmakers were all laid at her feet, and all found impotent to staunch her incense-streaming wounds. But the verse improved and improved, becoming more charged with feeling and more competently turned; and though there were people who said that it had become popular, and others who said that they liked poetry to be poetry, the great majority of the readers who were prepared to read it, regarded her as one of the few, most celebrated poetesses of the day. When a photograph appeared in *Vogue*, in which her lovely head, crowned with a wreath of violets, leaned against a fluted column, it was felt, among the few thousand people who saw it, that the seal had been set on her reputation.

Corinne Leeper felt that she and her sister belonged to the public. She herself had not so far published anything but it was understood among her friends that she would presently write a novel though she would probably have to undergo the Deep Analysis first. For the time being, painting and performing dance interpretations to the gramophone occupied most of her energies.

Evelyn Gresham, who felt Hunter Crankshaw's wrongs as Hunter himself no longer did, disliked Zenobia so heartily that he was prepared to dislike the Leeper family merely for being connected with her. Still the connection was one that in a small neighbourhood could not be ignored without open rudeness, and Imogen, always ready and hopeful where unknown people were concerned, made up her mind to call. Besides, though she too disapproved of Zenobia she felt about her all that uneasy curiosity and strong interest which women are apt to feel about others who are extraordinarily attractive to men.

She found Mrs. Leeper at home in the downstairs room on an oriental string-bed that stood a foot from the floor; on the walls hung several of Mrs. Leeper's paintings from which Imogen averted her eyes in nervous haste in case she should be invited to say anything about them. The room, which was a large one, occupying half the area of the house, was uncomfortably littered with family possessions. It was clear that the Leeper children had no nursery or play-room other than the family living-room, and that they had followed their mother's example in leaving things on chairs and windowsills or merely thrown down on the floor rather than putting them away. Mrs. Leeper was ebullient in her welcome, and delightfully pretty. Her head of curls tied up with ribbon bore an ominous likeness to the coiffure worn by Roman ladies just before the barbarian hordes overwhelmed the Roman Empire.

Imogen, after a few polite remarks, enquired after Zenobia. Corinne Leeper's bright face assumed at once a serious air. 'She is digesting the Corsican experiences,' she answered. Most people would have said that their sister had had a very good holiday in Corsica, but Corinne Leeper thoroughly understood her duties as the relation of an artist.

'She is writing, at present?' asked Imogen diffidently.

'Oh, my dear! Yes,' exclaimed Corinne, raising herself upright on the string-bed and fixing Imogen with a burning gaze. 'People envy writers and artists, but they've no idea of what it all means. She's *crucified* every time she writes a poem, simply *crucified*.'

Imogen was so accustomed, in her husband's absence, to imagining how he would receive people's remarks, that she felt a faint tremor of the uneasiness she would have felt if Evelyn had been present to hear this.

'Still, of course, one wouldn't change one's temperament,' continued Mrs. Leeper, sinking back with a renewal of complacency. 'And one does hope to inspire some sort of consciousness in the new building estates. My husband's awfully keen that there should be some sort of community theatre. At present all the dramatic activity of the neighbourhood is scattered about in little ineffectual spots – there's the play-reading society at Silverpath, I think they've got about seven members! And the Amateur Dramatic at Yew Tree End, and then of course the schoolchildren at Whitefield have a play once a year, and there are the Chalk Players, if they exist now – what we want is to have all the effort concentrated. Then we could get producers down from London, and probably work up to a festival before long.'

'But don't you think that people enjoy it more in this amateur way? The standard's never going to be really good, is it? It's the doing that's so enjoyable.'

'But the doing would be so much more enjoyable on a proper civic basis with outside professional help. And then – with all these new people coming from the London area—'

'Won't they feel that the cinema is – is more—'

Mrs. Leeper raised herself again: 'My dear! We must *show* them.' Imogen's eye wandered fearfully round the room. She wondered what Corinne Leeper had to show any working mother.

Then Tim had strayed in, so frail and light, so hesitant and unhappy that his method of getting himself into the room resembled the wind-blown progress of a dead leaf. Tim was so young that his face was still as round as a sixpence but his neck, arms and legs were like matchsticks. The first time he ate a meal in the Greshams' house, Imogen thought she could see why. He had never been expected to sit still at mealtimes and wandered away with a piece of cake in his hand to go on knocking a tennis ball with a racquet against the garden wall. Evelyn got up and followed him. 'One thing at a time, my boy,' he said. 'First it was tennis practice, now it's tea. After tea it can be tennis practice again if you like.' The kind, reasonable tone gave Tim no offence; he came back cheerfully. His method of eating was more difficult to improve. It showed all the signs of neglect from baby-hood. Tim would take a large mouthful, stare all round the room with his mind anywhere but on his plate, give one bite with his mouth open, then bolt the food and begin again. This way of eating, together with getting up and roaming about, or wandering away altogether if he didn't see anything he liked to eat, had made him so much under weight that he was perpetually low-spirited. As he came into the room on this occasion, his mother said sweetly: 'What are you doing, darling?' Tim said nothing but approached a pile of boxes at the far end of the room. He poked about while Imogen watched him intently. 'What are you looking for?' called Mrs. Leeper with slight impatience.

'My science set,' he muttered. Suddenly he gave a determined pull and dragged out a wooden box, but a second's examination of the contents disappointed him. 'It's gone!' he wailed.

'It must be somewhere, darling, whatever it is,' his mother asserted.

But the confusion before him was too much of a problem for Tim's weak and exhausted mind. He began to whimper, and then slunk out of the room, keeping close to the wall as if he were afraid of something. His mother sighed.

'He's so disorientated, I think we shall *have* to take him to a psychiatrist,' she said vaguely. Imogen could not trust herself to say anything. She did not prolong her visit and took her leave very soon after, saying it would be so nice for Gavin if he and Tim could be friends. She looked from side to side as she went down the path hoping to see Tim again. There was no sign of him, but in the branches of an ilex tree two scowling, dirty-faced little girls were crouched like monkeys. Their savage watchfulness gave Imogen an unpleasant sensation as she passed beneath them. Her feelings towards Mrs. Leeper, which had become hostile on Tim's account now softened a little. Their brother might be feeble but it was plain that Varvara and Ludmilla were tough. Whatever Mrs.

Leeper's shortcomings as a parent, there at least she was going to get the reward of them.

Evelyn, to whom Imogen retailed these experiences, could hardly contain his righteous anger. He exclaimed that Hunter was well out of that lot.

'Yes, if only he can think so,' said Imogen softly.

This annoyed Evelyn still more. 'Women all over!' he said testily. 'A broken engagement or a divorce and they think the fellow will never recover, when ten to one he's much better off than he was before. Not that I mean divorces are to be taken casually,' he went on. His voice, suddenly purged of feeling, assumed that impersonal tone she associated with his most serious utterances: a professional opinion, a deep conviction. 'But Hunter has a very good life,' he continued; 'plenty of friends, plenty of interests, plenty of money, an absorbing profession—'

'I sometimes wonder: do you think working in the Foreign Office can be very interesting?'

'Of course. Absorbingly interesting.' Evelyn, like many brilliant men, had a great veneration for the professions of which his own had not allowed him time to learn anything. 'Yes. On the whole,' he said, 'though of course one must regret a young man's marriage being broken up – deeply regret it, the real cause for regret is that he should ever have married that woman. As he did, the best thing he could do was to get out of it.'

In spite of Evelyn's thorough dislike of Zenobia, a dislike but too well justified by events, Imogen could not but remember one evening when she and Hunter had dined in Welbeck Street. Zenobia could seldom exert herself to take a genuine interest in the affairs of somebody else, but for men she could occasionally do it. When she did, it gave her beauty the stupefying influence of chloroform. Throughout the evening she had spoken to Evelyn about himself and his career. 'I suppose taking silk means you don't have any more of the dreary chores to do? You never thought any of it dreary? That's because you are a genius. You say you aren't, but I don't think there's a surer sign, ever, than when a man of your powers thinks *all* his work is interesting, even the parts other people think a dead bore. It must be so wonderful to feel you've saved someone from death, like a great surgeon, but more difficult in your case I should think, because surgeons have everybody working for them, and at least half the people are against *you*.' Imogen and Hunter had been obliged to sit quietly talking to each other like a pair of well-disposed cousins, while Evelyn, his head turned to Zenobia, white, intent, faintly smiling, had seemed scarcely conscious of what was handed to him, or said to him by anybody else.

Zenobia's marriage had ended within a year of that dinner party. Hunter had allowed her to divorce him, which his own friends regarded as Quixotic idiocy and Zenobia's circle of devotees said was the *least* he could do. Indeed, although Hunter during his brief spell of married life had been entirely faithful, and their final cause of disruption had been the mutual passion of Zenobia and a young man who practised folk dancing, she and her friends managed to consider that Zenobia was the injured party. Not that she ever abused Hunter. She would only say, faint-voiced: 'I don't think he'll *ever* understand what it was he did to me.'

'Very likely not,' was Evelyn's comment when this was repeated to him, 'but at least he allowed her to get away with his family silver.' For Hunter, returning to his flat after an agreed absence, had found himself not only without most of his furniture and all their joint wedding presents; he accepted this with resignation. It was more daunting to find himself without pillow-slips and sheets; but what really tried him was the disappearance of his George II spoons and forks. Hunter however was one of those to whom money has done no harm. He was not only rich but good-natured. He would have liked to get back his family spoons and forks for sentimental reasons but he would not embarrass Zenobia by appearing to notice that she had taken them. He soon forgave the injury but Evelyn Gresham never forgave it for him. It was with a gloomy satisfaction that the latter heard from time to time of Zenobia's goings-on.

Though he had felt some irritation at Imogen's going out of her way to call on the Leepers, he was obliged to admit that the acquaintance could scarcely have been avoided. He himself was too conspicuous a figure for either Mr. or Mrs. Leeper to overlook. Corinne Leeper had it on her sister's word that Evelyn had been one of the latter's conquests. She thought he was probably eating his heart out for Zenobia still. She determined to bring them together again. Not that she meant any harm to Imogen, though no one could be blamed if anything of that sort were to result; some things are stronger than oneself! Clifford Leeper had at first claimed Evelyn Gresham as an ally and supporter; he was resigned to the hostility of the neighbourhood to his enlightened schemes, it even stimulated him; but he took it for granted that anyone who could think at all must think as he and his friends and colleagues thought. Evelyn had not much time for sitting in the village pub but he enjoyed an occasional half-hour in the dark little back room of the Fisherman's Rest, where the windows were glazed with thick greenish panes that gave the light a watery quality, and where he, the postman, the station-master, the neighbouring farmers and shopkeepers would sit in a contented silence, so companionable that it seemed to an outsider they must be having some wordless intercourse like animals. To Mr. Leeper the Fisherman's Rest was a poky little hole that made no worthwhile contribution to communal life. He explained to Evelyn one evening as they walked home from it, his plans for a new public-house in the development area. The green in front of it would be covered with chairs and tables and gay umbrellas and here, not men only but their wives and families would congregate, drinking Coca-cola and ice-cream sodas.

'What will they do when it's wet or cold?' asked Evelyn.

Mr. Leeper mastered his displeasure and said: 'They will go inside.'

'I should concentrate on the inside if I were you,' said Evelyn kindly. He meant nothing but kindness, and as, unlike Mr. Leeper, he spent his holidays in England rather than in Spain, Portugal or the South of France, he thoroughly understood the English weather, but his manner did not commend itself to Mr. Leeper. When a foolish or inaccurate thing was said in Evelyn's presence, in court or during a consultation, it was essential that he should correct it at once, as decisively as possible, and the habit of instantly setting right other people's blunders and mistakes was perhaps carried with him into private life farther than he knew. Evelyn's singular acuteness of perception was as a rule directed to those feelings in other people which become translated into conduct. What had been done, what was likely to be done, was the object of his attention, and feelings which had no such outlet, mere states of mind, were not much regarded by him; since he did not find them interesting he was apt to ignore their existence. Occasionally however he underwent an involuntary flash of illumination, as on the present instance. He realized that Leeper had put his ability and his heart such as they were into the projects for the new community and that he was wounded by indifference and dislike in someone who, he felt, should have been able to appreciate him.

Evelyn told Imogen about it as they walked by the river's brink, waiting for the gong to ring for dinner.

'It's what Johnson said: "No man is pleased to have his all neglected." Do you remember?'

'Yes, I think so.'

'He felt that was what I'd done. I was sorry. I felt I'd been a brute.'

'I don't at all see why you should.'

'After all I dare say he's a well-meaning fellow. And probably he doesn't enjoy having a wife who's an ass.'

'I expect he does!' cried Imogen, 'else why did he marry her?'

Evelyn gave a married man's shake of the head.

FOUR

That summer of two years before was the beginning of the new era in their lives that succeeded the war. Evelyn had been on war service till 1945; the years immediately following his release, in which he had no sooner picked up his practice than he found it develop with great rapidity, opened the most hard-driven period of his career. At the same time, life became progressively easier for Imogen. The return of Miss Malpas to their household after absence on war work, being able to employ a gardener once again, and to have groceries sent home by the shops instead of lugging them back in a heavy basket that had to be set down many times on the way, above all the mere fact of Evelyn's being at home again, though in London for the middle of the week and irritable and preoccupied when in the house, all this brought back an almost forgotten ease and calmness. It seemed an irony of Fate that her own existence should afford leisure and self-possession once again just as the pace and strain of Evelyn's was increasing to an extent that was alarming, and causing him to settle down to domestic life on an iron ration of patience and self-control. The sense that something she had been longing and waiting for had slipped her grasp just as it had come within her reach, haunted her sometimes with an unnameable premonition of dread. No longer an idol, no longer young enough to have allowances made for her, she now had to devote herself to the task of making Evelyn's domestic background so smooth that it never aroused his unfavourable attention. This required just that efficient management of detail which she found difficult. Her anxiety was acute but only a small part of it was caused by a fear of his displeasure. She had an ardent sympathy for him over the hardness of his professional life. She had only once seen him come out of court after an important case. He had come down the steps of the Central Criminal Court, looking as she had never seen or imagined him to look, pale and sweating with exhaustion. Though she was to meet him there by his arrangement, though he had gained a verdict for his client, she could not go forward to speak to him. She stood at the side of the flight of steps, watching him walk down them and get into a taxi, oblivious of her absence. Everything about him looked unfamiliar. It was dreadful to her to understand as she afterwards did, that the condition in which her husband then was, at half-past four, did not mean that he stopped work. It meant only that when he got back to his chambers his clerk gave him half a pint of milk with a tablespoonful of brandy in it. When he had drunk this slowly and come to himself, he began to work on the case in which he would appear next morning. Some men carried on this existence with a carelessness and imperturbability which meant that nothing used up their nervous energy except the work itself. These were not men of magnetism, of histrionic ability and commanding physique. They were rather small men, spare and dry, witty and immune. Evelyn Gresham was of the opposite type, of formidable presence, severe but vulnerable.

Imogen felt that to love him now was the natural consequence of having loved him before, for now all the qualities were developed in him which had been foreshadowed then. His face now showed in the most distinct form characteristics of which it had once borne hints, then made unnoticeable by the handsomeness of youth. Now his face was plain to read, like a bold landscape revealed in the strong light of day. There was in it a strange contradiction between the regular mould of the features and something turbulent suggested by the jutting brows and a gleam, fugitive but startling in the clear, piercing eyes. Imogen thought that Wordsworth's sonnet about the boy whose character was influenced by the sight and sound of streams might have been written about Evelyn, who had, in fact, spent many holidays in the northern dales and loved to watch:

The sullen reservoirs whence their bold brood
Pure as the morning, fretful, boisterous, keen,
Poured down the hills, a choral multitude.

The cast of his mind suggested that it had been influenced by some clear, forceful, passionate element. He, too, might have said:

Maturer fancy owes to their rough noise
Impetuous thoughts that brook not servile chains.

There was never a doubt in her mind that to meet his demands was the most absorbing and the most valuable end to which her energies could be used. She tried hard to foresee what should be done and to carry out his requests; but she never acquired that unthinking grasp of practical matters that creates confidence. Evelyn never felt able to omit the precaution of saying: 'Did you telephone to the garage? I suppose you did post those letters? Has that coat gone to the cleaners?' And though more often than not she could say 'Yes,' it was never without an inward shudder and the thought, suppose I had forgotten! which made the occasion almost as painful as those on which she had. She could not remember any such strain of mind before the war; perhaps in those days Evelyn still had leisure to do for himself the things that now fell to her; perhaps her shortcomings then had been merely smiled at. Certainly his rare fallings out with her in those days had been lovers' quarrels between two people on equal terms, not the irritation of a master of the house whose requirements have not been met.

Another defect in her relationship with him had never weighed on her in the early years of their marriage. Her capacity for romantic affection was so great, the happiness of being the object of his passionate love was so enchanting, that for a long time she scarcely recognized her own deficiency in the sphere of physical passion. When she did realize it she hoped always that her capacity would improve, that what was bright already would become brighter, and what was sweet, wildly and unimaginably so. She had now to face the truth that the happiness of this relationship would never improve and could from now onwards only decay. Her own content would have been complete had she not known that he wished her to feel something more. Now that their relationship was no longer romantic, this knowledge, the sense of missing something herself and being subtly belittled and condemned because she did so, began to have a slow but fatal effect upon her happiness.

'It's an art, I suppose,' he had said carelessly. 'Some people have it.' The faint, unconscious note of contempt she thought she detected made her long wildly not only to be dead, but never to have been born. The tears flooded her eyes and welled down over her cheeks. Evelyn sighed, and caressed her kindly, absently.

Looking back to their life in Welbeck Street, she could see, by a comparison with the present, how widely the landscape of their emotional life had altered. On the evening when Hunter and Zenobia had dined with them, she and Evelyn had stood on the second-floor landing after the guests had gone. The staircase with its swanlike curve swept down before them. Far below in the darkness of the hall a thin streak of light showed beneath the door of Paul Nugent's consulting-room. On the landing where they stood, one lamp gave a dim radiance. Above their heads the roof opened in an oval glass dome, festooned with plaster wreaths. Through the glass, clouds and stars showed faintly. They rested their arms on the balustrade. They had often said it was like standing at the rail of a ship. Because of Evelyn's exacting hours it sometimes happened that the most intimate moment of their day would be one like this. Impelled by a feminine wish both to show Evelyn that she had noticed his preoccupation with Zenobia and that she was indifferent to it, she said softly that if women could have their choice of gifts, they would choose beauty such as that. He turned her about with his arm round her waist, and bending his mouth to hers, brushed her lips from side to side with his own, a habit of his, till the rough texture of his shaved skin made her mouth glow and burn.

'What silly things you say, don't you?' he said under his breath.

'Yes.'

'Don't you?'

'I said yes. Why do you make me say it again?'

'Just as well.'

Looking into her mind at their two figures standing at the stair, she seemed to be looking at them in another world.

There was so much in this of inescapable human lot.

'O world, O life, O time,' as the poets were always saying, that a thoughtful person could not rebel against it; besides, a great deal of the happiness of the marriage remained intact, and some new satisfactions appeared. During the war years she had been obliged to be entirely responsible for Gavin; it was now the greatest comfort and relief to be able to share this responsibility with Evelyn, indeed to feel that he took the greater part of it. She was privately convinced that Gavin was simply the handsomest, cleverest and most interesting child alive, but they did not get on well together.

She did not possess his confidence, and where a mother of robuster temper would have ignored this and ridden rough-shod over his reluctance and hostility, Imogen could not do so. She both respected and suffered from them. Gavin's brusqueness and lack of any inclination for her company sometimes wounded her, sometimes caused her irritation and even momentary dislike. She said wistfully to Evelyn that she knew Gavin had not much use for her: choosing her time for saying this when they were happy in each other's embrace, and she could rely upon her voice to recall the plaint of the wood-pigeon rather than the whine of an unoiled wheel. Evelyn's tenderness rarely showed itself in words; his terms of endearment were simple and few and used with an inarticulateness that suggested a boy rather than an experienced man. His moments of deepest intimacy and affection were marked not by what he said but by the lowness and gentleness of his voice, which at other times had a ringing resonance. It was in such a moment of enchanted quiet that he said, 'It'll clear up, my dear. Boys often haven't much in common with their mothers at Gavin's age. And I expect it's partly something he gets from me. I thought my mother was a fool. When I first went to school she sent me in shoes and all the other boys were wearing boots. So I concluded from that moment that she was a fool, and that women in general must be fools.'

'Because of your shoes?'

'Yes.'

'But you were fond of your mother?'

'Oh, very, in certain ways, on the whole. But I didn't feel any confidence in her after that. It was unfair, I dare say, but one's feelings are single-minded at that age – eight I suppose I was, seven or eight.'

'I have tried – I do try, so hard—'

'My sweet, I know you do. But it's the instinct he's inherited, not anything that's been developed by his environment.'

'He does think I'm a fool, I know.'

'Horrid little blighter. He's too young to know there are other kinds of intelligence beside his. But,' he continued seriously, 'you must – we must be very careful that we don't ever make him suffer what I – well, I've nothing to say against my mother. She was a much better mother than I was a son, I dare say. But boys *do* go through agonies of embarrassment and discomfort sometimes, if their parents make them conspicuous in any way. You can't be too careful how you treat a boy in front of his own contemporaries.'

'No, I know one can't.'

The eager willingness to put herself under Evelyn's influence made her subordinate many of her tastes to his as well as her opinions. Had her aesthetic sense not been guided by his she would never have used deep strong colours; as it was, she had interpreted his taste by choosing, for one room, a highly polished wallpaper of burnt scarlet, fading to chestnut, for another a scheme of pale yellow and violet. Evelyn would never have thought of these colours for himself, but was delighted when he saw them. Her secret preference was for rooms in twilight and for tangled thickets, but Evelyn had taught her that lighting should be adequate and well arranged, and that all corners of a garden should be kept as far as possible cleared, clipped and free of encroaching undergrowth. She had been largely cured under his influence of her readiness to buy an object that was elegant and graceful, however battered or impaired. Evelyn loved the arts of the late eighteenth and early nineteenth centuries, but a thing gave him no pleasure if it were not in mint condition. He had two boat-shaped dishes with arched arms, resting on a square base; they were of Sheffield plate and the silver was now so much worn that the copper showed through. This offended his eye, and he had several times spoken of having them re-silvered. Each time Imogen had implored him to leave them as they were. Their colour seemed to her exquisite; on the outsides the copper showed through the silver with the faint pink of a November sunrise, the insides glowed with a rose-coloured flame. So far she had been able to prevail with him. Their reading was sometimes a source of disharmony. Imogen read so willingly and so much and, where their tastes coincided, pleased him so greatly by her sympathy and intelligence, that it disappointed him when she declared she could not read Conrad or Herman Melville, or the more political of Disraeli's novels. Worse however was her addiction to those lesser works of literature that combine thrilling emotion with a grave deficiency of common sense. Evelyn had stigmatized someone in court as a 'gay Lothario,' and Imogen, seeing this reported in the newspapers, at once sat down to read *The Fair Penitent* and was absorbed and charmed by this vehement if unbalanced work. She thought it only right, in the circumstances, that Evelyn should read it himself. This he could hardly deny, and he accepted it from her, though with some misgiving. He sat up to read it and told her next morning that he had seldom been so glad to get to the end of anything. 'What miserable stuff!' he exclaimed.

'But didn't you think it *interesting?*' she asked. 'I see it isn't great, but I thought it so intensely fascinating.'

'My dear girl,' he said, 'you must be out of your mind. For heaven's sake read something worthwhile, if you must spend all this time reading.' The condemnation and disgust in his tone seemed to convict her at the same time of the folly and wickedness of the characters and the incompetence of their author.

They had however many pleasures in common, more than Evelyn's scanty leisure now allowed him to enjoy. There was not time now, for them to visit all the churches, castles, museums and exhibitions they would have liked to see. Such expeditions had been among their most delightful pastimes. 'I like to take you with me. I see more when I have you beside me,' he had once said, and the words filled her with elation, for his observation was so acute, it seemed scarcely possible that hers could assist him; yet this was one of those statements made between lovers, the sincerity of which is never in doubt.

They knew very few people in the neighbourhood; now that peacetime conditions made it possible to cultivate home life again and to entertain guests with comfort, most of their visitors came from London. Among the most frequent were three friends of Evelyn. Two of them, Mr. Cochrane and Mr. Ames came with their wives; they were barristers of Evelyn's rank. Their clever, good-tempered faces showed minds with some of the attributes of his, but temperaments much calmer if not less determined. The third, Mr. Justice Bannister, was a widower and somewhat older. In appearance he was straight-featured with bright, pale eyes; his manner was eminently courteous and forbearing, and he had a reputation for making lacerating comments in a silver voice, and for imposing severe sentences with an air of regret. Imogen thought him like the terrible crystal of Ezekiel. He was however a charming guest. Without conscious wishes in the matter, when she was in men's company, Imogen's intuition told her accurately whose emotions would be deeply stirred by her, whose might be in favourable circumstances and whose would never receive any but a superficial impression. These three men, all of whom were unerringly recognized by her as belonging to the latter class, were so kind, so pleasant, so well-bred, their company was so agreeable for what it was that she felt none of that obscure resentment that indifference sometimes arouses in a woman to whom emotional preoccupations are of great importance; and the unquestioned acceptance of their immunity gave her a sense of peace, of contentment even. No challenge was issued on either side, but every courtesy and attention was exchanged. It was delightful to have a relationship full of liveliness and charm, but entirely free from agitation. On these occasions, too, Evelyn appeared in an entirely fresh light; his conversation, though full of its own peculiar vitality and emphasis, was tolerant and calm; his manners were always good, but among these guests he was exquisitely courteous and good-humoured. With Mrs. Cochrane and Mrs. Ames, Imogen was on such pleasant terms as thoroughly well-intentioned and well-mannered women produce between each other. If Imogen tried rather harder than they did to maintain this comfortable state of things, they had the less need to try. Both of them were nearing fifty, and having married very young they had both lived through spare, strenuous years in their early married lives. Now the satisfaction and well-being brought about by their husbands' success had made them plump and settled. They did not think, now, of adapting themselves to anybody, but they were kindness and good humour itself to anyone who was adapted to them. Imogen really enjoyed their visits, and liked to think that the guests enjoyed them. It used to mortify her that Evelyn, after saying that some such week-end had been a great success, would add, as a rider, that of course Leila Ames and Dorothy Cochrane weren't *her* sort, but *he* thought them very nice women, both of them. Imogen's own friend Cecil Stonor, was another of their visitors, whom both of them were glad to see. Cecil worked in a publisher's office where her efficiency and meticulous regard for her duties were as much prized by the heads of the firm as they disliked her caution, coldness and self-control. Her habit of wearing neutral-coloured clothes with black shoes and gloves made Evelyn say that she got herself up like a Siamese cat, a creature whom with her pale and black-ringed sky blue eyes she somewhat resembled. Evelyn was amused and interested by her habit of carefully playing the stock market, saving half of each of her small gains and reinvesting the other half. He thought it excellent in a woman to be interested in making money as well as in spending it. Imogen was attached to her for an opposite reason. Imogen was the one person in Cecil's arduous and repressed existence who stood for grace and sympathy; Cecil loved her, and Imogen, though Cecil was far more practical, more experienced, more intelligent than herself, had a protective affection for her. She was instinctively very sorry for her, and loved to be with her and make her happy. Paul Nugent came to them fairly often, sometimes with his wife but often without, for Primrose was staunch to friends of the old Willesden days and had numerous engagements among them. Hunter Crankshaw completed their intimate circle and though Imogen was on speaking and even tea-drinking terms with most of their neighbours, she herself, absorbed in her domestic life, reading, writing long letters, and finding pleasure in a certain amount of solitude in scenery of such remarkable natural beauty as their own, made no effort to cultivate local friendships.

She could not have said exactly when she had become aware of how often their neighbour Blanche Silcox's name occurred in Evelyn's conversation as that of a woman immensely knowledgeable on rural topics, whose opinions on the ethics of tied cottages, drainage and poultry-keeping for profit called forth respectful agreement. To all such topics Imogen herself could only listen in silence. When they looked at buildings and works of art she and Evelyn were delightfully of one mind but their attitude to nature, in particular to the countryside, was not the same. Evelyn was deeply moved by natural beauty; one of his reasons for choosing a house in Berkshire was that he loved the landscape with its chalk uplands, bare except for the groups of beech trees that stood like sacred groves; but he looked at the scene not only as a devotee but as an economist. He scolded Imogen for any admiration of natural beauty which disregarded usefulness and sense, for admiring dead trees that raised their arms spectre-like against dark woods, or poppies and cornflowers among wheat, or broad verges and overhanging hedgerows that took up space which should have been under cultivation; he was irritated by her sympathy with the travelling deer that ate the young shoots in plantations and with the rabbits and squirrels that every sensible person regarded as pestilent.

'You talk like a townee!' he would exclaim. 'There's no room for sentimentality in the country; it's too big, too important, it's the basis of life itself; that's what you'll never realize. I love it – I love it as much as you do, but I respect it much more than you. I don't think of the countryside as a picture-book. I recognize it as something vital to our very existence.'

'I do see that. I do really,' she said earnestly. 'But that squirrel seemed to ripple along. It was outlined in silver light.'

'I dare say,' said Evelyn. 'Your mind is wrongly orientated, my dear girl. At least,' he amended, 'I expect I should not say "wrongly," but "differently from mine."' She stood still, aghast at the finality of his tone, and the civil apology which seemed to put them on the footing of strangers. They were walking among the trees one Sunday before lunch. A Spanish chestnut hung its dark, glossy, serrated leaves above them; at a little distance on the grey moss, a squirrel had left, neatly arranged, a collection of empty nutshells. The detail of the scene printed itself on her mind with alarming distinctness as if it would never leave her.

'Oh!' she said.

He looked back. 'Why are you stopping?' he asked impatiently.

She came on with light, fearful step. 'There seemed such a gulf between us when you said that.'

'For heaven's sake, don't be touchy!' he exclaimed. 'Don't make mountains out of molehills! The man I'm defending tomorrow – the motorist manslaughter case – you remember?'

'Yes. Tell me.'

'I don't think I shall accept another brief of that sort. I find I *loathe* people who have got themselves within range of being accused of dangerous driving with fatal consequences. The people in the other car – the man and woman both killed: their boy's still at Dartmouth.'

'Poor boy. How dreadful.'

'I shall think about that boy before I go into court.'

'I expect the client will think about him, too.'

'Lomax! If he gets out of this, I doubt if he'll give the thing another thought.'

They walked on, silent. The situation his words had called up had driven her own half-formed dread from her mind, but it had disappeared like some creature that turns a threatening face as it vanishes from sight. As they made their way along the towing-path to the stile at the end of their own lawn a series of shots echoed in the woods on the opposite shore.

'Blanche Silcox is shooting something,' said Evelyn. 'I hope it's squirrels.' They had barely reached the stile when the shots sounded again, lower down in the woods and muffled as they came across the water. To people who had lived through the war, the sound of shots naturally recalled it: there was nothing surprising in that, and as Imogen's thoughts on approaching the house concentrated themselves on the salmi Miss Malpas was making for Sunday lunch, she did not ask herself why at the back of her mind there rose the recollection of the photograph, printed by the newspapers, of a wall in Paris on which the retreating Germans had painted: '*Wir kommen wieder.*'

FIVE

Imogen was driven sometimes to wonder whether other people's children who appeared to outsiders so serene and biddable were, in the privacy of home, as awkward and difficult as Gavin; whether Billy Cochrane with the wide-apart front teeth and the engaging smile, secretly tormented his mother past bearing, or if the Ames' three daughters, serious young ladies with fair hair hanging down their backs drove their parents almost out of their minds when no one else was by? Everyone who came to the Greshams' house was impressed by Gavin as a remarkably self-contained and self-occupying child, but Imogen sometimes felt that the emotional condition between them was like nothing so much as an over-turned beehive. She tried with all her might to practise sense and self-control, but there were occasions when her temper was so rasped that she behaved as outrageously as he did. These lapses on her part always shocked her, but sometimes they seemed to do good.

One evening Gavin was sitting in his play-room, putting together the bones of a mouse which he had collected from owl-droppings picked up under the yew tree. The table was littered with sheets of paper carrying the different small bones. A book showing the diagrams of a mouse's skeleton was propped open against two other books, and Gavin, with a magnifying glass, a pair of eyebrow tweezers, nail-scissors and a roll of thin, glittering florist's wire, was articulating the bones of a leg. A benevolent stranger would have thought it an occasion for allowing bedtime to be postponed indefinitely. A mother's ears were shut from force of habit against the 'Just a bit longer!'; for Gavin was almost invariably occupied with some concern of absorbing importance at bedtime, and allowances of extra half-hours never meant that he was any readier to go to bed at the end of them. This evening however, the irritation he felt at having to stop what he was doing was even more acute than usual. He had nearly finished making the little hook and loop to attach two of the bones to each other; he would make a job of it in another ten minutes (or twenty, anyhow). A quarrel blew up before they could stop themselves, or rather before Imogen could stop; Gavin had no wish to do so. Imogen expended the whole of her remaining force on a command to clear up at once and come along, and then retired thankfully to the kitchen to be taken to task by Miss Malpas for not having remembered to buy the soap and starch needed for next day's washing.

'We shan't be able to get pegged out as early as I like to,' said Miss Malpas grimly.

'I knew I'd forgotten something,' said Imogen in contrite tones. 'How utterly silly of me!' Through the connecting doorway Gavin was heard saying in an affectedly low and musing voice:

'Well, if you *know* you're utterly silly, I suppose that's something towards it!' Like most parents, Imogen put up with a good deal of back-answering because her ear told her that though rude it was innocent, but the note of genuine insolence wounded and maddened her. She darted back into the play-room, losing all sight of the fact that she was dealing with a boy of eleven. In her vehement anger she could hardly fetch the words for her teeth chattered and her voice went hoarse.

43

'I think it *is* something towards it,' she stammered. '*You,* for instance, don't know you're beastly!' She rushed out again and took refuge in the drawing-room. Let him go to bed when he chooses, she thought, or stay up all night if he'd rather. She was sick of these scenes. But if Gavin sensed the opportunity of staying up till morning he did not take it. Presently she heard him bounce upstairs and set the bath-taps gushing at full tilt. A little calmer in mind, she went out to the play-room again.

'That boy's gone to bed without putting his things away,' said Miss Malpas. She was pouring blackcurrants, weltering in their rich Tyrian juice, into a bread-lined basin, whose contents would transform themselves overnight into a summer pudding.

'Oh, never mind,' muttered Imogen; 'anything to get him upstairs.' She approached the table, for she wanted to put back Evelyn's nail-scissors where he would expect to find them. One sheet of paper had no bones on it. Across the top, was printed in small letters: 'I am not beastly.'

Gavin's friend Tim Leeper was, though small, pale and unnoticeable, an important element in the Greshams' lives, for while Gavin had a boy with whom to fish, climb trees, explore, play with model railways, build fires, exchange comic papers and spend those long intervals of absorbing occupation to which the adult has no key, the question of his going to boarding school for companionship did not arise. It was arranged however that he should go to a preparatory school in Shropshire, in the coming autumn. Evelyn and Imogen paid a visit to Brackley Hill, and as much of it as could be seen on a visit they liked greatly. The common-room, dining-hall and dormitories were bright and airy, the schoolrooms and the laboratory were well furnished, and the boys' relations with the Headmaster and his wife were clearly those of the family kind.

'I liked it all *very* much,' said Evelyn as they drove home through Worcestershire, Warwickshire, and over the Oxfordshire border. Evelyn drove extremely well with safety, sureness and at high speed. The hum of the engine, subdued but powerful, enveloped them: beyond it, above and around them, was the transparent golden evening, the purple distances, the fields strewn with wreaths of early hay, the hedgerows starred with fragile, wide-open wild roses. As they flew onwards, the gold light died, leaving the sky a translucent, solemn blue; the scent of hay floated to them, the dimness rising from the fields threw up the roses as staring wraiths. As they drove past a dark and glassy horse pond, Imogen's eye caught a quaking glitter in its depths; she became aware that the moon had risen behind them.

'Yes,' she said. 'I did, too. I liked the way the boys spoke to Mr. and Mrs. Maude. You felt they had got the boys' confidence – a good deal of it, anyhow.'

Evelyn continued: 'I had a word with the maths master and the man who takes the science—'

'Did you like them?'

'I am trying to tell you. Maude got them to speak to me because Pringle had told him Gavin was something of a prodigy in those directions. I didn't want to look like the proud parent – I'm sure that sort of thing doesn't do a boy any good. I simply said I hoped they wouldn't find he'd been overpraised. Not that I think they will.'

'Nor do I,' she said softly. 'Oh! I *do* hope he'll be happy there.'

'If he's not happy there,' said Evelyn, 'I don't know where he could be happy.'

'No, certainly. I'm sure it's as hopeful as one could find.'

'But why not wish and hope that he'll do well, improve himself, get the foundations of a good education, my dear girl? All this talk about *happiness* – happiness is a by-product of doing something in a satisfactory manner. It isn't the object and end of existence, as you seem to think.'

'Yes, of course. I would have said what I meant more if I had said I hoped he would do well, fit in with his surroundings, go on developing – then of course he would be happy. It would mean the same thing.'

'Not necessarily. It might, one hopes it would. But the work of life can be done, is done often, without what *you* call happiness.'

She was silent, incapable of reply. In the gathering dusk, the flying shapes, house, field and farm, were touched with a weird glint as the moon climbed the vault at their backs. The landscape became familiar once more but it wore a frightening face, the pallid walls of a park overtopped with throngs of silent trees, black yews holding out their sweeping, fringed boughs between a blanched spire with glittering clock dial and a road of gleaming chalk. The question she longed inexpressibly to put, 'Are you happy?' she could not have unclosed her lips to ask, the weight of dismay and fear was so great. She dreaded to make the fatal movement that would bring down the avalanche.

By the time they were home, it was after nine, and Miss Malpas appeared in the hall, lighting a candelabra and enquiring calmly whether dinner would be wanted. It was laid in the dining-room, but she hadn't known whether they'd be stopping for some on the way? Evelyn, pausing before garaging the car, apologized for this lateness.

'That don't matter,' said Miss Malpas kindly. 'Only say if you want it.'

'Of course we *want* it,' said Evelyn apologetically.

'Very well; have it,' returned Miss Malpas. 'Soup and some cold fowl.'

'And some of that cheese,' added Evelyn hopefully.

'Naturally,' said Miss Malpas. 'Coffee likewise if you want all the particulars.'

'Delightful!' said Evelyn. 'I shall be ready in quarter of an hour. Shall we say 9.30? And I ought to be shot, having dinner at this time of night.' Miss Malpas maintained a noncommittal silence on this point and disappeared into the kitchen. Imogen went upstairs. She heard Gavin floundering in the bathroom and opened the door on a wild scene of dampness and disorder.

'You back, Mum?'

'Yes. Just this minute.'

'Oh. Is Daddy?'

'Yes, of course.' She began to wash her hands.

'What was the place like?'

'Large playing fields, and a swimming bath, and a carpenter's shop, and a tremendous science lab., and a very nice common-room with heaps of books. And the food we saw was very good.'

'What was it?' demanded Gavin suspiciously.

'It was a high tea, which they have instead of supper.'

'What were they having?'

'A spaghetti dish with tomatoes and bacon and mushrooms, very nicely done, I thought, and then ice-cream because it was Saturday.'

'What sort?'

'There were three sorts, coffee, chocolate and pink.'

'Good. No white. White's hopeless. I wonder what make it was.'

'It was their own make. They made it themselves in a very large refrigerator.'

'Sounds all right.' He slid under water. A solid wave slapped against the front of the bath. Its crest broke off, leapt in the air, and splashed at her feet. Imogen shrank against the wall. She would not disturb his amiability by the usual exhortations to mind out, and hurry up for goodness sake, and went back to her room, deep in twilight, with a brilliant prospect of the moon above the hanging woods. In the quiet, the brief tinkle of the telephone startled her. As she went downstairs she heard Evelyn saying:

'Only just got back . . . Very good run both ways . . . Oh, splendid, thoroughly satisfactory, at least as far as one could tell . . . I think he will . . . All right for Monday morning? . . . Good . . . So shall I. Goodbye . . . Goodbye.'

As they sat down to dinner, Evelyn remarked: 'Blanche Silcox is driving up to town on Monday and she'll give me a lift.'

'How nice.'

'I shall be glad to give my tyres a rest after to-day. We must have done nearly a hundred and thirty miles.'

'And you must be very tired. It wasn't a very good way to spend a Saturday, I'm afraid.'

'I enjoyed it. Besides, it had to be done. Still, I shall be glad to be driven on Monday.'

'I do wish I had ever been able to learn to drive. It would have been so useful now you haven't a chauffeur.' Once Evelyn had given her considerable encouragement to learn, arranging driving lessons for her with a school, making the chauffeur give her practice and sometimes supervising her attempts himself. Even when her incompetence and her dread of traffic made it clear that she would never pass a driving test, he had continued to urge her, saying it was only a case of giving her mind to it. The matter had never been entirely dropped, but now he said with decision: 'It's no use to think of it. You'll never do it now.'

'I'm afraid not.'

Perhaps the late summer evening conduced to melancholy; perhaps she too was tired with the long hours of driving though she had been only a passenger, but the sense of failure and frustration rose in her again, almost to tears. In their room, Evelyn again said that he was tired. She raised her arms to his neck and so gained a perfunctory caress. Then he went to his bed without a word. When he was not inclined for conversation or for making love, to sleep in the same room with him was almost like sharing a ship's cabin with a well-behaved stranger.

She lay watching the moon, brightening and still brightening above the woods whose greenish tint could be distinguished in the wonderful strength of her light, until the eerie radiance was so intense that the whole sky was seen to be hollow and filled with it. The sight became intolerable.

'What is the matter with me,' Imogen thought, moving hopelessly on her pillow, 'that everything seems wrong? Moonlight, the most beautiful thing in the world, now it seems dire to me.' Presently the moon passed from the window, bearing away her emptiness and death, steeped in cold and brilliant light, and the warm, living earth settled to sleep in darkness.

SIX

Evelyn's strong feeling for beauty, order and a regulated state of society made him value church-going as a social duty. When they were first married, Imogen, as the product of an intellectual but aimless society which valued Christian ethics in lackadaisical fashion but thought Christian doctrine quite exploded, had had to be induced to go to church by her husband, though she did so willingly enough. The practice had now grown on her and she went to church regularly just as Evelyn appeared almost to have given it up. He went to church at Christmas and Easter and occasionally at other times but from the point of view of social duty, it was perhaps enough if one member of his household went.

The comfort Imogen found in the Anglican services was so great that she dreaded to have it disturbed by the arguments of scientists, rationalists or materialists, for though she felt obscurely that there was an answer to them all, she knew she could never lay her tongue to it or convince anybody with it if she did. She was so fearful of attack that she shrank even from saying that she went to church, and when obliged to say so to acquaintances, she did it with bent head. She hardly bore to imagine what Saint Paul would have said to her.

During terms, even Sundays were not entirely free for Evelyn, but he usually took a walk while Imogen was at church. Often he went over to Blanche Silcox's house, where it seemed they had many points of interest to discuss, for Evelyn was now becoming much interested in rural topics, and he liked, too, to hear what Blanche Silcox could tell him of her experience of local government; he had never before met a women who had any. To Imogen one of the admirable things about his mind was his enthusiasm for collecting information and acquiring new insights into affairs which she herself regarded as so tedious they were to be avoided at all costs. The fact that Miss Silcox had actually and of her own free will undergone the experiences that provided the information did not give Imogen a moment's pause. She was amazed at Evelyn's concerning himself with such dead-bore work because she regarded herself and him as in the same sphere. Blanche Silcox she thought of, when she thought of her at all, as someone quite removed and having no part or lot in her own experience.

One Sunday morning Evelyn, feeling possibly that in a small community, all his visiting should not be confined to one house, called at the Leepers', where he knew he would find Gavin, to bring the latter home to lunch. The Leepers welcomed him cordially and Evelyn, a little touched by compunction, did his best to be very pleasant. Unfortunately, the uncongenial elements of Mr. Leeper and his professional activities came to the fore almost at once and staggered Evelyn in his good intentions. Mr. Leeper was a colleague of the architect who was responsible for the new school in the development area, which was so large that its window-cleaning alone cost the ratepayer £300 a year. This fact had been seized on by the inhabitants of Chalk as a focus of their dismay; the effects of closing down the village school and sending their children nine miles by 'bus to the enormous new one were more difficult to define though none the less acutely felt. A general sense that the children learned little in school because the classes were so large there was no vital relation between the teacher and the taught, and that most of what they learned out of school was undesirable, adding up as it did to a revelation that life in a country village was 'lousy' and 'out,' was making itself increasingly felt among the parents of the village. Mr. Leeper however was an enthusiastic admirer of the school, that is to say, of the school buildings, for to him they were one and the same thing. He admitted though that you would not see it at its best until the Ministry had sanctioned the rest of the plans; the theatre and ballet studio, the extensions to the science block and the installations for treating the pupils with sunlight lamps had yet to be built.

'They tell me there's to be no library,' said Evelyn, directing his piercing glance at Mr. Leeper. 'Is that so?'

'No, there is not.'

'I should have thought, when so much outlay is being planned on other things, a school library might have been thought of?'

'You'll find,' said Mr. Leeper gruffly, 'that nowadays, with a progressive educational authority, there is less emphasis on the bookish side of education and more on what we call the direct approach.'

'I see. But what happens to any clever children? Or are you assuming that you don't cater for any?'

Mr. Leeper sat bolt upright and exclaimed in a tone of bantering reproof: 'That is a most unsocialist comment!'

'Very likely. But in my opinion, you can't provide a sound education without good teaching and plenty of books. Has this school got either?'

'It's a matter of opinion.'

'My dear fellow, how can you say so? The ability of the teachers may be a matter of opinion, but either the books are there or they aren't. This schoolmistress here encouraged their reading. Are the children there given opportunities to read or aren't they? That's what I'm asking you.'

Mr. Leeper got out of his chair with a muttered exclamation. Evelyn continued, imperturbably but with great resonance and distinctness:

'The village parents are complaining that the children seem to have lost the power of amusing themselves. On Saturday mornings they hang about whining for money to go to the cinema – at twelve o'clock on a fine morning!'

'Oh, the *village* parents,' interrupted Mr. Leeper impatiently, as if any complaint from such a source were beneath the attention of a rational person.

'Village life is a most tremendous stronghold of obscurantism!' cried Mrs. Leeper brightly. She did not treat Evelyn Gresham with the severity she knew his utterances deserved, because he had a handsome and commanding presence and was so eminent that a good many of her friends had heard of him. Besides, she thought he should be treated with sympathetic consideration because he was one of Zenobia's victims, and handled carefully because he was an eligible one. She planned to give a party for Zenobia very shortly and the occasion would be momentous. Evelyn now felt that it would be improper to take a second glass of sherry from people to whom he could hardly bring himself to be civil in their own house. He got up.

'Imogen will be back from church,' he said.

Mrs. Leeper put her head slightly on one side and said with an air of scientific curiosity: 'Why does she go to church?'

Evelyn merely replied: 'We both go sometimes but this morning I stayed at home. Now I think I'd better find Gavin.' Gavin at once appeared from behind the iron staircase.

'Can Tim come back to lunch with us?' he said.

'We shall be very pleased to see him,' said Evelyn courteously, 'but you must ask his parents.'

'Well, can he?' said Gavin, addressing Mr. Leeper. The latter said gratefully, 'I'm sure he'd like to.' Tim, pale and smirched with the greenish grime from laurel branches, stole into view at Gavin's back. He said nothing but it was plain that he now regarded himself as attached to the Greshams' party. Mr. Leeper with real good nature took from a drawer some half-pound blocks of chocolate with different fillings and asked Gavin to choose one. Gavin's head was bent over the collection in avid scrutiny. 'Raisin, hazelnut, milk, coffee,' he mused.

'I think the milk will be best: won't it, Tim?' But Tim was already on the path to the garden gate, blissfully secure of lunch and an afternoon at Gavin's house instead of his own.

Imogen met them in the hall. 'Oh, Tim! How nice!' she said with sweet alacrity. Tim said nothing. His silences were remarkable and she thought they were becoming deeper. Gavin was sometimes taciturn but Tim was frequently almost mute. His reserve suggested no lack of friendliness however. When she went out to tell Miss Malpas he had come and to collect a cover for him, he followed close at her heels, stopping when she stopped and returning to the dining-room in her wake. When she had laid his place she went out to see if Evelyn were in the drawing-room or if they must ring the gong. Gavin came into the dining-room as she left it and she heard him say: 'Decent of your Pa to give us that chocolate. It's about half a month's ration for one person.'

After a slight pause Tim said languidly: 'He is fairly decent, in some ways.'

Gavin's voice rang out in encouraging accents, 'He's better than your mother, anyway!'

Imogen gasped. The serious caution she had so often had from Evelyn not to make the boy feel a fool in front of other boys (mothers, she herself admitted, being prone to do this in a way beyond the powers of any other relative) was violently brought into collision with an anxiety that Tim should not be distressed. She stood in miserable indecision, and Gavin's voice was heard again:

'Are your sisters good or bad?'

A pause followed, so long that Imogen thought Tim must have decided to ignore the question, but at last his little voice said tonelessly: 'I don't mind them.' At that moment Evelyn walked in from the verandah. Her relief was great. Either Gavin's indiscreet remarks would be checked by his father's presence, or if he made any more, Evelyn would know how to deal with them, without exasperating him.

Tim's table manners had improved greatly since his first teatime in their house. He would not have dreamed, now, of leaving the table before the end of the meal; he accepted everything that was offered, and Evelyn's good-humoured scolding had almost cured him of bolting his food without chewing it, or of packing it in the side of his cheek and washing it down with a gulp of water. When the pudding was begun there was a moment's silence, and Tim broke it suddenly and unexpectedly.

'What is a psychiatrist?' he said.

'A psychiatrist?' repeated Evelyn. 'He is a doctor who cures people's minds, or does his best to.'

Tim stared at him with eyes almost black with panic. 'But what's the matter with their minds?' he demanded.

'How long is a piece of string?' asked Gavin sarcastically. Imogen was on the verge of telling him to be quiet, but Evelyn, ignoring him, said in his kindest voice, warm, gentle, authoritative: 'It may be any kind of thing, quite a little thing like a sprain or an earache; just something you'd be more comfortable without.'

'But what does he *do*?' said Tim wildly. 'Does he cut your head open?'

'No, indeed he doesn't! I expect you'd think he was doing hardly anything to earn his money! But you know how sometimes, if people have a worry, they feel better if they talk it over with somebody?' Tim nodded. 'Well, that's rather the way a psychiatrist cures a person.'

'He just talks to them?'

'He talks to them, and lets them talk to him.'

'But suppose they don't *want* to talk to him?'

'Then they can tell the old fool to shut up,' cried Gavin with cheerful abruptness. 'Mum, can I have some more pudding?' Imogen silently refilled his plate.

'I don't admire Gavin's way of expressing himself,' said Evelyn, 'but as a matter of fact, that's just what they *can* do, if they feel like it! A psychiatrist can't do anything for a patient unless the patient wants him to, and helps him to do it.'

'*Can't* he?'

'Not possibly. He can try to persuade the man to have the treatment, but if the man won't have it, nobody can make him.'

'Not *whatever* they did?'

'Not whatever they did. And besides, the psychiatrist wouldn't do anything. The patient must pay the five guineas or whatever it is, but if he's decided not to let the doctor do any work for it, that's his look-out. They can just talk about cricket or stamps until the time's up. Very nice. I wish I had some clients like that.'

'But,' said Tim, still anxious, 'the patient might not have all that money; it might be a boy.'

'Well, then the boy's parents would be paying, wouldn't they? But it would still rest with the boy to decide whether he'd let the psychiatrist try to help him, or not.'

'Jolly good sucks to the parents if they went on paying and paying and the boy went on going and going and he and the old geyser never talked about anything except stamps! Are there any third helpings?' Gavin wound up.

'There haven't been any second ones yet, except to you,' Imogen pointed out. 'Evelyn? No? Tim, do have some more. Then we can let Gavin have the rest.'

'Yes, please,' said Tim eagerly. His usually pale cheeks were filled with a deep clover pink. He took back his plate and began to wield his spoon with such a will that Evelyn exclaimed: 'Now then! No need to choke yourself!'

'It was quite slow really,' said Tim apologetically. 'This pudding is inclined to slip down your throat.'

The moment everyone had got up from the lunch table, the boys disappeared as if they had sunk into the ground. Imogen was used to these instantaneous vanishings, particularly when Gavin and Tim were in each other's company.

'Gavin saved us then,' said Evelyn gravely. 'If Tim had asked me about the psychiatrist by himself, I couldn't have turned it into a sort of joke as Gavin did. He did just the right thing without realizing it. Boys are so good for each other! Nobody else can take their place. But his manners really are shocking – that rude way of shouting for more instead of waiting, not a please or thank you to his name. Surely he's old enough by now —'

'Quite often he gets to the stage of behaving properly and then he seems to go right back to the beginning again. It is disappointing – one has to start nagging again when one thought all that was finished. I didn't say anything then because I didn't want to interrupt you.'

'I'm glad you didn't, that time. Those Leepers! It's the mother of course. I don't *like* Leeper but I'd trust him with the boy, ass though he is. I wouldn't trust that woman farther than I could throw a battleship.'

Imogen repeated what she had heard of the boys' conversation and Tim's moderate tribute to his father. 'I wondered if we ought to give Gavin a hint about not criticizing people's parents to them?'

'If he does it in front of you, certainly. But I think in private we may as well leave him be. He won't hurt Tim's feelings, and it may give a relief.'

'It was wonderful to see how relieved he was when you'd explained that he couldn't be psychiatrized against his will!'

57

'Poor little fellow.'

'Can *you* see any need for psychiatric treatment?'

'The only thing I can see any need for, is for that bitch to tidy up her house and have proper meals served punctually four times a day. And to keep her mouth shut,' Evelyn added.

SEVEN

Mrs. Leeper's party for her celebrated sister was announced for the first Saturday in July, thereby causing Evelyn Gresham acute annoyance. During terms, taking a Saturday off meant working most of the night and sometimes it could not be done at all; but he had seen his way to a day's racing on this date and had asked Hunter Crankshaw for the week-end to go to Hurst Park. Hunter had been a keen racing man since the age of sixteen when his house-master had complained strongly of the number of book-makers' circulars that arrived for him by post. Since the break-up of his marriage, his favourite pastime had become a mania. He had been heard to say in a solemn manner that if it had not been for his marriage ending when it did, he might never have come fully to understand the importance of the Turf. Evelyn greatly enjoyed a day's racing in Hunter's company. He found a charm in the society of a congenial man who was a good deal younger than himself and Hunter's conversation delighted him; it was extremely knowledgeable on the subject in hand and for the rest it was a blend of worldly wisdom and hare-brained wittiness that Evelyn, exacting and overstrung, found keenly refreshing.

The fact that his former sister-in-law lived in the neighbourhood was no bar to Hunter's staying with the Greshams. He merely took care not to run into Mrs. Leeper. But he would not come when Zenobia was known to be there. If Corinne Leeper knew of his presence, she would make a point of inviting him to come with the Greshams to a party given for her sister. Such a thing would be in accordance with what she called 'one's idiom of life.'

Evelyn's sense of grievance was partially assuaged by finding that both his arrangements and Hunter's allowed of their changing the day for Hurst Park to the Saturday before the one originally chosen. Not that the change of date was entirely indifferent to Hunter: it would be too much to expect that to a man of his science any one race meeting could be just the same as another. He said regretfully that they wouldn't now see Porphyry, whom he'd hoped to have a look at, but he was interested to note that Clever Dick would be running, a horse that had made a promising appearance in April in the Berkshire Handicap. Did Evelyn remember its performance?

'Vaguely,' said Evelyn impatiently.

'Vaguely!' exclaimed Hunter in shocked reproof. 'That sort of attitude won't get you very far!'

'I rely on you to get me anywhere,' replied Evelyn.

Hunter made an early start on Saturday and drew up his car on the Greshams' drive soon after eleven. Imogen heard the crunch of wheels and ran out. The sun was dazzling on the lamps and bonnet of the car. Beyond it the lawn and the woods were still lying in fresh morning shadow, though at one point at the lawn's edge there was a perpetual glitter where the river entered the flinty reach, and on the bushes by the drive the cobwebs were strung with burning diamonds.

Hunter was a welcome guest to any hostess; for unlike some guests who come, self-absorbed and prepared to act the part of human vampires, it could be seen at once that Hunter came to amuse and be amused, to give and to enjoy.

Imogen led him to the drawing-room, whose french windows opened to the lawn and were entirely filled with a prospect of green, for alders closed the end of the view, and on the left hand the oak woods rose in massive leaf, silent and still, while at their feet the river slid, bright and smooth.

'How beautiful!' said Hunter. 'Nothing but a race meeting would make me leave it on a morning like this. You're coming, I hope?' he asked, as he took a glass of sherry from her hand. Imogen shook her head. It was difficult to give a convincing reason for staying at home other than the real one, which was that Evelyn's pleasure would be spoilt by the presence of an ignoramus in a specialist's expedition, and of a woman in what would otherwise be a day of particularly enjoyable masculine companionship. She felt it so thoroughly right and appropriate to stay at home that she scarcely regretted doing so, although three minutes of Hunter's society acted upon her like good food on someone who has been strictly dieting: it reminded her of how delightful were the carefree attentions of unattached, cheerful men who liked women enough to spend a lot of money on them, and gave her a sharp appetite for more of the same thing. However she looked forward very much to the rest of his visit. Hunter was peering eagerly at her dress, a Swiss muslin dotted with yellow, clasped by a grey and yellow belt.

'This may be a matter of great significance,' he said.

'What may?'

'Your wearing this dress. Grey and yellow are the colours of the owner of Clever Dick, a horse I've been thinking a good deal about.'

Imogen laughed. 'More sherry?' she asked.

'Perhaps I'd better. It's hardly safe for me to drive without at least a couple of glasses of sherry inside me.'

'Are you driving, or is Evelyn?'

'I don't know. The pronouncement has not been made.'

A sharp, tinkling sound showed that someone had finished a

telephone conversation and a moment later Evelyn came out of his study. Delighted to see Hunter, full of enthusiasm for the day's pleasure, there was an indefinable air of strain about him none the less. Pale as he naturally was, his pallor now looked like the effect of the heat. His clothes were immaculate as usual but they looked as if he must find them hot.

'Which of us is driving?' asked Hunter presently.

'Oh, my dear chap, that's the thing. Neither of us has to. You remember Blanche Silcox, our neighbour? She's going, and she'll take us in her Rolls. We should have met her there anyway, as I'd asked her to have lunch with us, and she suggested giving us the lift. There's no point in taking out two cars.'

'Well, that's very nice of her,' said Hunter temperately.

'She's looking forward to meeting you. She'd like to have your advice, I'm sure. She takes racing much more seriously than I do.'

Hunter made a movement of his head as if to admit that this was all to the good; then he looked directly at Imogen and said: 'Why don't you come and make a four?'

Imogen hesitated: before she could answer Evelyn said, 'Imogen isn't interested in racing, are you? You don't want to come, do you?' His tone suggested surprise at any such idea.

'No,' said Imogen at once. 'I really won't this time, thank you.'

'We shan't be late,' said Evelyn kindly. 'In fact, if you like to give us tea about five, we should be back for it.'

'Good.'

'It would be very pleasant to have it on the river bank,' he added.

'Yes. And do ask Miss Silcox to come in this time. She is so very kind in all the things she does but I never seem to see her.'

'I will. Hunter, I think that's the car in the road now. Are you ready? I don't want to hurry you.'

'I'm quite ready, thanks.'

They all went out on to the drive. The bend with its over-hanging evergreens concealed the road where the Rolls-Royce was drawn up. Evelyn hung his binoculars on his shoulder, and felt to make sure of his wallet. He walked on with his firm, rapid pace, his head bowed a little.

Hunter's head had still the erect carriage of a young man's and when he turned to smile at her he gave a luminous effect of light hair, greenish eyes and brilliant teeth. His suit of the lightest summer weight in a pale tan and his holland shirt looked as cool as women's clothes. She did not follow them round the shrubbery but stood in the middle of the gravel ring and waved goodbye. Hunter turned and raised his hat. He then hurried after Evelyn with loping steps like a dog bound for an outing.

As she walked back to the front door she met Gavin and Tim coming out with jam-pots hanging from strings. They were making for the river. She told Tim to come back for lunch, and as she went indoors to her household tasks she was saddened to think how much he was going to miss Gavin when the next term took the latter to Brackley Hill. She would have him at the house as often as he liked to come, but of what use would the house be to him without Gavin? The boys, she could see, were now at the water's edge, stooping, intent. Tim knew of the coming separation, but the autumn, which was near enough to chill an adult with its prospect, was divided from him by a long, glorious summer's morning, an afternoon of more brightness, tranquillity and heat, and by more such days after that, melting each into each. At his time of life, the present was a shining barrier beyond which the future was nothing but an empty threat.

When Imogen came through the hall again she noticed Hunter's pigskin suitcase at the foot of the stairs, and carried it up to the spare room since he was not there to forbid her. The elegance of the case, its well-used but pale and rich appearance and the sight of the blond car on the drive below had something romantic about them that reminded her of her young days when she and the girls she knew had been ceaselessly occupied with ideas of men as lovers or possible husbands, even when these ideas were disguised as preoccupations with dresses and hats. In those days they had practised among themselves and on everyone they knew a kind of sexual rating. When they spoke of a match they could decide immediately, to their own satisfaction at least, which of the parties had had the luck, which should consider themselves as only too fortunate and be prepared to conduct themselves accordingly. Money and social standing modified the sexual rating a little, and it was considered, too, that the woman in order to equal the man in this calculation must have a higher level of charm and desirableness than his, because there were too many women, and because often the man was going to become steadily more eligible long beyond the point at which the woman would begin to be less so. Most of them could smile now as they looked back to that era of their lives, fanatically fashionable and intense. They no longer slaved over the care of faces, hair, hands and clothes, though such toils had been unnecessary then and would have been reasonable now; but the ingrained habit of cautious assessment was never outgrown, and Imogen, like the rest, was always ready to look at other women with an objective eye, to ask herself how much prettier, more charming, more interesting they were than she and where the difference was in their favour, to admit, academically at least, that in a drawn battle they would come off victorious.

She had not known Hunter in this period of her life, and when she had first known him, he had been so unhappy that the expression of his eyes had made him look as if he suffered perpetually from a severe headache. It was only since he had cast off responsibility and grief that he recalled to her the atmosphere of her own youth. He had now become a most charming companion to his women friends. He had said to Imogen on the one occasion when he had spoken to her about his past, that now he was like Charles the Second, determined not to go on his travels again. From being intensely concentrated upon one woman he had become gaily affectionate to many; yet he was never called a philanderer; he was too lively for sentiment.

By quarter to five, tea was laid on the small, sloping stretch of turf that covered an old stone arch in the river bank, the remains of a seventeenth-century boat-house. Very tall plane trees with their mottled boles shaded it and two massive stone urns stood one at each side of it, now filled with scarlet geraniums. It was a good place for a picnic, for it had all the beauty of the riverside and the woods, and being raised a few feet above the water's surface, it was out of the way of some at least of the insects.

Imogen was in the kitchen cutting cucumber sandwiches, when rather sooner than she had expected she heard the car on the drive, not the well-known sound of Evelyn's Bentley but the softer, more resonant note of a Rolls. A moment later while she was hurriedly rinsing her fingers under the tap, Evelyn's step and voice entered the hall. 'Imogen!' he called. 'Blanche can't stay to tea. Come out and speak to her.'

Imogen hurried into the hall. Hunter and Evelyn were outside, lifting field-glasses, packages and evening papers out of the car. On the front doorstep, with a curious, pecking movement of the head, Blanche Silcox stood or rather hovered. She had removed the jacket of her suit and was wearing a tweed skirt and a blouse and a round straw hat whose crown rose like a beehive. Imogen noticed this almost unconsciously: what impressed her most was that Miss Silcox was extremely pale. She came forward quickly, thinking the visitor might be feeling ill, and begged her to come indoors, but Miss Silcox resolutely refused to advance a step. She stood, pushing her chin forward and withdrawing the rest of her person, and spoke in a breathy, toneless, staccato voice that showed unmistakable agitation. What she said was difficult to make out, but 'Must be back' Imogen heard, and 'So kind of you.' Miss Silcox then turned abruptly and scuttled back to her car.

Imogen followed her at a run and stood at the driver's window. 'Do you feel all right? Are you sure you won't come in for a minute?' she asked, mystified and concerned.

Blanche Silcox looked at her from the driver's seat. Her face, still very pale, showed signs of some strong feeling. As she was sitting down the absurd shape of the hat was less apparent; its brim framed her face and under its shade her eyes had for the moment the look of a much younger woman's. There was something touching in their expression. In a voice much deeper than usual, almost croaking, she replied, 'No thanks. I'm *perfectly* fit. We had a marvellous day but I must get back.' The big car started at once with a sudden glide, and disappeared in a second behind the shrubbery.

Evelyn and Hunter were standing at the front door. Gavin, grimy and half naked, burst out of a syringa thicket. 'If you want to have tea with us,' said Evelyn, 'go and get washed and put a shirt on. Has your friend Tim gone home?'

'No,' said Gavin. This was seen to be true, for Miss Malpas was bearing the tea-tray across the lawn followed sedately by Tim, carrying two plates.

'Why don't you both have tea in the kitchen with Malpas?' suggested Evelyn hopefully.

'We've had it there. We thought we could have some more with you.'

'Good heavens! Very well, but you must make yourselves respectable.'

On the turf, the slope made a comfortable seat for the grownups. The boys hung over the top of the arch, stirring the water with sticks until Gavin, bringing his up with a flourish, sprayed the party with water from a mass of slimy weed. Evelyn told them to take a piece of cake each and get away. The day's racing had been so good however that as they departed with wistful backward looks, he stopped them and added cucumber sandwiches. The racegoers had all had an unusual run of luck, except that Clever Dick had not been placed. 'Oh!' exclaimed Imogen, 'my colours!'

'Nothing in that,' said Hunter encouragingly. 'Don't give it a thought.'

'Did *you* back it?' she asked Evelyn.

'No. I was altogether fortunate, thank you. Blanche and I backed New Venture for that race and we collected a nice little win. In fact the only money any of us lost the whole afternoon was what that fellow laid on Clever Dick. The beast hardly showed a leg. Your system wants overhauling, my boy.'

'Not at all,' said Hunter. 'This afternoon was just one of those things God does from time to time to remind the racing man that He's got His eye on him.'

Imogen leaned back against the stone urn. The slight jar rocked it on its pedestal and the geraniums showered down scarlet petals on her hair, her shoulders and her lap. Hunter leaned over and began carefully to pick them off her.

'I do wish we had some white ones,' she said. 'I long for white geraniums in the dining-room.'

'Surely that isn't impossible, if we give our minds to it!' Hunter exclaimed.

'Not in the least,' said Evelyn, 'but she's never mentioned it till this moment.'

Hunter went on: 'There's a glass-house by the road, belonging to that nursery garden that you pass after Rose Hill. It's full of geranium plants, I noticed to-day. There may be white ones.'

'Oh, I should love some!'

'If the chap is about on a Sunday, we might try to-morrow morning.'

'She goes to church on Sunday morning,' Evelyn said.

'I could go in the evening instead.'

Evelyn turned on his side. He and Hunter were about the same height but Hunter was so slight that nothing but his height was noticeable. Evelyn's figure was at the perfection of mature masculine beauty. He himself regarded any such tribute as absurd and brushed it aside impatiently. He could no longer play football against Guy's Hospital, therefore he professed to regard himself as dilapidated. He was looking much better than in the morning. The alert look never left his face: even in sleep he looked as if a touch would bring him to instant consciousness, but now he had a slight, contented smile and his pose on the grass suggested sensuous enjoyment.

Imogen wished for a second that even the welcome Hunter were not there, that they could be by themselves, to walk away into a thicket and dissolve into one of those close embraces that were for her the most exquisite moments of their life, when she was able to give and be all that was asked of her, and her passion increased his own. As her eyes recognized the opposite shore again, she heard Evelyn saying:

'We'll drive over to the glass-house and call in on Blanche Silcox for a drink before lunch. She has very good sherry.'

'One would think so, judging by her car,' said Hunter. 'She has a lot of money, I suppose?'

'A good deal. Her father was the senior partner of Silcox and Boone. Do you know them?'

'The stockbrokers? By name, of course.'

'The firm is carried on by the Boones now, but of course she and her sister were left very well off.'

'Miss Silcox struck me as having a very good business head,' said Hunter meditatively. 'She should have gone into the firm herself!'

'Oh well, for a woman, you know. Still, nowadays – and you're quite right about her business sense. It's wonderful. I dare say she would have been very successful at it.'

'What does she find to do now?'

'Any number of things. She practically runs the neighbourhood.'

'Does she?' exclaimed Imogen, astonished. 'I never seem to see her.'

'Of course you don't,' said Evelyn brusquely. 'When do you ever put your head outside your own house except to go to London! You have nothing to do with the Girl Guides or the Women's Institute, or any of the local institutions. Blanche is on the Board of Management of the Home for Incurables at Silverpath, and she's the Treasurer of the New Turning Club that takes in girls who are having an illegitimate baby – she's done any amount of voluntary work.'

Imogen was taken aback at the sternness of his tone and remained silent.

'She seems a good sort,' said Hunter. 'Pretty shrewd eye in the paddock, too. She picked out Lunar Rainbow, I noticed.'

'When her father was alive they did a lot of racegoing,' said Evelyn casually. 'He used to do it *en prince*, she was telling me.'

Hunter nodded, staring at the water. It seemed motionless, dark, glassy green, but now and then a small leafy spray, a straw or a dead rush was seen to float by, carried on by invisible force.

EIGHT

Imogen, who thought she had, and was generally considered to have, great insight where emotional situations were concerned, thought it possible that Hunter and Cecil Stonor might come to like each other. She knew that in the ordinary way a man accustomed to such beauty as Zenobia's would not be liable to notice her plain little friend, but in this case she thought the opposite principle might work. Men, even those who had been exasperated and finally bored by Zenobia, still felt the power of her beauty, all except one. To Hunter it now meant no more than a picture postcard. Cecil's force of character, reserved and blameless, her reliability, integrity and common sense, might draw him, if only he were not repelled by her caution and coldness. Cecil was so much repressed, even Imogen could only guess at her probable feelings, but Imogen held the thoroughly feminine view that Cecil would be almost incapable of indifference to so eligible a man if he showed any attachment for her.

They set out for the glass-house on Sunday morning in Hunter's car, with Imogen sitting beside Hunter, and Evelyn in the back seat. The conversation was naturally for the most part between Hunter and herself, and she said casually that she had hoped to have had Cecil there for the week-end of his visit but that the change of date had made it impossible. Hunter replied sincerely that it would have been very nice if it could have been arranged. Imogen wanted to continue talking about Cecil to him and was slightly hesitating for a topic when Evelyn's support was given in a most welcome manner from the back seat.

'What a sensible young woman she is!' he observed. 'It's refreshing to find a woman who is interested in making money as well as spending it. Not that one would like it if she were mean, but she's not. She's honest and careful, and generous as far as her funds allow.'

Imogen turned her head in surprise. 'That is all absolutely true,' she exclaimed, 'but how did you know? You see her so seldom.'

Evelyn gave a small shrug. 'I suppose I've trained myself to be observant,' he said carelessly.

Hunter said: 'I was rather shocked when she said she wouldn't bet because she wouldn't run the risk of losing money; but I was reconciled when I found she played the market.'

'But is taking risks with your money a virtue?' asked Imogen, puzzled, 'especially when you have only a little!'

'The less you have the nobler it is.'

'Cecil doesn't enjoy the risk,' began Imogen, hoping she was not lowering her friend in Hunter's eyes. 'She accepts it as something unavoidable in that way of making money.'

'So it is,' said Evelyn, 'but study of the subject and a good head, and self-restraint, all tend to minimize the risk. You can talk to Blanche about it. She has the whole thing at her fingers' ends. I think Cecil would get on with her like a house on fire.'

Neither of the others spoke. Hunter was scanning the road for a turning: Imogen had already decided that if it lay with her, Cecil should do nothing of the sort.

The nurseryman had several pots of white geraniums among his rose-pink, flesh colour and scarlet, though he seemed surprised that anyone should ask for them. As Hunter had taken charge of the expedition, Evelyn remained in the car, while Hunter and Imogen entered the small, flashing glass-house. The sun smote them through the panes, and drew out a scent of dampness and geranium flowers from the plants ranged in tiers upon white duck-boarding. They chose three plants, their earthenware pots cold as a well from the damp black mould inside them, the thick, quilted green leaves downy with almost invisible silver hairs, the stems drooping like the arms of candelabra before they rose to support the white heads.

'We shall have to be careful,' said Hunter. The stems spread and swung, that was their great beauty, but it would be difficult to transport them without damage. Hunter paid for them, and while the nurseryman with the expert's carelessness took a pot under each arm, he himself carried the third in both hands towards the car.

'Is this Birnam Wood?' exclaimed Evelyn.

'You'd better let her sit at the back, then she can look after them.' Imogen sat in the back seat and two pots were put at her feet, the third beside her. Evelyn's driving proceeded without a jolt, but the mere motion swayed the flower-pots and made leaves and stems knock against her. Every one of the velvet touches against her leg or side caused her apprehension, and she was so much occupied with fears for the safety of flowers and stems, and with breathing, delightedly, the faint, delicious scent, that they had turned into Miss Silcox's drive before she was aware of it. She had only seen the house from the back as it was approached from the woods, and this aspect was quite foreign to her. The house was a large oblong, built, appropriately enough, in what is known as Stockbrokers' Tudor.

'It seems so odd,' Imogen thought as she got carefully out, 'that it should have been here, so near to us all the time, and that I should never have seen it before.' The idea lent a strange interest to the scene as if it had been suddenly disclosed by magic, and the sensation persisted in spite of the commonplace nature of the scene itself. The garden was shaved and trimmed and intersected with paths freshly coated with loads of expensive yellow gravel. Indoors the house was light and spacious. The drawing-room to which Evelyn led the way, had the benefit of light walls and large windows, and numerous small gilt radiators showed how effective the central heating would be when it was on. The chairs and sofas were extremely comfortable, as squat and overstuffed as modern manufacture could make them. A few beautiful objects were discernible: a looking-glass surmounted by an urn and ears of wheat hung over a mantelpiece of pale blue tiles; two small chairs with the Prince Regent's feathers carved on their backs were almost lost to view in the welter of blue velvet upholstery and gilded cane. The Chinese do not make many ugly carpets, but one of their few had been unerringly chosen; it had a pattern of green and mauve on a mustard ground.

Imogen was so eager to see and to take in, that it was some seconds before she could grasp the many impressions offered simultaneously to her view. Blanche Silcox, standing in the middle of the room, seemed very glad to see them. Hunter she now greeted like an old acquaintance: Evelyn it seemed required no greeting. He was asking after the Bristol Milk, pouring it out and recommending it to Hunter. Imogen was looking about her so intently that she could not afterwards remember how Blanche had greeted her. She came to herself to realize that the latter was leaning towards her holding out a glass of sherry. That strange agitation of the previous afternoon had disappeared from Blanche's manner; she now looked at Imogen, pleasantly, but in a composed and remarkably searching way. Imogen took the glass. The sherry was the strongest she had ever tasted: her heedless swallow burned her throat and set up a ringing in her ears; through this she studied Blanche as the latter moved to talk to the other two. Until yesterday Imogen had never seen her at close quarters; this was the first time of their being in a room together.

Blanche Silcox's manner was unassuming but she gave, none the less, the impression of a remarkable degree of self-confidence. She was now fifty and made no attempt to appear younger, though this would have been by no means impossible to her, for the something ungainly and frumpish in her appearance was the result more of mental than of physical characteristics. The effect of her figure with its bloated waist, in contrast to which her small legs and her feet in pointed shoes, looked like the slender forelegs that unexpectedly support a bull, could have been minimized by a woman who knew how to dress, but her tweed suit did nothing to disguise it. The skirt was very short, in that style that had always been ungraceful on an elderly woman even when it was fashionable, and now it was not fashionable. At the same time the calmness with which she seemed to assume that nothing was amiss with her appearance, coupled with the dignified absence of any attempt to make an effect with it, was in itself an attraction. In ways not connected with personal appearance however, she seemed to Imogen very much concerned with making an impression. Her voice was toneless and rather harsh but in a vehement utterance it would sink suddenly to a low register of great warmth. She was now at Evelyn's side, exclaiming tensely and laughing in a throaty manner at his every other word, the enthusiastic hostess whose drawing-room, prepared with luxurious masses of flowers, large silver cigarette boxes filled to the brim, layers of glossy periodicals and the imposing array of bottles and decanters on a massive silver tray, reflected a radiant welcome.

Imogen was no sooner aware of these surroundings, so unfamiliar to her, than she realized that they must be thoroughly familiar to Evelyn. Miss Silcox sat at the end of the sofa nearest to his chair and he was smiling upon her with bent head as he listened to her complaints of the local labour available for gardening.

'It's quite extraordinary,' she was saying. 'You'd think they were doing you a favour. And of course, colossal wages. I really don't know what they *do* expect nowadays.' Hunter, seeing that the conversation was not to be general, attached himself to Imogen and they stood looking at the bookcase. It had a complete set of *The Shooter's Magazine* for 1884 and a miscellaneous collection of single works. Hunter pulled out a guide to the aquarium at Naples published in 1912, and then *The Head Hunters of Borneo*. Imogen looked as usual for novels and found some fascinating Edwardian relics in their olive-green covers: *By Their Fruits, One Poor Scruple, Half in Earnest*. The shelf below was full of books about dogs, ranging from the fictional or philosophical treatment to the strictly practical, *The Jack Russell in Health and Sickness* and *The Dog Owner's Vade Mecum*. Hunter drew out an expensive rose-grower's annual with coloured plates.

'Oh, Evelyn has that,' exclaimed Imogen softly. 'He swears by it. He chose all our new roses out of it.' She stooped to look at the lowest shelf. Hunter flicked open the title page, closed it and pushed the book back. The page said, Evelyn Gresham. Imogen rose, flushed, from the bound volumes of *Punch* and the county guides and saw that a new arrival was in the room. This was Miss Silcox's stepsister Marcia, who often came to spend the week-end with her. It was understood that these visits were, above all, to give Marcia 'a rest.' Those who knew that Mrs. Plender was the wife of a wealthy man with a well-staffed house, and that her three children were at boarding school for three-quarters of the year, sometimes asked themselves from what she could be resting. In the school holidays it was more understandable; then the children usually came by themselves, while their mother rested at Sunningdale or Frinton.

Marcia Plender was short, plump and middle-aged. She was also excessively feminine, but so far from throwing her stepsister in the shade on this account whatever she might have done when both were girls, she now acted as a foil to her, though one would have been as far from suspecting it as the other. Marcia took great care of her person and appearance though she had allowed herself to become fat. As her constitution required her to rest in bed till half-past twelve and drink two double gins before lunch, it was difficult for her to avoid increasing weight. Upstanding curls marched across her head in a kind of *cheval de frise*, under which she blinked and stared with kittenish artlessness except when she darted a look of keen watchfulness. Her hands were loaded with platinum and diamond rings and clattering charm-bracelets, and she exuded the bland scent of expensive soap and bath essence. The assured, formidable appearance, combined with a sugary air, fluttering eyelids and die-away voice, made the beholder turn to Blanche with relief and even a sort of admiration. Blanche's abruptness and half-strangulated accents were not charming, but they were a great deal better than Marcia's efforts at charming.

Mrs. Plender immediately assumed control of the conversation and Hunter's face took on a melancholy expression, while Evelyn's wore the look that reminded Imogen of Gavin's when he was sickening for something.

'Did you come through the woods?' she asked, rolling her eyes at Evelyn, then at Hunter.

The latter answered: 'No: we drove round by Rose Hill to get some geraniums for Mrs. Gresham.'

'From Seaton?' asked Blanche. 'The man with the little glass-house?'

'You know him, do you?' said Evelyn with a return of animation.

'Yes. He's been there a long time. He used—'

'There used to be a mahvellous place near there,' Mrs. Plender interposed. 'Mahvellous. We used to get mahvellous pot-plants there, cut flowers, too, in Mother's day. 'Member, Blanche?'

'Hawkins, you mean? Yes; but he went out of business a long time ago.'

'Oh, I dare say. Seems like yesterday. I always think having kids makes you forget how time goes. Mine keep me young, I always say. Have you any, Mrs. Gresham?' For the first time Mrs. Plender spoke directly to Imogen, and in doing so, exchanged her artless gaze for a sharp stare. Blanche immediately said: 'Indeed they have. You remember Gavin, surely?'

'Oh, yes. Quite a big youngster, isn't he?'

'Eleven,' said Imogen.

'Oh yes. Does he go to prep. school?'

'He will next term; he's going to—'

'Mine goes to Eaglescliff. It's a first-class school, one of the very best. Costs the earth, of course. But I always say it's short-sighted to save on your children's education.' She turned. 'Don't you, Mr. Gresham?'

'Certainly.'

'Not that brains are everything. But they must be with people of the right sort. And nowadays you can't rely on that unless you pick a really expensive school, that's the only way to be sure it's exclusive. Sounds awful I dare say, but when your children's future is at stake you just *have* to be realistic.'

No one could think of a reply to this before Mrs. Plender began again.

'Same with the girls,' she said. 'My two are at Whyteladies. They have a particularly nice class of girl there. When I saw the headmistress, I said: "Candidly – I'm not crazy about examinations. They won't have to earn their living, but they *will* be expected to know how to keep their end up in society."'

'Do they like the school?' said Imogen.

'Mavis and Shirley? They're crazy about it.'

'I didn't think Mavis was,' said Blanche, surprised.

'Oh, she is,' said Mrs. Plender carelessly. 'They both are.'

'Perhaps when Mavis is stronger she'll enjoy it more,' said Blanche doubtfully. Imogen looked at her with sympathetic enquiry. 'She has rather bad backaches at present,' Blanche explained. 'But they say it's nothing serious and she'll outgrow it.'

'Oh my dear,' exclaimed Mrs. Plender, shifting on her hams and flinging ash into the fireplace. 'I've given up worrying about Mavis's backaches. I worried myself sick at first, until the doctors told me I simply must take a pull and realize there was nothing *to* worry about. Simply nothing. Mothers are awfully silly. Aren't you often told that, Mrs. Gresham? I'm sure your husband thinks you're frightfully silly sometimes.' She rolled her eyes, then blinked them rapidly several times.

Imogen smiled. 'I expect he does,' she said.

Evelyn got up.

'Must you go?' Blanche murmured, rising also. 'I wish we could have asked you to lunch but the cook's on holiday and my old parlour-maid is single-handed.'

'Oh my dear,' exclaimed Mrs. Plender, 'you're much too slack with Parker. Why shouldn't she put herself out for once?'

'She has a weak heart,' said Blanche, looking down.

'She's had that ever since I can remember.'

'Then it's not likely to be any better now, is it?' Evelyn suggested.

Mrs. Plender looked for once genuinely astonished, not, however, offended. She said goodbye to them with good-humoured indifference and remained in the doorway while Blanche accompanied them to the car. The latter admired the geraniums while Imogen established herself once more among their leaves, and exchanged a few abrupt and cheerful words with Hunter about meeting again at Hurst Park. She said goodbye, and Hunter and Imogen repeated it, but Evelyn said nothing. This was not from absence of mind, for he was looking fixedly at Blanche while the others spoke. He was silent on the way home.

Hunter was to return to town after tea. At lunch Evelyn

suggested that he and Imogen should take a walk along the river bank past the weir and follow the tributary until they came to the reach where there was trout-fishing; part of this was preserved by Miss Silcox and Evelyn said he had arranged to share it with her.

'Next time you come down you must bring your fishing tackle,' he said cheerfully.

'I haven't any,' said Hunter with a harried air. 'I practically never fish.'

'You must take to it,' Evelyn urged. 'There's nothing so soothing. It needs just enough concentration to prevent brooding, and allows you to relax at the same time.'

'I think the mind wants stimulating rather than relaxing,' said Hunter, 'and you can't concentrate on racing if you're thinking about fish; it stands to reason.'

'Did you never take to it?'

'I used to do a bit of salmon-fishing with my uncle up in Yorkshire —'

'You did? I can't think how you came to leave it off.'

'I've got more important things to think about. Besides, I do it when I'm up there.'

'I should have thought it would have been your chief hobby.'

'You talk as if it were yours. I never knew you were so keen on it.'

'Nor did I,' said Imogen. 'I never heard you mention it before.'

'I did it a good deal as a boy,' said Evelyn, 'and Blanche Silcox's being such a keen fisherwoman reminded me how much I used to enjoy it. She's got all her father's rods at that house. She won't let me buy one. She would certainly lend you one if you want to join in next time you're down.'

Hunter did not go through the formality of saying this would be very good of Miss Silcox. He became somewhat silent for the rest of lunch, but this was the less noticeable as Gavin began to ask questions about the trout, and drew upon himself a strict warning against playing in that part of the stream, and instructions to convey the same to Tim Leeper.

'Tim won't do it if I don't,' said Gavin confidently.

'Very well, then don't you.'

'I expect Miss Silcox wouldn't mind if we did. She didn't mind the time we made the dam.'

'It wouldn't be a question of her this time. I am paying half for the fishing rights, and *I* should mind very much. In fact, I should be very angry.'

'Oh, all right. I never said we *would* do it.'

'And I don't like your arguing like this, Gavin. I don't often tell you not to do something. When I do, you might as well take it without making any bones about it.'

Gavin said nothing. Imogen wished that he would say 'Sorry.' The merest mutter would be enough. Evelyn with his impressive presence and his severity was formidable, but the edge to his tone, his rising colour and his frown showed that he was hurt. She longed to be able to say something that would soothe or distract him, or failing this, she wished to be able with one word to prevent Gavin from giving any fresh offence. But she could think of nothing to say to either of them that would be certain of effect. It struck her, so forcibly that she could no longer ignore it, that she was now altogether lacking in self-confidence in her attitude to them both. She had often felt this at different times in relation to one or the other but never till now towards both together. The absolute necessity of asserting herself somehow in the face of this realization made her leave the table somewhat abruptly and say: 'Then Hunter and I will walk along the river and have a look at the trout. When must you go, Hunter?'

'Soon after tea, I'm afraid.'

'Perhaps we'd better say tea at four, then. Gavin, if you want your tea with us, will you be ready and clean by then?'

'I will if I do,' said Gavin and made one of his instantaneous disappearances.

The walk along the bank led them for half a mile or so through meadows, over stiles, along a towing path and at last to the great grove of aspen trees that surrounded the weir. The trees were of unusual height. Against the pale blue sky their myriad leaves, now grey-green, now silver, shivered and whispered. Beneath, the river slid on, dark and clear, till it rounded over the weir in a glassy, greenish curve, then splintered into flakes, tresses, sheaves of foam that poured, thundering, to gush into the stream below. The lower waters, shaken unceasingly, sent reflections like watered silk over the bank and up the trunks of trees. Under the spangled branches could be seen fields of pale gold oats, turning to silver as the breeze wandered through them. Wind, shade, water and light made an enchanted place. It was not till they had turned to the right along the bank of the tributary stream, with tall fields of oats shutting them in with the sluggish water, and the sun beating on their heads and drawing out sickly-sweet scents of river plants, that Imogen began to speak of their visit before lunch. She picked a dock leaf and waved it as she walked, to dissipate the clouds of insects that rose from the water's edge to attack their faces.

'That Mrs. Plender—' she began.

'A corker, wasn't she?' Hunter slapped the back of his neck smartly as he felt a sting.

'I thought it made Blanche Silcox seem very nice, that she didn't seem to see how awful Mrs. Plender was.'

'Miss Silcox *is* very nice, I should say.'

'Yes, of course. But she must be very dull?'

'It depends. I've only seen her on an afternoon like yesterday. She doesn't seem dull if she's doing something with you that she knows how to do.'

'I suppose not.'

'And being that sort of age, she knows the ropes pretty well, and of course she's got a good deal of money and does everything very comfortably. That makes her pleasant to go with.'

'So I suppose her lack of attractiveness doesn't really matter?'

'Well, in what way?'

'To men – to their liking her.'

'Not to their enjoying an afternoon on the course with her. So far as I'm concerned, nothing else has been in proposition.'

Imogen laughed, but she continued soberly: 'It does surprise me that Evelyn seems to like her company so much. He is so very – as a rule, so *very* exacting: hardly any women really please him, I often feel I don't.'

'Oh come, that's absurd.'

'It's true.'

'A very busy man, in such an extremely exacting profession, he probably doesn't show his feelings, except when he's annoyed—'

'I am not complaining. Only I do sometimes feel that I don't soothe and interest him, as I wish I could. So it makes me the more angry with myself that somebody so unprepossessing should be able to amuse him – *him* of all people – and now this fishing will begin, hours and hours of it, I expect.'

Just before them a white post was stuck crookedly into the bank. The board attached to it said: 'Private. Fishing rights reserved.' They walked round a screen of alders and a charming reach of the stream opened before them. The muddy bottom had given place to chalk once again. The bed had been cleared of the mare's-tails, water-buttercup and arrow-head which were growing thickly in the reach they had left, and the banks were freed of reeds and rushes. To look into the depth for a moment was to see the dart and quiver of a fish.

'Very nice,' said Hunter. Imogen said nothing. Presently he went on: 'If you take a woman fishing, it has to be a dull one. Anybody lively scares away the fish. There's a special type of woman, in fact, who is chosen for fishing holidays. My uncle had a friend, old General Mather, who used to take a particular woman away with him twice every year, simply to fish with.'

'And was she boring?'

'To madness, in ordinary life. But just the thing for fishing. And being in the open air all day made him very sleepy, so he needed someone dull to sit with him in hotel lounges in the evening.'

'Yes, I see.'

'Various people said: "Isn't this a bit out of line, all this staying in hotels with Maud Buggin?" But my uncle always would have it that when they said that it just showed they didn't know what was what. Maud and the General were simply doing what they said they were, neither more nor less.'

'I suppose your uncle was very experienced?'

'Pretty well. Besides, he was very fond of fishing.'

'Yes. And of course I wouldn't dream of saying that Blanche Silcox isn't very pleasant in her way.'

'She certainly cuts a very good figure beside that fearful step-sister.'

'I agree. But, you know, I was surprised how amiable Mrs. Plender was when Evelyn gave her that snub about the maid's weak heart. I wouldn't have expected her to take it so good naturedly.'

Hunter looked thoughtful and then said slowly: 'I expect there's a good deal of solidarity between them – Blanche and her. She obviously meant to make the visit pass off well. In fact she probably thought she was being captivating, and alluring us all to come again!'

'She didn't mean to allure *me*, I think.'

'Perhaps that was natural.'

'I got the feeling—' Imogen spoke with sudden determination – 'that Blanche Silcox was very much attracted by Evelyn.'

Hunter was silent.

'Did you think so, from seeing her yesterday?' she added.

'Yes, I did. One could hardly be surprised, I suppose.'

'No, not in the least. I believe I heard that as a girl she was engaged to somebody who died – poor thing. And after that, I suppose no one took any notice of her until now.'

'When you say "*notice*",' said Hunter somewhat hurriedly, 'you mustn't imagine from anything *I* said that there's anything cooking between her and Evelyn!'

'Oh no! How *could* one. But I suppose I am a thoroughly contemptible character – I can't make myself do the things he enjoys, but I dislike other people's doing them with him.'

Hunter put his arm round her waist and they walked back through the blowing cornfields to the weir again and the temple of trees whose thousand tongues were always speaking. Their messages were so loud and urgent, the sense almost transcended the unknown language. Imogen felt for a moment that something of intense importance to herself, some revelation, some warning even, was being uttered in the heights of the silvery and sibilant leaves; but as they walked on through the sunny, open meadows where all was still again, the sensation was calmed and lost sight of in the halcyon spell of Hunter's affection. He usually showed it at such a time, the last opportunity of a visit that was nearly over. He lifted her over each stile and kissed her in the shade of the hedgerow before they went on to the next. With each stop their kisses became longer and more numerous, but his love-making was so gentle and affectionate that when they crossed the last stile on to the lawn, Imogen felt quite able to meet the eye of anyone who happened to be about. No one was except Gavin and Tim, whose heads were raised from the groups of wild iris that sheltered the little harbour for toy boats. Imogen stopped.

'Where's Daddy?' she asked.

'He won't be long,' said Gavin. 'He just took the car round to old Silcox.'

'Darling, *don't* call her that. Miss Silcox, or Blanche, if you like, but one or the other.'

'Oh, all right.'

'But why did he take the car there?' Gavin had crawled into the flags and only the soles of his shoes were visible, but Tim was upright; after a second's pause he came up the bank towards her, a dripping boat in each hand and said: 'Miss Silcox is going to drive Mr. Gresham to London to-morrow. So the car's got to be at her house. At least it may as well be.'

'I see. Then he'll walk back through the woods, I expect. You might go and meet him while tea's getting ready.'

'I expect she'll drive him back, in *her* car. That's what they did before, anyhow.'

'Before! When?' Imogen would have checked the words in any case, but Gavin poked his head out of the reeds and shouted: '*She's* the cat's mother.'

'That's all very well,' cried Imogen, 'but how did *you* speak about Miss Silcox?' The reeds were silent.

Hunter went indoors to pack and Imogen began to make preparations for tea. She had it all laid on the sloping turf, the boys had been induced to wash, and Hunter had brought down his suitcase, but there was still no sign of Evelyn. Imogen made a point of waiting for him at meals; it was a courtesy she liked to pay, and he was so punctual in his habits that as a rule it never entailed more than a few minutes' wait. But some smothered irritation now made her determined to begin. Tea had been arranged early for Hunter's convenience, and it could not reasonably be delayed.

'Aren't we waiting for Daddy?' asked Gavin, surprised, as he saw the long, glassy spout of tea pour into the shallow cup.

Imogen added milk and handed the flower-wreathed cup and saucer to Hunter. The china was Worcester, and it was reckless to bring it out for tea on the grass, where Gavin had once trodden on a saucer, but she loved to have such things in daily use. 'We can't wait,' she said rather shortly. 'We're having tea early specially for Hunter.'

Halfway through the meal, Evelyn came walking across the lawn.

'Did Miss Silcox drive you back?' asked Imogen. 'Why didn't you bring her in to tea?'

'She has her own tea waiting for her,' he answered.

'This is cold,' said Imogen. 'I'll fetch some more.' He laid a restraining hand on her arm. 'Don't,' he said. 'This'll do.' One of Evelyn's particularities was smoky China tea, brewed in a pot from which boiling water had been poured through the spout not more than five seconds before the tea was made in it. He liked the latter operation to be performed with both hands, almost simultaneously, the tea shovelled in with the left hand, the kettle lifted with the right. Miss Malpas made no pretence of doing this: Imogen did not always do it, though she never neglected it without a pang of guilt, but both of them managed to bring the tea to table in what he called a drinkable condition, and he sometimes gratified them by saying he never got tea as he liked it except at home. Now however he drank a tepid brew with too much milk in it to correct its being overdrawn, and seemed to relish it, pouring himself another half-cup from the dregs.

Once or twice during Hunter's short visit, Imogen had realized a fleeting wish to be alone with her husband. It made her feel compunction as they saw Hunter off, and put unusual earnestness into her invitation to come again as soon as he could. When his car had disappeared from the drive, and the boys had flown away, there was an hour before going to church, and nothing to prevent her from having her wish. She put her arm in his as they walked back into the hall. The drawing-room looked particularly beautiful: the bunches of translucent leaves round the verandah columns and the deeper green of the lawn were all reflected in the looking-glass, while the chandelier was a wreath of watery brilliance in the sinking light. Imogen hoped he would come into the drawing-room but at the door he stopped and withdrew his arm, and, saying he must write letters, went into his study. The door was shut; there was no reason why she should not have followed him, asked him to whom he meant to write, begged him to hurry, and sat down in the same room to wait till he had finished – no reason except the certainty that he would have found such conduct highly irritating, and therefore she could no more cross the hall to the study door than if a bar of iron had been before her chest. She had no heart to sit in the drawing-room: she went upstairs aimlessly, thinking that there was no point in washing up the tea things until it was time to get the supper ready. Miss Malpas, out and away to Reading with old friends, would not be back till late at night, so there was no fear of her pouncing on the used crockery and washing it in what should have been her free time. Imogen came to the head of the stairs and was about to walk into her bedroom when the ringing of the telephone made her stop. A feeling of annoyance at the likelihood, the almost certainty that it would be Blanche Silcox telephoning Evelyn made her dread to go into the room where the telephone extension stood between the two beds. Too late, she now regretted her scrupulous habit of avoiding the telephone when Evelyn answered it. The natural, the normal thing, she now saw, would be to pick up the receiver to find out who was wanted, and replace it if the call were not for her. That was what was done in other households; but she had never done it when she might and she was absolutely prevented by self-consciousness from doing it now. She walked up and down the landing, looking out of the windows, feeling restless, disturbed, very nearly wretched. She came to the window in the end wall, overlooking the river, and stepped out on to the small leaded balcony which was almost embowered by yew branches. The geraniums, awaiting some rearrangement in the dining-room, had been stood upon a greenhouse table immediately underneath. To the left was the flat brick wall of the outbuildings, and against this, Gavin and Tim were hitting tennis balls with a couple of old racquets. A good deal of dexterity was needed, as the run-back on the dark, mossy path was so narrow; before now they had landed up to their knees in the river. The tendency therefore was to hit a good deal sideways. Imogen leaned over the little balcony, to implore mercy for the geraniums, and before she could speak, Gavin's ball had crashed into the little grove of foliage, with a soft, tearing sound and a clatter of earthenware pots rocking on their saucers.

'I say!' said Tim, aghast. 'Will she *do* anything?'

She paused to hear what Gavin would say. He picked up a broken white head, and threw it down carelessly. 'Oh no,' he said, 'she never does. She just *suffers*.' The contempt in his tone stung her to madness. She rushed along the landing with rugs sliding under her feet and hurled herself down the stairs, reaching the hall just as Gavin appeared at the front door, dangling his racquet. He might have come to explain, to apologize even – she did not care.

'Gavin!' she cried passionately. 'How *dare* you do that to my geraniums? How *dare* you? You saw they were standing there! How dare you play that idiotic game just where they were?'

'*I* couldn't help it!'

'You could!'

'I couldn't, I tell you!'

'I'll teach you to help it another time. I shall take away your yesterday's pocket-money for it.'

'Daddy will give me some more if you do.'

'No, he won't,' shouted Imogen, beside herself. 'Not if I tell him not to!' The study door opened and Evelyn came out.

'What on earth—?' he began, in an astonished voice.

Imogen faced him with unusual red in her cheeks and a haughty carelessness that was equally unaccustomed.

'Gavin was deliberately knocking his ball where my geraniums were standing, and he's smashed one of them to bits.'

'That was disgusting of you, Gavin. Why couldn't you have gone somewhere else?'

'I didn't do it on purpose.'

'I'm not saying you did, but you should have had the sense to realize—'

'You may think it was just lack of sense,' Imogen broke in. 'I say it's simply that nothing belonging to *me* is worth bothering about. And I say he ought to give up his week's pocket-money for it.'

'So he shall, my dear, if you say so.'

Imogen turned abruptly and walked upstairs again, clinging to the banister, for her legs trembled. It had ceased to matter to her all of a sudden either that the geranium was broken or that Gavin despised her. She heard Gavin say urgently: 'Can't I have *any* money this week!' and Evelyn reply in an almost conspiratorial tone:

'I don't know. You and I shall have to mind our P's and Q's, my boy!' Then he walked back to the study. As he went she heard him give the laugh that was between a chuckle and a clearing of the throat. It sounded as if he were amused and in a state of high enjoyment. He took unusual pains to be pleasant and conciliating that evening, and she consented to Gavin's being mulcted of half his pocket-money only: not that she now cared whether he paid anything at all; but since Evelyn pleaded with her with great earnestness, gentleness and a sort of deference, even, she did not like to appear to have abandoned all interest in the matter, and when he suggested half as reasonable, she agreed at once.

In bed she clung to him like a drowning creature. The night was very still, and she woke several times to realize that it was, yet her dreams had been loud with the voices of the aspens and the weir.

NINE

The school sent a list of the clothes that would be needed to set Gavin up for the autumn term, and Evelyn read through the lavish particulars of shirts, underclothes, sweaters, shoes and stockings with mounting indignation and dismay. But when Imogen began to look at the items to see whether some could not reasonably be done without, he said No. Since that was what was asked for, that was what Gavin must have.

'But it's ridiculous, all the same,' he added, looking at the list again. 'They must think I'm made of money.'

'So you are, very nearly,' said Imogen, smiling, for she loved to talk about his success, 'only most of it is taken away again.'

'What's left then?' he asked. 'If money is what I'm made of, and the money is taken away, what is left?'

'*You* are,' she said illogically, but with a world of emotion in her eyes.

'Now, now,' he said, 'don't be silly.' His manner was pleasant but abrupt. He bent over the list once more.

'You will be sure to get exactly what it says here, won't you?'

'Yes, of course I will.' He teased her. 'Nothing fanciful, nothing to make him look pretty?'

She shook her head, unsmiling. It was decided that she should begin the shopping at once. It would take time, and in the summer holidays they would be away. Imogen said she would spend a day in London in the middle of that week. Paul Nugent was coming on the next Saturday and Primrose had been asked too, but had been obliged to refuse. It was Old Girls' Week-end at her school. Imogen thought that as Primrose would not be there at the week-end, it would be as well if she asked her out to lunch when she herself was in town. But it turned out that Primrose could not manage this either, for on this Wednesday she was going to Willesden to spend the day with her mother. Primrose was a person of numerous engagements and though these were almost all such as sounded as if they might have been postponed in favour of something of a more rare and eventful kind, Primrose thought otherwise. An invitation to *Tristan* at Covent Garden on a night in May would have caused most people at least to try to rearrange their engagements, but Primrose had been known to refuse it because 'my friend from the Training College' was going out with her that evening, to a cinema and coffee and sandwiches afterwards. This was wholly admirable. It was also, to many people, incomprehensible. Imogen had been brought up in a circle where a great deal of importance was attached to engagements of a glamorous nature, and she would never have thought the worse of another woman for throwing over a previous engagement with herself to go to something extremely eligible of a social or personal kind. The inconvenience would be honestly regretted on the one side and forgivingly borne on the other. But Primrose never considered such a thing. Nor were her rejections of the Greshams' invitations a demonstration of independence against Imogen, for with unswerving integrity she treated everyone alike. At least, she tried to do so. When Paul told her that the Lady Mayoress was giving an At Home at the Mansion House for the Greater London Council for the Prevention of Tuberculosis, Primrose got as far as saying: 'The 29th? Mum and Auntie Beat were thinking of coming here that afternoon.'

'They must think again,' said Paul with unusual terseness. Then he added: 'Give your mother my love and say I need you to come with me that afternoon. Ask her to bring your aunt another day. I know she won't mind.'

Otherwise, when left to herself, Primrose acted with strict impartiality. First come was first served. Imogen naturally did not expect that invitations from her should take precedence over immutable fixtures such as Old Girls' Week-end, but whenever she realized that a dinner in town with herself and her distinguished husband, a week-end at their house with an afternoon of watching polo thrown in, or a matinée of some extremely popular play with herself as escort, had been refused because Primrose had arranged to go and watch a tennis tournament at the club she used to belong to at Willesden, or Auntie Carrie hadn't been up to town for quite a while and had chosen just that afternoon, she bowed her head and felt that it was a chastening experience. She made no complaint now, and left it for Evelyn to say, as he did not fail to do, that Mum, who had nothing to do except keep house for a retired husband, could have had her daughter to lunch any day of the week, and would probably have been glad to make the change at that.

Since Primrose could not come, Imogen made another plan, much more agreeable to herself, to lunch with Cecil Stonor, and as the latter was entitled to a free afternoon, to spend it with her in helping her to buy a dress. Cecil had never in her life made a light-hearted, frivolous purchase. Since she had come to be interested in dress, the matter, as one of those in which she was now making good after a girlhood of gaucheness, plainness and blank social failure, demanded every effort of intelligence and will. She invoked Imogen's aid with the sober concentration she would have used on some problem of her office work. Imogen made the engagement with her for Wednesday, but on this Tuesday evening Evelyn telephoned with an unexpected scheme for a lunch party the following day. He would not be in Court on Wednesday afternoon though he would have to be back in chambers at half-past two; but he had an invitation from Blanche Silcox for the whole party to lunch in the private dining-room of Messrs. Silcox and Boone; he had arranged with Paul Nugent to join them, as Primrose was not to be at home, and so if Imogen—

'Of course I should love to,' said Imogen, 'but Cecil—'

'That's the point. Blanche Silcox will be very pleased to see her, to see you both. I've told her about Cecil's addiction to the stock market and of course she was interested. I'm sure Cecil would be interested to see this old place—'

'Yes, I'm sure she would.'

'And they do themselves amazingly well from what I hear – they put on a lunch fit for an Emperor.'

'It's so awfully nice of her to ask us all. If you're sure – of course we'd love to.'

'Very well, my dear. Then you'll arrange with Cecil to be there at one?'

'Yes.'

'She's always punctual, I know.' He paused, as if wondering whether it might be as well to enjoin punctuality none the less.

Imogen said: 'She *is* always punctual, but I'll tell her you've got an appointment for immediately after lunch.' He sounded relieved, telling her the address of the place, and then gave her an affectionate good night; he was not perfunctory or brief, but she could divine the intense preoccupation with a pile of documents that lay behind his words.

The firm of Silcox and Boone had offices in an angle of Farringdon Street and Ludgate Hill; their front windows looked down on the ceaseless movement of vehicles and foot passengers; into the back ones, the dome of St. Paul's loomed with startling nearness. The firm, like many old-established concerns, maintained its premises in something like the comfort of a private house. There was a dining-room where the directors lunched and to which with notice they could bring their friends. Though the face of the block and a good deal of its interior had been completely modernized, this room was part of the core of the original building. It was possible to stand inside the fireplace and look up the chimney to the sky. The sideboard supported two ebony knifeboxes like funeral urns; the wallpaper was covered with wreaths of vine, once perhaps green on a white ground, now changed by age, smoke and successive varnishings to a dark vine on a ground of deepest saffron. On the glazed surface there hung a signed photograph of Queen Alexandra, an enlarged photograph of old Mr. Silcox with rod and creel, holding an enormous fish by the gills, and a group of directors and their wives coming away from the Royal Garden Party. There were also several framed certificates and an oil painting of shire horses looking over a fence.

Blanche Silcox though not a director herself had the *entrée* to the directors' dining-room as in her father's lifetime. The housekeeper and the waiter were in the relation of family servants to her, and when any advice or help was wanted in the domestic field, the two brothers of the Boone family, and the third partner who was their cousin, usually applied to her rather than to their wives, since she knew the requirements so thoroughly, was very able and had time on her hands.

On the day of her lunch party, Evelyn and Imogen arrived before either Cecil or Paul Nugent. Blanche greeted them in her usual manner of awkward goodwill; a long table was already occupied but a smaller one was reserved for her party. Imogen was eager to be pleased, knowing how much Evelyn liked his friends and their belongings to be appreciated, and how quick he was to notice any failure on her part to come up to an enthusiastic estimate of his own; but she was so genuinely delighted by the room that she forgot everything but the pleasure of examining it. Blanche Silcox seemed anxious to depreciate its features. She showed Imogen how to get a glimpse of the sky up the chimney – made the room awfully cold in winter, she said, always a draught. When Imogen exclaimed with admiration at the knife-boxes, Blanche said gruffly: 'Funny old things, aren't they?' while as for the wallpaper: 'My dear, did you ever see anything so frightful? Even in my father's day, they were always saying it must be scrapped, but it never got done.'

'You won't get any support from Imogen over that,' said Evelyn. 'She has a passion for the oldest and dirtiest wallpaper she can find. You've seen our drawing-room one? A perfect disgrace.' But he was pleased by Imogen's spontaneous enthusiasm, and when she turned and demanded his sympathy at the astonishing sight of the great dome, coloured like a thundercloud, for they were on a level with the square balustrade from which rose the columns that supported it, she met a look of amused, indulgent tenderness on his face. It disappeared quickly, for she wanted to put her head out of the window, but that would have showed too much *entrain*. He did not want, in a dining-room full of strangers, to hang on to her heels while she launched herself over Ludgate Hill. He checked her in an impatient undertone. 'Covered with smuts,' he said irritably.

The waiter now showed in Paul and Cecil, who had arrived independently with equal punctuality. Evelyn introduced Cecil to Blanche Silcox with a genial allusion to Cecil's interest in the stock market.

'Oh, you follow it, I hear?' said Blanche. She gave Cecil one of her extremely keen, prolonged glances. It was almost a stare.

'Yes,' said Cecil composedly, as they sat down. 'I am an amateur. Of course you are a past mistress of it.'

'I don't do much now,' said Blanche.

'You keep an eye on your investments, though?' said Evelyn.

'Well, yes, but the buying and selling I leave to our broker. Of course I keep abreast. He doesn't do anything without discussing it with me first.'

Cecil raised her eyes of Arctic brightness, considered Miss Silcox an instant and lowered them again.

'I'm quite sure he doesn't.' Her unspoken comment was picked up by Imogen as plainly as if it had been put into words.

Paul Nugent had to be at hospital by quarter-past two and therefore the taking in of an appropriate quantity of food was his first concern. The meal was of an almost historic excellence: large but delicate slices of cold roast beef, baked potatoes with pats of butter pushed into their slit skins, hearts of celery, apple pie and clotted cream, the last made by the housekeeper from quarts of milk, in a machine provided by Miss Silcox for the purpose. Blanche apologized for the food: 'Very plain and ordinary. I hope you don't mind,' she said. Paul would rather have eaten inferior food at home than join a lunch party when he had to be present at a resection of the lung in an hour's time, but he could seldom withstand any suggestion of Evelyn Gresham's, and Imogen's presence made him desire the meeting. Through the noise of conversation in the room, the muffled din outside the windows and the cares and preoccupations of his brain, the enchantment diffused itself. He spoke to her now with almost brusque cheerfulness, enquiring after Gavin, and she told him of her successes and reverses in shopping for the school outfit. Evelyn went on talking to Blanche Silcox. When the beef was put before them, the waiter brought a thick dark red wine, which surprised Evelyn because he thought it was port. He had not realized the extent of the hospitality which his presence occasioned. It turned out that this was Constantia wine, fine old Constantia, imported not later than 1840 when the Constantia vineyards had ceased to bear, a few bottles of which remained in the cellar acquired by the late Mr. Silcox.

The wine was sweet and heavy and Imogen thought that if port were considered a dessert wine, Constantia should be treated as such; but Evelyn, whatever he might have thought in other circumstances, was ready now to drink it as if it were claret, extremely gratified by an attention so rare and costly. Paul did not much care for wines of the kind described by wine merchants as full-bodied and of generous bouquet, but he drank off half a glassful in a businesslike way before he settled down to his plate of beef. It was a little too potent for Imogen or Cecil to drink with pleasure, so proper appreciation was left to Evelyn, who sipped and smacked his lips, and showed such vivid enjoyment that Imogen felt a creeping dismay invade her as she realized that nothing she was able to do for him would produce that degree of satisfaction. Then she scolded herself for the all-too-feminine trick of referring to herself everything she noticed, and gave her whole attention to what Paul was saying.

Evelyn interrupted their conversation about Gavin's winter-weight vests by saying:

'I told Leeper you would be with us over the week-end, and he and his wife are very keen you should go with us to their party on Saturday evening.'

'My dear fellow!' Paul expostulated. 'What on earth should I do when I got there?'

'I don't know,' said Evelyn. 'My method is just to show up – speak to the host and hostess to prove I've been there – and then cut off as quick as I can. It's not difficult in a big crowd. But *you* can stay and keep Imogen company. She enjoys these things.'

Imogen saw Blanche Silcox regarding her with an appraising look.

'I'm not as fond of them as all that,' she said in a self-excusing tone. 'I don't want to go if nobody else does.'

'Paul will enjoy it,' said Evelyn in a decisive, not to say dictatorial manner. Then he laughed and said: 'I was joking. Of course we don't want to drag you there. We shan't stay long. At any rate, *I* shan't.'

'It's very kind of your friends,' said Paul in tones of acute discomfort, 'but I can't feel that I should have the slightest *locus standi* in a thing of that kind—'

'Of course you would!' cried Evelyn bluffly. 'I've explained to the Leepers who you are. Tuberculosis ranks very high as a social asset, I assure you. Gynaecology is first, I should say, but tuberculosis is undoubtedly second. I should say tropical medicine would rate about the lowest. Wouldn't you?' He turned to Blanche Silcox, before he recollected that this was not the sort of question on which she was likely to have any answer. She gave a throaty laugh however, and Paul said hopefully: 'Couldn't you say that I'm *devoted* to tropical medicine in my spare time? That I really can't talk about anything except parasitism?'

Evelyn said: 'If you start talking about ticks to Mrs. Leeper, ticks will be all the go with her.'

Paul sighed and got on with his lunch. Cecil meanwhile had used the opportunity to study Blanche Silcox. Imogen had described the latter to her with great earnestness but the description had conveyed little of what Cecil now found to be the reality. Imogen had said that Blanche Silcox was obviously much attracted by Evelyn, and that she was so thoroughly kind and useful to him it was only natural that he should appreciate it. There was nothing in it on his side, naturally. When Cecil had the people concerned before her eyes, she began to doubt the truth of this judgment immediately. She doubted it even though Blanche Silcox's appearance was beyond anything she had been prepared for. Imogen was by now accustomed to Miss Silcox's manner of dress and did not pay more than a passing attention to the fact that on this occasion Blanche's hat threw into the shade anything which she had seen her wear up till now. Cecil however had not had the preparation of the hats Blanche had previously worn. To her startled eye the present one, in black velvet, of lofty and copious design, recalled the sable helmet that descended with a crash upon the pavement of Otranto, 'a hundred times larger than any casque made for human head.' But she had not expected, either, anyone so forceful as Blanche, so quietly determined, so full of magnetism, of heat. The impression Blanche made upon her in the first few moments was like that of the indrawing draught of a furnace. Had this quality been, as it were, unregulated, it might well have frightened a man off; but here it was accompanied by the awkwardness, the diffidence, the modesty, of an inexperienced elderly woman. What the combined effect of these qualities might produce, even in the most unlikely circumstances, was by no means easy to decide. Cecil was fonder of Imogen than of anyone in the world, and though this was not saying very much, it said everything of which she was capable. Therefore when she roused her powers of observation for Imogen's sake, her mind became so alert that everything she saw and heard told her something. She noticed that when Blanche Silcox spoke to Evelyn it was in a slightly lower tone than she used to anybody else.

The beef was replaced by the apple pie, aromatic with clove, and the great dish of clotted cream. Evelyn said he did not as a rule care for a sweet at lunchtime, but this was so excellent he must have a spoonful. When he lunched with men only, he usually took cheese instead.

'Oh, but there is cheese for you,' said Blanche Silcox. 'They can put it on now if you don't want any pie.'

Evelyn's deprecation was ignored, and the waiter brought a variety of biscuits, and a wooden board on which several kinds of cheese were arranged.

'What are these?' asked Evelyn, examining them with intense interest. 'I don't recognize anything except the Gruyère.'

'That one,' said Blanche, 'is just a milk cheese. I thought the ladies might like it. But you must try one of these, either this, which is made of goat's milk, or the yellow one; they're both local cheeses from the Warwickshire Cheese Fair. It was almost given up during the war but now it's going again, I'm glad to say. I go every year just to see what they make, and I buy as much as I think will keep.'

Evelyn had cut himself a sliver from each and was now tasting their pungent flavours with critical delight. A woman who understood so much about cheese and would go to such trouble to get it exacted his homage. The whole lunch party felt that this was so. Miss Silcox's role of hostess took on a kind of classical success like that of the Virtuous Woman in Proverbs who brought food from afar. Coffee was sent for at the same time, as Paul was pressed. When it came it was black, burning hot and of strong fragrance.

'I am exhausting my stock of adjectives,' said Evelyn as he swallowed his first mouthful. The pudding plates being removed, the rest of the company were invited to take cheese.

'You'd like the milk, I expect?' said Blanche to Imogen with one of her intent looks. She pushed the board towards Imogen so that the milk cheese was decisively presented to her.

'Thank you,' said Imogen. 'It's just what I do like.'

'And you?' said Blanche to Cecil. The latter was listening to a remark of Paul's. She merely smiled in the direction of Miss Silcox without meeting the latter's eye, and silently helped herself to the heavy-flavoured local cheese.

'Won't you find that too strong?' asked Evelyn, surprised and amused.

'No, thank you,' answered Cecil carelessly. 'It's very good.' She turned her attention to Paul again.

The party lunching at the other table showed signs of breaking up and a florid lady in black, decorated with a striking display of pearl necklaces and diamond brooches, crossed the room and spoke to Miss Silcox on her way out.

'Not stopping a moment. Don't get up,' she cried to Paul and

Evelyn, fruitlessly, for they had stood up and remained standing with their napkins in their hands, 'but we shall be in your part of the world next Sunday, my dear, and I wondered if we could come on to you for tea?'

'I'm most awfully sorry,' said Blanche, 'but I shan't be at home. I shall be in town.'

'Oh well!' The lady seemed resigned. 'Better luck next time. *Must* fly—'

'I'm most awfully—' Blanche repeated, but the lady was no longer there. The men sat down again and Blanche exclaimed· 'What lies one does tell!'

'Shall you be in town?' asked Evelyn curiously.

'No. I shall be at home,' she said. Cecil looked at her. A woman of Blanche Silcox's homely appearance would as a rule be given credit for speaking the truth, she thought. To find that she lied aptly, spontaneously, just as if she were another sort of woman altogether, gave Cecil a good deal to think about.

Paul drew out his watch and looked at it in the palm of his hand. He got up. 'Thank you very much for such a pleasant lunch,' he said to Miss Silcox. 'It was most kind of you to include me in your invitation. I must apologize for having to leave so abruptly.' The goodbyes, repeated thanks and lookings forward to meeting at the end of the week were gone through, and Paul retreated hurriedly. Imogen's face and the moss roses pinned to her jacket carried in one reach of his mind, the rest of it concentrated upon the hope of picking up a taxi as soon as he came out into Farringdon Street.

Imogen was about to sit down again as Paul left the dining-room, but she changed her purpose when she saw that Evelyn remained standing. He too now took out his watch.

'You and Cecil had better be starting on your shopping or whatever it is you want to do, hadn't you?' he said. 'You have only a certain time to do it in, haven't you?' he asked Cecil. 'Hadn't you better be off right away?' Cecil looked at him silently but smiled. No one who saw her could suppose her to be tongue-tied; as Evelyn was not her husband, and she was a stranger to Miss Silcox, her silence was natural, becoming, even.

Imogen however took the cue at once.

'I suppose we had better,' she said. She thanked Blanche Silcox warmly for the delightful lunch – such superb food, the room so interesting, such a charming occasion altogether.

'You must come again,' said Blanche. She sounded very much in earnest. Her eyes were lowered, with a troubled expression.

'I should simply love to. And we shall see you very soon, I hope.'

'Such near neighbours, practically next door,' said Blanche with the same slightly harassed air.

'You'll take the 5.45 down, will you?' asked Evelyn.

'Yes, nothing later than that. Shall you be on it?' Imogen turned to Blanche Silcox with a friendly enquiry.

'No, I am staying up here for the night. It's my stepsister's birthday, and she's having a dinner party and we're all going to a show.'

'I do hope you'll enjoy it.'

'I suppose we shall. I've forgotten the name of the thing though they did tell me.' They all laughed.

Evelyn then shook hands with Cecil. 'You must come down to us for a week-end soon,' he said. 'Imogen, get her to choose a date.' He kissed Imogen's cheek. 'Goodbye, my dear. I'll be down for lunch on Saturday.'

He came with them across the room and saw them out of the door.

They came out in silence and rounded the corner, then stood still, looking towards the great flight of pillared steps that crowned Ludgate Hill.

'Let's go up the dome,' suggested Cecil.

'Yes, do let's! But don't you want to begin your shopping?'

'Not so much as this.' They walked across the open space,

skirting the statue of Brandy Nan. It seemed that all memory of the lunch party they had that moment left had been banished by mutual consent.

'How interesting all this part is!' exclaimed Imogen. 'And I hardly know it. Of course I've been to the Old Bailey once or twice to listen to Evelyn but I've always gone and come away in a taxi. I'd like to get to know all these streets by walking. It's so thrilling to see their names! Paul's Churchyard and Newgate Street – I remember how excited I was when I saw that Wood Street really did come out into Cheapside.'

'Had you thought it wouldn't?'

'Well, but "The Reverie of Poor Susan," you know! You can see the very corner where the thrush's cage must have been hanging! So of course

Bright volumes of vapour through Lothbury glide
And a river flows on through the vale of Cheapside.'

'Of course it did. But I should have thought Wordsworth's saying the streets are where they are makes it less surprising to find them there, not more?'

'Yes, in a way. But when anything is very delightful or interesting, I find it almost hard to believe.'

'Does it work the other way? Do you find a thing hard to believe if it's very bad?' But now they were walking up the nave, so lofty, so vast, so hushed, so light, it was natural that conversation should die. When they had reached the staircase that led to the dome and were climbing the seemingly endless spirals of shallow, beautifully curved wooden stairs, Imogen said:

'There is so much I want to hear – about the office, and all.'

'Don't ask now, it'll keep.'

'This does fill one's head, certainly.'

As they mounted, purer and stronger light poured in through

the oval windows; the sense of airiness, brightness, vastness increased the higher they went, until the climax burst upon them, dazzling, as they stepped out on to the Stone Gallery that ringed the base of the dome, breathless with the climb and with the impact upon their brains of fathomless light above, the city below, and immediately in front of them the pale pillars of the parapet that striped the prospect.

'I thought there was a great sound as we came out!' cried Imogen, but all was silent, until, gradually, muted noises from below rose one by one.

'Don't let's go up to the cross and ball,' gasped Cecil. 'There's no need to be fanatical. We only want the view.' They held their hats on and began to move round the walk, lingering between the pairs of columns in the balustrade. Along to the left the river carried the eye to Tower Bridge above its spit of pebble beach. Returning, the gaze was caught, almost immediately below, by a great sea-green globe, the weathered copper dome of the Central Criminal Court.

'Look,' said Cecil, 'there's St. Sepulchre's just opposite. Are you going to fall down in a heap because it really and truly is just outside the site of Newgate? And they really and truly could hear the bell tolling for their execution as they stood in the Press Yard, waiting to set out for Tyburn?'

Imogen said: 'Yes, I shouldn't wonder if I did.' She clasped her hands round a pair of pillars, craning between. 'Down Newgate Street, down Holborn, down Oxford Street,' she murmured. 'What a long way, going slowly! It does sometimes seem, apart from war, that there is *nothing* to be frightened of now, compared with then.'

Cecil said nothing. Presently they had completed the circuit. As they re-entered the doorway and began to go down the stairs which seemed almost dark now, well-lighted as they were, Imogen said: 'I had not quite realized how very near the Old Bailey is to Ludgate Hill.'

'Just a few minutes' walk.'

'Though when Evelyn is in court he always lunches there. The judges and the leaders all lunch together. Otherwise that dining-room of Miss Silcox's firm would be a very convenient place for him to lunch at.'

'Yes, very. Where does Miss Silcox stay when she's in town?'

'I don't know – at a hotel, I suppose. Oh, Cecil, *do* let us arrange a week-end for you to come down to us. I want you to so much.'

'And I want to.'

'I'm sorry that you and Hunter couldn't manage the same one.'

'I'm just as glad it didn't turn out like that. You and I shouldn't have seen so much of each other. And I do see him fairly often now.'

'And I hope that's pleasant?'

'Yes, it's very pleasant,' answered Cecil tranquilly. They were in a taxi now, speeding down Fleet Street, to reach Piccadilly and Bond Street. Imogen squeezed Cecil's hand.

'What sort of dress must you have?' she asked eagerly.

'For sherry parties, dining out. Not a long skirt. Black, I think—' Cecil showed herself in one of her very rare moments of uncertainty and confusion. A black dress would be the best from many points of view but she did not know if she really wanted a black one. Imogen however would know how to choose. She luxuriated in the rare sensation of being able to leave a decision to somebody who was more capable of making it than she was. Two hours later, the frock had been bought, conforming to the requirements Cecil had laid down but presenting a romantic variation on them; for the skirt was not long, but it was spreading, and the colour was dark, but a dark greenish blue sprinkled with small gold stars. Imogen's own parcels were now collected, and arranged round her in a carriage at Waterloo. She and Cecil had arranged that the latter would come to Chalk the week-end after next.

'You'll have all about the Leepers' party to tell by that time.' Imogen looked surprised as if she had forgotten this impending event. 'So I shall,' she said. A guard now motioned Cecil off the carriage step and she retreated some paces. From this distance, she saw Imogen seated in the far corner, turned away from her to answer some question from a man opposite about the carriage window. Imogen looked very elegant and graceful, prosperous, poised. She would have looked almost unapproachable had it not been for the gentleness and simplicity that formed such a charming feature of her appearance. But then Imogen turned to look through the window for the last of Cecil. Her face might have belonged to a different person; it was troubled, searching, and looked on the verge of tears. Cecil evaded the guard and pressed forward again, waving. Imogen's eyes lighted up and she kissed her hand with an eager, affectionate gesture, as the train started. Cecil walked slowly out of the great station, now filling with the crowds who used it at this time every evening. She took a taxi to the Post Office in the neighbourhood of Long Acre which her business experience had taught her stayed open late, and here she was able to consult an up-to-date edition of the London Telephone Directory. In it, she saw that Miss Blanche Silcox had an address in Halkin Street.

TEN

On Saturday morning Evelyn's clerk telephoned to say that Mr. Gresham wouldn't be able to get home in time for lunch after all. Work had come in which would detain him most of the day. Would they therefore not expect him till they saw him? Dr. Nugent however would be with Mrs. Gresham for lunch as arranged.

Paul had never relinquished his principle of not being alone with Imogen if he could help it, and since a solitary afternoon with her was now forced on him, for it could not be expected that Tim and Gavin should give up their activities to keep the grown-ups company, he determined that the time should be spent in work rather than in loitering. He was interested in collecting evidence from novels of the nineteenth century of the raging development of tuberculosis such as Imogen had told him was to be found in the novels of Charlotte Yonge.

He decided that this afternoon should be devoted to a compiling of references. Immediately after lunch he told her to collect the novels about which she had been telling him, so they brought down *Hopes and Fears*, *The Trial* and *Pillars of the House* from the bookcase on the landing and carried them out to the river bank, where the distant calls and splashes of the boys and the frequent passing of canoes and launches did away with any sense of solitude. Imogen turned over pages and read out paragraphs, described characters and related incidents, until Paul felt that if anything could have induced him to read his way through the densely populated novels of Miss Yonge, it would have been Imogen's eyes fixed on him while she assured him how interesting he would find them. However, after an afternoon's reading and listening, he admitted that Charlotte Yonge's description of tuberculous subjects showed unusual observation, and that she had shown a grasp of the relation between disease and temperament which he had never seen bettered in a lay writer. Most novelists, he said, imposed consumption on a character as if it were a broken leg. He was divided between admiration of her powers of observation and dismay at her indifference to cause and effect. Imogen meant to make his flesh creep with Dr. May's saying when his son Tom married a girl so prostrated by tuberculosis that she could not get up off the sofa: 'I have liked none of our home weddings better,' but before she could direct him to this passage in *The Trial*, Paul was deeply immersed in the first chapter, where Dr. May and Dr. Spencer were arguing about the origin of a scarlet fever epidemic. When Paul found that, though Miss Yonge had stated the epidemic to be scarlet fever, she made Dr. Spencer perform a tracheotomy as if it had been diphtheria, his enthusiasm knew no bounds.

'The date!' he exclaimed, 'the date this was first published! Can you find it?'

'I think I can – indoors. Do you need the *actual* date?'

'Of course. We want to know how much before Jenner this is. You see, *she* doesn't distinguish between typhoid, scarlet fever, diphtheria, it's all "the fever" to her – to a woman as knowledgeable as that! Do find the date if you can!'

Imogen rose, a little unwillingly, disinclined to stir and a little piqued at finding the interest of her society superseded in Paul's mind by the interest of what he was reading. With Evelyn, such an idea would not have occurred to her; she would have darted away to do his bidding, delighted at the chance; not that she showed any unwillingness now. She found the date of the publication of *The Trial*, 1864, and Paul said: 'Then what we need now are the dates Jenner's lectures were published – the *Identity and Non-identity of Typhoid Fever*, and *Diphtheria, Its Symptoms and Treatment.*' He looked at her speculatively.

'Paul,' she said, 'there is *nowhere* in our house that I can find that.'

He smiled, and said, 'A pity. However I think we should be fairly safe in putting them both somewhere between 1850 and 1860 – there or thereabouts. So it was quite excusable in the general public – even the intelligent section of it – to know nothing of the differentiation of fevers in 1864.'

He gave Imogen his pen while he took the pencil from his diary and between them they copied out the striking parts of the passages they had discovered. At least, he thought, he had kept her little nose to the grindstone. As for himself, what a baseless notion it was that a woman who enchanted him would appear less enchanting because she was busily employed beside him! They stood on the sloping turf beside the stone urn, the papers and books collected, ready to take indoors. The extraordinary beauty of the river and the woods, the garden in the afternoon sun, absorbed them both. A vanished launch had left the water stirring; glassy waves slapped the bank, the scum of minute water plants rolled on gleaming circular ridges, then spread flat and swayed to and fro; the leaves of great plane trees on the bank mottled the water; the water sent quivering gleams of light up the dappled tree stems.

'*The shadow of my dear delight stood trembling by my side.*' He did not utter the words, but asked her if she were fond of Blake's poetry? Yes, she said of what she could understand; she could not read the Prophetic Books. 'I am inclined to think,' he went on, as they began walking towards the house 'that the one thing all great poets have in common, is the power of saying a great amount in a very short space. Would you?'

She paused. 'Yes, perhaps I should,' she said. 'What were you thinking of in Blake's poetry that reminded you of that?'

This sympathetic reply – was it social aptitude, a personal sympathy with himself, or could she really want to know? Perhaps the question came from all three motives. To have it asked at all gave a sense of soothing and exhilaration to a man of his arid domestic climate.

'What made you say that?' she repeated, looking round.

'I was thinking of

How the youthful harlot's curse
Blasts the new born infant's tear
And blights with plague the marriage hearse.

Volumes of social history, morals, hygiene, all in a line or two.'

'Yes, and sufferings too – "*The youth pined away with desire, And the pale virgin shrouded in snow.*"'

'I see! You would rather talk about the sufferings of love than of economic exploitation?'

'Yes, actually. But I was not meaning to turn the conversation, it was just that those words slipped into my mind.'

Miss Malpas was bringing the teapot into the drawing-room. 'They rang through again from New Square,' she said. "E'll dine in town and drive down afterwards. But you and the Doctor are to go to the party without 'im.' Paul looked aghast.

'When did they telephone?' asked Imogen.

'About an hour ago. I didn't fetch you in as 'e wasn't speaking 'imself.'

'No. Thank you. Shall you mind going to the Leepers' very much?' she asked.

'I really never understood that I was meant to – I haven't brought any dress clothes—'

'Goodness! You wouldn't need them in any case—'

'Well of course if you really want an escort—'

'I don't think I could go without either you or Evelyn.'

'But surely, nowadays, a woman—'

'Oh yes, as far as that goes – but you see if she's been expected to come with one or other of two distinguished men – and then comes by herself, she's a disappointment, and she's an extra woman, too, and that's never very acceptable unless she's particularly dazzling.'

Paul smiled indulgently at what he thought nonsensical, but if she really wanted his company he had not the heart to refuse it, and if he were to do so, she might stay at home herself. It was better to spend the time with her in uncongenial surroundings than in the solitude of woods and water and failing light.

Over tea, Imogen said suddenly: 'We might ring up Blanche Silcox and ask her to come round for a drink before dinner. I ought to do that sometimes. I will.'

'She lives near, does she?'

'Quite near if you cross the river beyond our stile and walk up through the wood. It's farther by road, but then it takes only a few minutes by car.'

Gavin came in very late, dirty and wanting tea; he flopped down with an air that said he was too much exhausted to go and wash. Imogen was in the act of carrying out the teapot. She knew advantage ought not to be taken of his father's absence and nerved herself to say: 'Go and wash. You'll just have time while I'm getting fresh tea.'

Gavin opened his mouth to say he couldn't, when Paul added: 'Yes, cut along. Then when you've had some tea you can show me the mouse skeletons.'

Gavin made out of the room and across the hall like an athlete in training for a walking race. Interest had banished in a fraction of a second every trace of muscular fatigue. Paul noted the small miracle such as nature was for ever performing before his attentive eyes. When tea was finished he and Gavin went out to the playroom and Imogen who had followed them into the kitchen with the tray heard Gavin say in the low tone of concentration which reminded her so much of Evelyn's: 'This is the one I can't fit in. I can't see where it goes.'

After a moment Paul said: 'Part of it's missing. That's why you didn't recognize it.'

'I ought to be certified,' Gavin muttered in disgust.

'Not yet,' said Paul; 'you haven't given yourself time to learn all the bones, that's all. Let's look at the others.'

Imogen went back to the drawing-room. She found she did not know Miss Silcox's telephone number. It was time she learned it. When she made the connection she was answered by Miss Silcox's parlourmaid. Imogen asked to speak to Blanche and the somewhat quavering old voice replied:

'Miss Silcox was to have been home to lunch, ma'am. We expected her home to lunch. But now we hear she's staying in town till later and she won't be down till some time this evening. Can I give any message?'

'No, thank you,' said Imogen. 'I'll ring later.' She walked out to the verandah and lifted a drooping mass of the china rose that was growing up one of the pillars. She came in again and went upstairs for a piece of thread to tie up the cluster in case its weight should pull down its sisters after it. As she bound and knotted the thread round the stems and the pillar, she did not even try to tell herself that Blanche Silcox might have been detained in town for any number of reasons. She was convinced that Blanche had stayed to drive down with Evelyn after dinner – to drive him herself; no doubt she had offered to do so. But how had she known he was to be detained? Perhaps they had lunched together. Blanche must have remained in town considerably after her stepsister's birthday dinner. Well, that was not an out-of-the-way thing to do. At all events, Imogen determined she would ask Evelyn about it at the first opportunity. If Miss Silcox had been a different sort of woman, the situation would begin to look threatening. As it was it was not reassuring, for Imogen was already sure that Blanche Silcox's own emotions were deeply stirred by Evelyn, and the vague but powerful impression Imogen had received of her strength of character, her intensity, her determination, and added to all this, her nearness, made up into a threat of some sort to their peace of mind, indistinct but menacing.

Gavin was enjoying himself so thoroughly in Paul's company, Imogen decided they would all three have dinner together at eight instead of Gavin's having his supper separately as he usually did. She did not dress until after the meal, so that between dressing herself and getting Gavin first into the bathroom and then out of it, it was ten o'clock before she came downstairs, in palest yellow, with some of the yellow china roses tucked into her bosom. Paul raised himself from the sofa where under the lamp he had been reading *The Trial* with mixed feelings of censure and admiration. Imogen straightened the cushions, thinking of Evelyn's arrival, and said: 'We could find quite a lot of illnesses and deaths in her other books, only they wouldn't be from consumption, I'm afraid.'

'I prefer the ones attributable to consumption,' he said, smiling.

'You wouldn't like one due to a miscarriage, brought on by the person's tripping over a croquet hoop?'

'That's rather off my beat, I'm afraid, but she seems to have envisaged every aspect of the medical position very thoroughly.'

'Oh yes, and there were sunstrokes too, and all sorts of accidents.'

'I noticed the sunstroke. The chorister, you mean, in *Pillars of the House*. It's strange the dread of heat they had in those days. Their clothes made it formidable, of course – and then, too, possibly—'

He paused. Imogen waited a second but when he did not go on she excused herself and went out to ask Miss Malpas to expect Evelyn at any time now. This was a mere gesture, since Miss Malpas was doing that in any case, and was ready to produce iced coffee, iced beer or hot China tea, which ever Evelyn might fancy as soon as he came in.

Paul had been going to say that perhaps the present mania for heat and sunlight in the population was a sign of sinking vitality, but he was glad to have been prevented. His mind was permanently depressed by his view of human affairs, but he had the doctor's instinctive caution in saying anything that might perplex, mislead or be uselessly distressing to the laity.

He and Imogen now set out for the Leepers' house. Imogen said: 'I expect Primrose is in the middle of her party by now. I hope she's enjoying it.'

'I hope so. I expect she is. She's a loyal little person,' he added, as a vision of the Old Girls rose before him; though was this party likely to be any improvement on theirs, to a rational mind?

A good number of Mrs. Leeper's invitations had been accepted. The village street was choked with cars, from Oxford, Wiltshire, London, and their lights gave a strange air of wakefulness and dreamlike excitement to the scene. This was intensified as they drew near the gate under the ilex trees; lurid lights from orange-coloured lamps filled the huge oblong windows of the Leepers' house, inside which figures circled silently like the inmates of an aquarium. As Paul and Imogen went up the path however sounds began to reach them of talk and laughter, occasionally rising to a shout and a tinkle of broken glass. Imogen was eager to see the sights but approached with diffident step; Paul, secretly reluctant, walked with a firm tread. They saw at once that Paul had no need to apologize for his clothes; though the women were in full evening dress, few of the men had adopted even the formality of a stiff collar. Mr. Leeper, who was operating near the threshold, wore a flannel suit and a scarlet cummerbund. Paul and Imogen, encouraged by his jovial shout and gesture towards the far side of the room, made their way past the iron staircase to the doors that led out into the garden.

There should have been a moon but it was concealed behind webs of murky cloud, and as the windows of the house gave little light on the back garden, it was both dusk and chill. Paul felt that no one with experience of English summer nights could have reasonably depended on anything else. Some fairy lights however traced the path with their wan illumination and led to the lawn where a man sat, wearing a toreador's hat, and surrounded by a tense group to whom Paul and Imogen joined themselves. The man was singing an exclamatory song in an unidentified language, accompanying himself by a stringed instrument. After a few harsh, rallying cries, he ceased dramatically, and everybody clapped. Imogen's heels were now sinking into a flower-bed and she clutched Paul's arm for support. The night grew darker and a vagrant but searching breeze played on the backs of their necks. Paul said: 'I think we had better go indoors.' They re-entered the house by a door which led into a smaller room, opening off the one through which they had come into the garden, and realized that they had now penetrated to the heart of the gathering.

This room also was lit with orange-shaded lights, but it was so full of people, nothing else about it could be noticed. There was a hum of conversation in the ranks nearest the door, but as Paul and Imogen urged their way towards the bright head of their hostess, they became aware of a hush and an immobility.

On a low settee Zenobia was sitting. Her dress was a mass of darkest purple gauze; her heavy moonstone necklace was more translucent than her neck but scarcely paler; on her inky hair she wore a very small black cap studded with brilliants and silver. She looked like a princess in a Persian miniature. Beside her sat Lord Fingal, whose collection of musical snuff-boxes was world-famous, whose cats slept in eighteenth-century catbaskets shaped like four-poster beds, whose town and country houses were favourite subjects with the photographers of *Vogue*, *Country Life* and *The Connoisseur*. The poise which all these possessions had helped to confer, however, availed him nothing under the impact of his first meeting with Zenobia. He had the look of a man who has been hauled out from the wreckage of a car smash. For a few instants following the remark that Paul and Imogen had arrived too late to hear, Zenobia maintained her complete stillness, pensive, remote. Then she unclasped her hands and slowly spread them on each side of her purple lap. Lord Fingal sighed as if under great oppression, and seemed to come to himself. A man approached with a loaded tray, and Zenobia, taking a small glass that sparkled like a ruby, turned to smile mysteriously at the men behind her. The crowd pressed more closely round the sofa to hear what she said.

'. . . saying to Lord Fingal,' they heard. 'I don't know how one ever recovers from the experience, but one does. I have come to *dread* knowing that I am going to write a poem – and yet, of course, that is what one lives for.' Lord Fingal's eyes were closed. He groaned. Then he opened them suddenly and took a glass off the tray that was still proffered at his elbow.

Imogen was riveted, like a child with an absorbing picture book. She would gladly have stood, gazing and listening with all her might; but, regretfully, she could tell without looking that Paul was not entertained. Out of doors he had been cold; here it was too hot. He was surrounded and pressed upon by people of a sort whom he didn't like; in all the horde there was only Imogen whom he wished to talk to, and here he was almost prevented from talking to her. He had been led and shoved through a crowd to look at a famous beauty; now that he had seen her he would have liked to go back to the Greshams' house. Deliverance could not be had as soon as that he knew, but he murmured to Imogen that perhaps they ought to make way for somebody else, and she put her hand inside his elbow and let him lead her towards the outer room.

They passed Corinne Leeper, on this evening only less beautiful than her sister, startlingly moulded in white satin that at a distance made her look like a naked neo-Grecian statue. She smiled graciously. 'I must see that you have a word with Zenobia presently,' she promised. She laid her hand on the arm of a gaunt lady wearing the sort of necklace dug out of the tombs of the ancient Britons, to whom she said: 'This is Dr. Nugent, my dear.' The lady's hollow eyes fixed Paul intently. 'You are a consulting physician to the Metropolitan Chest Hospital!' she stated. Paul guardedly admitted as much. 'I must talk to you about these mobile X-ray units for mass-radiography,' she said passionately. 'Such a splendid thing, don't you think? But the apathy of the Ministry of Health, and the local government – The idea has barely got going. It's up to you doctors to throw your weight into it, you know. Surely you agree?'

'About the advisability of X-raying everybody? I'm not sure that I—'

'Not sure!' exclaimed the lady indignantly. 'What a reactionary person you must be!'

Paul bowed slightly.

'I *think* you'll find,' said the lady with quiet dignity, 'that all the *really big* men agree with it, like Sir Henry Bond, for instance.' She named the man whose pupil Paul Nugent had been, whose colleague he now was. It so happened, that though some eminent physicians were in favour of mass-radiography, Sir Henry Bond was not one of them, for he thought its material advantages were offset by its psychological ill-effects. Sir Henry thought, and brought up his students to think, that subject to rational precaution, the less people were encouraged to think about their lungs the better: their lungs or any other part of their anatomy, but the lungs were his personal concern. Paul could not but remember some of Sir

Henry's comments on the subjects who had been X-rayed by mobile units, and had then been to their doctors for nerve tonics to keep them up while they waited to hear the results.

One of the differences between himself and Evelyn Gresham was that the latter would undertake to enlighten and put down anyone who made a crass misstatement, in whatever circumstances they made it. Although from where Paul now stood, the noise of talk was so loud and steady that it was no longer broken up into words but made a continuous sound like that of pressure on an electric bell, Evelyn, undaunted, would have taken the lady to task at once apropos of Sir Henry Bond and administered a sound drubbing. Paul almost never corrected anybody unless professional duty obliged him to do it. As to attempting it here, it never occurred to him. He bowed again and wished himself away. Imogen with what he thought of as uncanny responsiveness to his state of mind, allowed the passage of the white-coated man with his tray of empty glasses to separate them from the lady with the torque, and used the brief respite to gain cover in the crowd again. The lady was no doubt willing to let go of such a reactionary, but he was inclined to give Imogen credit for everything that fell out well, just as he could never bring himself to blame her for what was admittedly her fault.

While Imogen looked about vaguely to see someone she knew, Paul's eye was attracted towards an erection that was a cross between a gibbet and a hat-stand, from whose arms dangled contraptions made of wire, the latest and most significant development of the art of Willy Quinn. Following the direction of his impersonal gaze, she saw the entrance of a guest, tall and loose-limbed, with long, waving hair, who flapped his arms and jutted his chin as he approached, with the air of a greyhound in the slips. This was the editor of a Left review who had just returned from a journalistic mission to a sphere of great unrest in the Middle East.

His arrival was greeted with rapture by Mrs. Leeper, who felt that it conferred diplomatic status on her. She at once established him at the foot of the copper staircase with a drink, meaning him to stay there while she collected a few privileged guests whom she meant to lead up to him with a murmured word about this wonderful opportunity. Unhappily, the editor's ebullience was so great that the instant her back was turned, he darted out and started making his way round the room, exclaiming to right and left with a wide grin, 'I'm just back from Persia. I'm just back from Persia.' Paul said to Imogen that he should have worn a ticket in his hat to say so, like Corsica Boswell. Poor Mrs. Leeper being frustrated in her first design, collected her élite and drove them after him, catching up with him under the gibbet. It was clear that the editor was in so effervescent a mood that he would defy all control, the more so when fortified by Mr. Leeper's whisky which he was now gulping down.

Paul Nugent's powers of self-improvement were not equal to his opportunities. He showed no anxiety to be enlightened by the editor on the Persian situation, and as it was a matter outside Imogen's ken, she felt it no sacrifice to walk away with him in hope of finding him distraction. The supper table was the most cheerful object in view and several guests were converging towards it. The food was very good, both hot and cold, and very well set out; but as the guests approached with pleased anticipation but polite restraint, two figures interposed between them and the food and drink: only two in number but so avid and ferocious that as they ran up and down the length of the table, they had the effect of a Tartar invasion. Ludmilla and Varvara, aged thirteen and eleven, appearing barefooted in their nightgowns among their parents' guests might have been a touching spectacle; in fact they were terrifying. The nightgowns were crumpled, torn and much outgrown; their legs and feet were grimy, the nails completely black. The same was true of the hands and arms they stretched out to claw the dishes, while their matted hair hung round faces that were set in a savage determination. The impression they made was that they were not only after food, but engaged in a punitive expedition against society.

Imogen instinctively looked round for their mother. Mrs. Leeper, all unattending, was standing some way away in the middle of the room, her gleaming white dress throwing up the striking beauty of her tall and taper figure, the vital glow of her skin apparent even through the thick coating of paint. Her head was turned in the opposite direction; her husband however had come to the scene and was trying to persuade Ludmilla and Varvara to be content with their spoils and go upstairs. Ludmilla said to him: 'Shurrup. I want to find the lobster salad. I'm not going, blast you. I shan't go till I've had some lobster salad.' Her younger sister made no reply at all; she merely snatched sausages on sticks, *vol-au-vents*, mushroom savouries and *petits fours* from their dishes, reducing the delicately poised heaps to tumbled disorder, crammed the food into the lap of her cotton nightgown and then attempted to balance two plates of ice-cream on the top. As she moved on her predatory course, the plates slid out and ice-cream and broken glass strewed the floor. Her sister trod on a fragment and shrieked out curses, then started to limp towards the staircase, leaving small patches of blood on the composition floor. Paul said to Mr. Leeper: 'Would you like me to see to that foot?'

'It's jolly good of you,' said Mr. Leeper earnestly, 'but I expect she'll be all right. They're always hacking themselves about.'

'Still, broken glass can be rather nasty.'

'Well, thanks very much, if you think it's indicated.'

'I do.'

Paul started to mount the spiral stairs in Ludmilla's wake; Imogen followed, looking down as she did so on the heads of the crowd now seething round the buffet. The somewhat low-pitched ceiling treated with copper foil, both muffled and amplified the noise. In the rooms upstairs the effect was of an eerie booming. Ludmilla had accepted Paul and his services at once, and led him into a bathroom. Imogen glanced into all the bedroom doors until she found Tim, propped up in a bed that looked as if it had remained unmade for weeks; his eyes had a glazed expression. The muffled reverberation from below filled the small room, but he also had a wireless programme going full blast from a set attached to his bed's head. He gazed at Imogen for a moment unseeingly and then shifted in his bed and smiled as he realized who she was. She did not wonder at his stupefaction; the noise was deafening.

'Tim,' she said, leaning over to make herself heard. 'Wouldn't you like this turned off now?'

'Oh no,' he said vaguely. 'I always have it on.'

'*Always?*' she said, astonished. 'Even when they aren't keeping you awake?'

'They aren't keeping me awake,' said Tim simply. 'I always have it on till it closes down.'

'Doesn't it make you very tired?'

'Sometimes I go to sleep a bit, then I wake up and hear more of it.'

Imogen saw that nothing could be done. She smoothed and straightened the bed, however, pulling taut the undersheet and blanket which had formed two cable-like ridges down the centre of the mattress, and shaking the pillows, one of which was a cretonne-covered cushion pushed into a pillow-case. As she finished her pulling and tucking, Varvara appeared in the doorway, her laden lap held up in one hand, while with the other she ate a sausage on the end of a stick. She sat on the bed and displayed a confusion and crumbling collection of food.

'Would you like some?' she asked her brother. Tim eyed the heap languidly.

'You can put something by my bed and I'll have it in the morn-ing,' he said.

Varvara sorted out two broken *petits fours* and two sausages and laid them on his bedside chair. Imogen looked down at the bent, tousled head and the dirty little hand, now occupied with a work of love.

'Are you sure you don't want one now?' Varvara asked in some surprise.

'No, I don't.'

Paul at the door gave Tim a look and said, 'Would you like a drink of water?'

'Yes, I would,' Tim said. He was lying back now on his reno-vated pillows, but his brilliant eyes looked incurably wakeful. Paul reappeared with a plastic beaker from the bathroom. While Tim drank, he exclaimed: 'Bless the boy, he's got his window shut!'

Tim paused in his draught. 'It's bust,' he said, hopelessly. Paul went to the window, which was made to open and shut on a some-what complicated system of screws and sliding bars. It was true that the apparatus resisted a first attempt on it. By wrapping the screw in his handkerchief however and using a good deal of force, he managed to get the window open; he then screwed it tightly in that position, hoping it might now stick open as it had stuck shut. He did not see anything more that could be done for the children, and he thought he might as well take Imogen away; if he did not make some such move she would stay up here indefinitely. He told Varvara that her sister was in bed and suggested that she should go back to bed herself. Varvara looked at him in silence but went calmly into the bedroom she shared with Ludmilla, who was lying with eyes staring over the sheet.

'Quite comfortable?' Paul asked.

'Yes, thanks,' she said.

They said good night to her and to Varvara. The latter only looked at them. She seemed too much surprised to say anything.

As he came down the stairs after Imogen, Paul murmured: 'It's after eleven. Do you want to stay much longer?'

'Oh no. I should be quite pleased to go now,' she said. They accordingly made their way to Mrs. Leeper, and just behind her, came face to face with Zenobia, with Lord Fingal in attendance. Zenobia at once greeted them with enchanting cordiality. She was enjoying one of those moments particularly favourable to herself, when lavish and spontaneous admiration had the effect on her of warmth and moisture on an orchid. When she was receiving so much that she did not need to demand anything, she herself could give, and the charm of her giving was extraordinary. It made Imogen feel for the moment that she had misjudged Zenobia in thinking her selfish and egotistical. Such pleasure at the sight of them, such tender interest in their affairs – she remembered Paul so well from having met him in Welbeck Street – even he thought Zenobia was being very pleasant; though to Paul, the fact that someone should show pleasure at meeting Imogen again was only to be expected.

'I hear Hunter was with you last week-end,' Zenobia said.

Imogen was taken aback and scarcely knew what to answer though the only possible answer was Yes.

'Don't mind me, my dear,' said Zenobia in her low, thrilling voice. 'If I could only feel that he was happier himself, I should have no regrets.'

Imogen felt it was fortunate that it was Paul and not Evelyn who was with her on this occasion. Paul could be relied on for a diplomatic silence; Evelyn would have assured Zenobia straight away that Hunter was as jolly as a sandboy. As it was, Paul's decent forbearance and Imogen's confusion passed the moment off in a suitable manner. It was characteristic of Zenobia that she not only endured but even welcomed a public reference to feelings that other people thought of as private, and indeed she carried off such references with great style and effect. She was never impetuous, never incoherent; she said things of sensational interest or star-tling indiscretion and she said them very well. She now fixed her wonderful eyes upon Imogen and said: 'And how is Evelyn?'

'He's very well thank you, but very busy.'

'Such a pity he couldn't come to-night,' put in Mrs. Leeper. Zenobia slightly shook her head. The graceful movement brought her dark cloud of hair a little forward and sent a gleam over the little scattered diamonds on her cap. Her great eyes looked for an instant to be bright with tears. At this access of sensibility, Lord Fingal seemed, in his gentlemanly way, to be going almost frantic. Zenobia's lips parted; she said with an exquisite, elegiac cadence:

'I'm glad he didn't. Evelyn is one of the strongest men I know.'

Paul felt that he had at last found his feet in this conversation. He said that Evelyn was indeed a man of very vigorous character and that there was almost no one whom he, Paul, wouldn't sooner face in a cross-examination. Had they seen the paragraph about Evelyn in yesterday's *Evening Standard*, he asked. 'Judge's Tribute,' it was headed.

'Yes, I noticed it.' Lord Fingal, emerging one moment from passion's trance, showed himself a kindly and courteous man. 'Mr. Gresham is your husband?' he said to Imogen. 'You must be very proud of him.'

'I am,' she answered.

Lord Fingal smiled at her. Zenobia moved again, making an ampler gesture, in which not her jewelled head only but her hands, her waist, her dark, spreading, vaporous skirt were all employed. The movement presented her beauty to the eye afresh; it was impossible to look at or think of anything else. Their attention and that of everyone round her was received by Zenobia's consciousness like rays of life-giving warmth.

'I've followed his career with the utmost interest for the last year or two,' she said. 'And I would have got in touch with you many times.'

Imogen said rashly: 'I do wish you had.'

But Zenobia shook her head once more.

'No,' she said. 'No. One learns, for oneself, and other people. It wouldn't be fair – however strong he is, or thinks he is.'

After one instant's burning silence, brilliant in gems and tears, like the incandescent phoenix, forever born again out of fiery suffering, Zenobia vanished from their sight. A rapid turn in the opposite direction brought the masses of her cloudy skirt floating about her, as if her shape had risen in fumes at some magician's invocation, and her wake was filled up by the people who crowded after her.

Stupefaction so possessed Imogen that she found herself walking through the gate under the ilex trees with Paul by her side before she could utter a word.

'How perfectly extraordinary!' she said, dazed, while Paul held open the gate and closed it after her.

'It all seems to have gone to your friend's head a little,' said Paul kindly.

Imogen recovered herself with a laugh. 'Not but what she is so *very* beautiful,' she said; 'one could not be surprised at any man's falling in love with her – it is simply that Evelyn is not, and I really don't think he ever could be.'

'No.'

'Well, I'm sure it's a lesson to us all.'

'Indeed? In what way?'

'I don't mean to you – I mean to women. Not to think men are in love with one when they aren't.'

'I don't think sensible women need such lessons.'

'Of course if you are as beautiful as that – and have such an effect on men – Evelyn was certainly bowled over by her on just one evening. I suppose she could really be excused for being mistaken. She can't be blamed if she takes it for granted a man has fallen in love with her, when so many actually do.'

'Are you sure you know what men fall in love with?'

They were turning out of the silent, star-lit street, into the lane that led to the drive. All noise of the party was left behind them; but from some way away, in a direction not easily located, the diminishing hum of a powerful car came through the dark air; it receded until the resonant throb lingered among unseen hedgerows like that of a giant hornet.

'Perhaps I don't,' said Imogen: 'I only know what they *look* as if they fall in love with. Lord Fingal, for instance!'

'He had something the matter with him, certainly. I'm only questioning the diagnosis. I doubt if it's what one would call love.'

Imogen sighed. 'How tired I am!' she exclaimed. 'I feel as if we'd been there for ages. I think perhaps we'd better not tell Evelyn what Zenobia said—'

'My dear child, I shouldn't dream of doing so.'

'No, I suppose you wouldn't. Men are so much more discreet than women. Men of our class, at least. I don't know about others. I should love to tell him, in fact I even may, if I see a very good moment some time – but I ought not to. I hope I shan't. He might turn savage, indignant – he does dislike her so. No, I must not.'

'I scarcely think he would be that, but I don't think it would amuse him. And perhaps, anyhow, the subject of falling in love is apt to be rather overdone? After all, very busy men don't have a great deal of time to think about it. That's where women are inclined to mistake, I think. Women never seem too busy to think about being in love, but men really are too busy, quite a lot of the time.'

'Yes.' He had been afraid he might have sounded prosy or to be laying down the law, but her reply, sweet, cheerful, eager in agreement, reassured him.

As they came up the drive, light glowed softly within the open hall door and the drawing-room windows. Evelyn met them, a glass of beer in his hand. His greeting was all cordiality and warmth. They went into the drawing-room, and in the bright light he said kindly that Imogen looked tired, and had better go to bed.

'I will when I've had a drink,' she said. She leaned against the chimney-piece, holding a glass in both hands.

'I suppose Blanche drove you down?' she went on carelessly. 'I telephoned her house at tea-time to ask if she'd come in for a drink before dinner, and the maid said she wasn't coming down till this evening.' She paused, standing so nonchalantly that she was almost lounging against the hearth. She did not look at Evelyn, so studied was her unconcern, but she was conscious of his giving her a sudden, surprised look, before he answered in tones of relief: 'Yes, she did. It was very good of her, I couldn't give her any dinner till long after the proper time. But we went to that little place in Greek Street and had some of the old fellow's *terrine de lièvre* that you and I used to like so much. Do you remember?'

'Of course I remember. What a peculiar thing to ask.'

'I'm sorry, my dear! I didn't mean any offence.'

'None taken. But naturally I remember one of our favourite things. Was it as good as ever?'

'It was very good. And that place is so pleasant because they never mind how late you come in. It was nearly ten – it was very good of Blanche to wait all that time for me.'

'Well, I don't know,' said Imogen, putting down her glass. 'I expect it was very exciting for her. I don't suppose people take her out very often; a dinner alone with you would be well worth wait-ing for, and the chance to drive you down here afterwards.' She turned to Paul, who was now standing on the verandah, examin-ing the stars with great attention. She thanked him for coming to the party, hoped he would be comfortable and wished him good night. It was plain to her perceptions, always acute in relation to other people's emotions towards herself, that so far from wishing to keep her beside him, Paul was now urgently wanting to see her out of the room. There was no need to say anything to Evelyn, since he would no doubt be coming upstairs in a few minutes, yet if it had not been for her having uttered those words a moment ago, she would unthinkingly have found something to say as she passed him to the door. Her silence as she now did so made the occasion marked.

She was lying in bed when Evelyn came into the room. He did not put on the light but the sky through the undrawn curtains showed the sharply defined bulk of his looming figure as he stood at the bed's foot.

'I want you to understand,' he said, 'that Blanche Silcox is a woman for whom I have a great respect and whose friendship I value very much. What you said downstairs was utterly uncalled for and if you can't prevent yourself from making disagreeable remarks about her you'll hurt me and make me very angry.' He went out of the room again before she could say a word. The racing of her heart made her feel faint and giddy and a dreadful sense of unfamiliar evil invaded her veins, so that as she moved her head on the pillow, she could hardly distinguish between the sense of physical and mental sickness. Fright at having roused his anger and a sense of degradation from indulging in what was vulgar and base clashed violently in her brain with the straightforward view that what she had said of Blanche Silcox was literally true, however uncharitable and inelegant it might be of herself to say so. These exhausting variations of feeling occupied her whole mind, for how long she did not know. Evelyn had still not come up to bed, when she realized that she would not be able to sleep unless she took something to make herself. There were some tablets of Evelyn's in one of the drawers of the chest; she had used them once but could not remember whether she had then taken one or two. She now swallowed three to make sure, and having exceeded the proper dose, deprived herself of the benefits of the drug, for after a sleep of not much more than an hour she woke with a fearful start in the chill dimness of early summer dawn, and realized the utter stillness of the room. That Evelyn should still be away – had he even left the house? – when had she last heard that menacing, hornet's hum of a retreating car? – overcame her with fright and misery. She sat up and gave a great sob.

'What is it, Imogen?' he said, getting up from his bed.

'I thought you weren't there,' she gasped. He stroked her hair and laid her down on the pillows again.

'I'm so sorry I was so rude and hateful!' she exclaimed.

'Never mind, my dear,' he said gently. 'Let's go to sleep now.' The enormity of making a scene at this hour and keeping him awake controlled her as nothing else could have done. The making of her apology had a better effect than the sleeping tablets. She turned on her side and lay comfortably, becoming warmer, happier, more drowsy, until she opened her eyes again in bright morning light and heard sounds of activity all about the house, and the ones which now seemed especially enjoyable to her ear, those made by Evelyn's walking about in his dressing-room, pulling drawers open and clearing his throat. She was half dressed when he came out, looking hale and cheerful, and gave her a hearty kiss.

'Hurry up!' he said. 'I can smell the coffee.' A staccato rattle of percussion caps made her fly, bare-armed, to the window.

'That's Gavin!' she exclaimed. 'I do hope he hasn't wakened Paul with those things!' But Paul was up already and he and Gavin now came into view, walking up from the river bank.

At breakfast Evelyn was in a jovial mood and everyone at the table seemed to draw increased vitality from the comfort of his presence. Gavin's irruptions into the conversation were like the gambols of a young dog. He kept trying to impart to Paul the knowledge he had gained from a first-aid manual, disregarding the evident wishes of the rest to talk about last night's party. Tim had told him those parties were the edge, and he had dismissed the affair as not worth hearing about.

'Do you know what I should do if I found a chap who'd bust his collar bone?' he demanded.

'No,' said Paul apprehensively. 'Let's hear.'

'Yes,' said Evelyn in resigned tones, 'we may as well have it first as last.'

'I should roll up my handkerchief and shove it under his armpit, the side the bone was bust, and then lash his arm to his side with the longest thing I'd got, say a scarf or two ties.'

'That would hurt him a good deal, wouldn't it?' said Evelyn uneasily.

'He can't help that,' said Paul. 'It's in the book!'

'It would be the right thing to do, wouldn't it?' exclaimed Gavin defensively.

'It might be the right thing to do,' said Evelyn, 'but you wouldn't be the right person to do it.'

'I don't see why not – if I *know* what to do—'

'But one thing you wouldn't know is how much you'd be hurting him every time you touched him,' Paul said. 'If you find somebody who's broken a bone, the best thing is to leave him where he is and get the school doctor as quick as you can.'

'Oh well,' said Gavin in an affronted voice, 'that's what the book said, anyway!' He left the table.

'Most irresponsible, these catchpenny books,' exclaimed Evelyn, 'making boys of Gavin's age think they can treat compound fractures, haemorrhages, anything you care to name—'

Gavin reappeared in the doorway. 'There was a piece in the paper,' he said severely, 'about a girl who was shot by brigands, and a chap that knew first aid dug the bullet out of her head with a latch-key.' He disappeared again.

'I wonder how Ludmilla's foot is this morning,' said Imogen, holding out her hand for Evelyn's coffee cup. 'Did Paul tell you how he—?'

'And another thing,' continued Gavin, putting his head into the room once more. 'It said how a chap on board ship saved another chap's life by taking out his appendix with a tablespoon.'

'Gavin,' said Evelyn, folding the *Sunday Times* over and over with great force, 'if you must give us this lecture, come in and get it over.'

'It doesn't matter now,' said Gavin, going out again. His tone conveyed that they had forfeited their chance of something very valuable.

'If he wants to take up medicine, all well and good,' said Evelyn.

'He has assembled those mouse bones very well,' Paul said.

'It's interesting – very interesting – to see what appeals to him,' said Evelyn absently. 'As far as one *can* see, that is. He may have all kinds of interests we know nothing about.'

'School will probably give his ideas a channel – you may be able to see his bent very clearly in a year or two.'

'Yes. And I think it's time he went; I'm glad we've made this arrangement at Brackley Hill. He's been fortunate so far in having Tim Leeper to play about with, but he needs the companionship of a lot of other boys, and I should like to see him put into the way of getting much better games than they can get at Endfield. Their football is pitiable; they've got nobody to give them any style. I fancy Gavin might be a really useful scrum half or outside forward one day; he's extremely fast.'

'Yes.'

'He'll go and stay with other boys, perhaps, and bring them here. All this mucking about with Tim Leeper has been very good for him up till now, but we must try and start him on more serious amusements soon – he can fish with Blanche Silcox – she'd take them both, I'm sure. I'll get him a light rod – it's time he did something else beside fishing for minnows in jam-jars. I don't know if there's any hacking to be got in the neighbourhood, but Blanche will know if there is. He could take some lessons in the summer holidays if he'd like to.'

'I should think he'd love to,' said Imogen. She blamed herself severely that instead of the vision of Gavin enjoying riding lessons, as he undoubtedly would, what had first risen in her mind was a pang of pity for Tim Leeper. But the next moment the knowledge smote her that what had really stood in the way of her instantly welcoming the idea of fishing and riding for Gavin was the prospect of Blanche Silcox taking so important a part in the scheme: in a role where her robustness and directness, her experience of country pursuits, her money, which had accustomed her to following them with the most expensive amenities, would tell to the greatest possible advantage.

'She is a great acquisition as a neighbour,' continued Evelyn. 'She can do all those things that make living in the country so much more agreeable.'

Paul was silent, filling and lighting a pipe, pausing in the operation however to say to Imogen: 'Have I your permission!'

'Please do,' she said. 'Sunday breakfast is so nice, isn't it, with nobody in a hurry?' Then, afraid that Evelyn's remarks about Miss Silcox had seemed to be pointedly ignored, she said: 'It would be very useful if she could find out about riding lessons for Gavin. I wonder if her sister's children ride when they're down here?'

'You might find out,' said Evelyn.

'I will.' Anxious to maintain this better atmosphere, she went on: 'What an extremely good lunch that was she gave us on Wednesday, wasn't it?'

'Very,' said Paul.

'I never asked whether you got to hospital in comfortable time?'

'Just about, thank you. And I hope you and your friend had a successful afternoon?'

'Yes, we did. We went up to the dome of St. Paul's first. It was the most amazing view. Do you know, I had never realized how near we were to the Old Bailey till I saw that green copper ball just below?'

'My dear girl,' said Evelyn, stupefied, 'do you mean that you had to climb up to the dome of St. Paul's Cathedral to find out that the Central Criminal Court is within a stone's-throw of Ludgate Hill?'

'Yes,' she said, 'yes: it sounds silly, I know, but I had.' He half shook his head, reduced to silence. Imogen got up. 'I suppose I learn things the hard way,' she said; 'but once I have learnt them, I—' She paused, unable to complete the sentence, and turned away.

'Tired out,' said Paul, getting up and walking casually to the french window. 'That party was enough to prostrate anyone. Perhaps she could sleep a little in the garden.' He walked out and remained on the verandah. Evelyn came up to her and took her by the elbow.

'You must be extremely tired,' he said gravely, 'or you wouldn't burst into tears over nothing at all.'

'No, should I?' she said, wiping her eyes. 'I'm sorry, it's too idiotic. But I took too many of those tablets, I think, and they had the opposite effect.' He made a sound of disgust and concern. 'Do apologize to Paul for me!' she cried, blowing her nose. 'I'm going to finish the coffee.'

Paul came in again. 'How many did you take?' he asked.

'Three.'

'Two too many, I expect. However, I think you'd be dead by now if they were going to kill you. Come and sit on the bank, and then if Evelyn and I leave you and take a walk, you might sleep for a while.'

'It's colder this morning,' she said. As they passed through the hall she took up a garden coat that she had not used for weeks.

'I'll bring a rug,' Evelyn said. When, after some minutes, he joined them on the sloping turf, she was touched to see that he had brought not only one of the plaids to lie on, but a light Shetland shawl to wrap round her. The attention gave a sweetness to the moment out of all proportion to the amount of consideration that had inspired it.

'That was Mrs. Leeper on the telephone,' Evelyn said.

'Was it?' Imogen exclaimed. 'I didn't hear anyone.' Both tired and soothed, she had, she realized, lost for the time being that morbid acuteness of hearing.

'Yes,' Evelyn continued, stretching out his length on the turf. 'She wanted us all to go round before lunch and meet Zenobia.' A slight smile animated his features. It gave the effect of his having said something very urbane and witty.

'What did you say?' asked Imogen eagerly.

'I said I thought you'd be too tired to go because you'd had a bad night, and that Paul was leaving us early, and that I was very busy.'

Imogen laughed aloud.

'What is there funny in that?' he asked. 'It's all true except that Paul won't leave as early as all that, I hope.'

'Hope and insist,' said Imogen. She paused, not quite knowing how, in Paul's presence, to explain the joke; but as she was committed to some sort of explanation, she said: 'I think Zenobia will feel that you are avoiding her because you are afraid of her fatal fascination.'

Evelyn said: 'She's welcome to think so if that provides me with a watertight excuse for never seeing her again! How Hunter – But it's no use talking about that now. But do you know that creature couldn't even boil an egg? Of course they had a cook – but once when something had happened to her, Zenobia produced a tin of sardines and some potted meat.'

'Well, after all,' said Paul equably, 'he wasn't marrying her for her cooking.'

'No,' said Evelyn, 'but it made her all the more abominable that she starved him as well as everything else. A brilliant young man like that to be so misguided – amazing.'

'Such beauty as that is usually supposed to explain anything,' said Imogen softly.

'It explained everything in poor Hunter's case, no doubt,' said Evelyn. 'It created a blinding infatuation that was extremely short-lived. But women as a whole, in my opinion, attach much too much importance to the effect of beauty on men. If they used their eyes, they'd see it isn't beauty that is the attraction. Consider that woman as a case in point – she can give a knock-out blow, but once the chap has picked himself up again she can't do anything else. However,' he added, 'the subject of sexual attraction remains a mystery.'

'Yes,' said Paul, 'we were agog. We thought you were just going to give us the answer.'

'*I* am the last person to give the answer,' replied Evelyn lightly. He stood up and Paul followed his example. 'We shall be back well before lunch,' Evelyn said to her. 'Of course if you want to go down to the Leepers' there's nothing to stop you.'

'I *don't* want to!' cried Imogen.

'Very well. Then I should try to get some sleep, as Paul says. I'll tell Malpas to see that the boys don't disturb you.' They walked away. Imogen began to wish fervently that she had said nothing in admiration of Zenobia. She saw or feared to see a fatal alignment in Evelyn's mind of herself with what was specious, irritating, contemptible, and opposite to her, those admirable, attaching qualities which were so conspicuous in Miss Blanche Silcox, whose drawing-room, whose sherry, were even now, no doubt, ready for the reception of Evelyn and his friend when they should call in during their morning's walk.

ELEVEN

At the end of July it was Evelyn's habit to go for a fortnight's walking holiday before he returned to take Imogen and Gavin to the sea. He would join two or three fellow benchers and go to Yorkshire, Cumberland or Scotland. He loved to sleep in white-washed cottages or small inns, never out of the sound of water, to walk in the hills, indifferent to rain and mist, to sit through clear, still evenings on the parapet of a bridge over a loud-gurgling stream, or at the door of the inn among fuchsia bushes. His friends shared the same tastes and needed the same sort of recuperation. At this point, the end of their exhausting year, they none of them wanted the presence of their families. All they wanted was to enjoy complete repose in unexacting masculine society.

Imogen understood this perfectly. Evelyn would send her picture postcards and letter-cards written in country post offices, saying where he was, what weather he was having, and how he was recovering, sleeping better, eating more, and looking forward to seeing her and Gavin very shortly. It was a time during which she scarcely even missed him in any painful sense, the postcards gave her so much satisfaction.

The first fortnight of the summer holidays was intensely enjoyable to Gavin; it meant unlimited hours of playing with Tim in the garden and by the river, and for the time being he even enjoyed the quietness of the house in his father's absence, with no one there to make him do anything he had absolutely determined not to do. This interregnum left him all the more enthusiastic for Evelyn's society when the latter came back. Evelyn used to bring him a collection of presents from his northern tour: specialities of the district such as the sweets made to look like seashore pebbles from Berwick-on-Tweed, and the burning peppermint ice known as Kendal Mint, besides things which could be bought in any town, which he had happened to see with Gavin in mind: a cricket ball, a toy microscope. Once Gavin had passed the stage of painting books and clockwork toys, Imogen had not been successful in her choice of presents for him. The toy theatre and the fort had lain about the play-room untouched, making her feel very silly. Now she always asked him what he wanted, not trusting her own judgment any more.

At the end of this July, Evelyn announced an innovation in his holiday plans. He, Sir Francis Bannister and Mr. Cochrane were going away together; they would put up at a small village on the Tay, but Blanche Silcox, her stepsister and the latter's husband would be staying at a hotel a few miles off. Mr. Plender and Miss Silcox would be salmon fishing, and Evelyn would join the sport. Cochrane also would probably take a hand, since he was something of a fisherman. 'But not Sir Francis!' thought Imogen wildly. 'There must be *somebody* to keep Marcia Plender company!' She pictured Mr. Justice Bannister in this taxing role. The prospect of his sufferings gave her, most unfairly, a keen satisfaction. She was the more hurt and aghast because she had thoroughly sympathized with the character of these holidays up till now, realizing the benefit, the need, of some such retreat. That another woman should be allowed to join them even from a distance, made it an insult that she should not be allowed to go herself. But on the heels of this idea came the perception of how well fitted Blanche Silcox was to join such a party without disturbing it by any recognizably female element. Blanche Silcox, crowned with one of her large-domed felt hats, battling with a frantic salmon, was not, on the face of it, a sight to seduce errant affections, and her conversation in general company, consisting as it did of brief and sensible, if trite, remarks, delivered in a manner whose brusqueness did not conceal the intention to be pleasant, would make her acceptable, or at least unobjectionable, in a society where no other kind of woman would be found tolerable. All the same, the idea of her joining Evelyn was very disagreeable, and Imogen wanted intensely to know with whom it had originated.

She could not bring herself to ask Evelyn this question; her emotions were so much involved in it, the mere asking would imply some sort of criticism of the plan. Evelyn was now in that state of overwork which made it possible for him to be polite and calm only by a strong effort of self-control. He was retained for a case, among others, concerning the claim of a client to a large share of his adopted father's estate. The claim rested on a verbal arrangement only and the dead man's heir refused to ratify his father's promise. It was said that at one of the interviews during which the arrangement had been agreed upon, there had been present in the library the ancient Marchioness, the present Lord Mountjoy's grandmother, whose evidence, in the absence of any written agreement, would presumably be of very great importance. The Marchioness however was in her eighty-fifth year, and though still a woman of commanding personality, she was now so irascible and unpredictable that each side trembled at the idea of calling her, for fear that she might do more harm than good. Evelyn had to make up his mind whether to call the old woman or not. He was tired, and it was unfortunate that the case of Mountjoy *v.* Mountjoy, which presented several complications, should have been the last in the list. For some weeks he had been in that state of nervous fatigue in which reverses, however slight, affected him more sharply than any intimations of success. In this frame of mind, he would relate to Imogen how a solicitor had disagreed with the method of cross-examination he had proposed to employ, or how opposing counsel had claimed, without a shadow of reason, that he had been unscrupulous. Even when these instances had occurred in cases in which he had secured a verdict for his client, he would still minutely recollect the obstruction, the adverse criticism, and repeat it with stretched lips and narrowed eyes as if he tasted something bitter. The praise, often bestowed on him, he spoke of very briefly. It was in this condition that he now had to decide whether he could afford to call his most important witness. He asked his client searchingly whether the Marchioness were fit to appear. He was told that she had her good days and her bad days, and that while the good ones were fairly good, the bad ones – here Mr. Mountjoy broke off. 'Quite so,' said Evelyn. The safe thing, undoubtedly, was to leave her alone, but if the gamble succeeded the success would be very great. The idea that an appearance in court would excite the old girl too much and send her completely round the bend, Evelyn himself scouted. To find herself the centre of a group of men all hanging on her words would, he thought, if anything, have the effect of reassuring the Marchioness and making her feel at home. There was the awkward possibility that if he succeeded in getting from her the evidence for which he hoped, a ruthless cross-examination might reduce her to such an unstable condition that the court would feel disinclined to place any reliance on what she had previously said. He accepted that her appearance would be a risk, and his interview with her showed him that the risk was very serious, yet when she left him, he was the more inclined to take it. He felt a strange sympathy, a sense of attraction towards this extraordinary old being; it was like having in his hands some miraculous piece of antique clockwork, so damaged by age that it was altogether unreliable. If it could be made to work, the effect would be tremendous.

The pros and cons of this question, added to the others that filled his mind, kept Evelyn in such a state of nervous tension that Imogen felt any idea of discussing – let alone seeming to cavil at – his holiday arrangements, to be out of the question. During this fortnight he spent the chief of the time in London. At home he was mostly shut up in his study, and he had the bed in his dressing-room made up for him. He had once or twice before slept here when she had been ill, and on one or two occasions when he himself had had an attack of sleeplessness. He had never before occupied the dressing-room for so long together; but then, he had never before been obliged to work for so long at such a cracking pace.

The case of Mountjoy v. Mountjoy opened on a Thursday. The court did not sit on Saturday and Imogen expected that Evelyn would be down on Friday evening to a late dinner. It turned out however that he had to spend Saturday morning in New Square and would come home after lunch. Blanche Silcox was not staying in town. She telephoned to Imogen on Friday evening with the address of a riding school where Gavin could take lessons, and showed a very friendly and practical interest in the matter, telling Imogen where his jodhpurs could be bought, for she suggested that there was no point in having breeches made for him just yet; he would outgrow them so fast. The conversation was pleasant, and Imogen saw how very much Blanche Silcox was improved by having something practical to talk about. The awkwardness of her manner disappeared when she was being authoritative and helpful, and her depressing lack of conversation went unnoticed when she enumerated copious details of addresses and prices and the sort of information her experience enabled her to give. Imogen felt she could not ring off without saying something about the visit to Scotland – it would look conscious, odd; but her feelings were so much involved in the matter she hardly knew how to approach it. She plunged abruptly into the topic, saying something about Evelyn's so much looking forward to getting away and how nice that Blanche and her sister could join the party. Blanche Silcox replied with equal incoherence about its being such a good thing Evelyn had taken up fishing, so good for him, just what he needed. Imogen then said she knew Blanche would excuse her if she rang off but this was just about the time Evelyn usually telephoned from London, and they said a hurried good night to each other. Evelyn rang up a quarter of an hour later, sounding extremely tired. He said the case was going well so far. He had decided to call the Marchioness. She would appear on Monday.

'Oh!' said Imogen softly.

'Don't talk to me about her, will you? I feel I don't want to say a word till it's all over.'

'No, dearest. I shan't speak about the case at all.'

'That's right. Good night, my dear. I'll see you to-morrow.'

As Imogen went upstairs, though it was barely ten, she felt suddenly overborne with that sort of pleasant tiredness that comes from a complete relaxation of the nerves. A light showed under Gavin's door. She went in, and, too impatient for her bed to coax or argue, took the book out of his hands and switched off the lamp.

'I don't see why I can't read in bed for a bit!' Gavin exclaimed, flouncing under the bedclothes.

'Daddy says you're not to do it after quarter to ten. It's nearly ten o'clock now.'

'If I could do it till ten I wouldn't want to do it any later.'

'Well, you'd better tell him that to-morrow.' She could not exert herself to remind him that his proper time for putting out his light was half-past nine and that Evelyn had given him the extra quarter of an hour as a concession. As she undressed and got to bed the delicious approach of sleep came on so fast she had barely time to think of anything once her head was laid on the pillow;

but her last conscious thought was one of gladness and relief that Blanche Silcox was down here in the house behind the trees, and that Evelyn, in London, was either by himself or with people who did not in the least matter.

At breakfast the next morning she saw that one of Gavin's eyes was inflamed and watering. She telephoned to ask the doctor to come in before he began his round, for she thought it was probably conjunctivitis, and besides wanting to be told what to do for it, she was anxious to hear whether Tim should be kept away. The doctor confirmed that Gavin had pink-eye, and said that if he and Tim were rubbing shoulders Tim would almost certainly contract it. The only safe thing was to keep them apart for the next fortnight. Faced with the annoyance of Gavin and the despair of Tim at this prospect, Imogen thought that Tim's developing conjunctivitis would be the lesser evil. He should perhaps in that case come and stay with them, so as not to risk giving the infection to either of his sisters. She went to the gate to intercept Tim for he would be certain to appear at any moment now, and she thought she had better explain the position to him before he and Gavin laid their heads together over the aquarium or their stamp collections. As she stood in the gloom of the evergreens just inside the gate, the deep hum was heard that now always conveyed some sense of alarm to her and in a few seconds Blanche Silcox sped by in her Rolls, driving very fast. A moment afterwards Tim appeared, walking through the grasses and sorrel at the roadside on a slightly wavering course but coming much faster than he ever went anywhere else. Imogen began to explain to him that Gavin was likely to give him a sore eye and that it would be much safer if he were not to come for the present. As she said all this Tim was walking straight up the drive to the front door and she had to follow him to get her explanation out. Tim said nothing at all but walked through the hall into the kitchen and on into the play-room, where Gavin with a lint compress and a green shade over one eye was sprawling on the window-seat, working out a chess problem.

'Oh, good man,' he said as Tim came in.

'Well, if you're going to stay together, remember not to put your heads near each other,' said Imogen resignedly. 'You mustn't play chess or cards, and if you're working on the stamp collections, you must sit at opposite sides of the table. Can you remember that?'

'Yes,' said Tim. The round, flat little face on the stalk-like neck had an almost Chinese impassiveness. He had shown a determination in getting himself where he wanted to be that would have suggested a much stronger character. Now that he was there, he was tranquil and silent. He had nothing to say.

Imogen felt obliged to telephone to Mrs. Leeper and explain the position and offer such assurances of care and precaution as she could. She rang up the Leeper house but she had forgotten that her own pedestrian habits of early rising were not everybody's. A muffled voice answered her in bemused accents. 'Oh yes, my dear, just as you like; we want you to feel *quite* free.' The receiver sounded as if it were dropped askew in the act of replacing.

Imogen could spend no more time on the matter of the boys' isolation for she had the Saturday morning's shopping to do, always important but this time of particular importance; the idea of Evelyn's wanting something the house was found to be without would be at the present crisis appalling. He usually bought the sherry and gin himself but now the bottles were dangerously low. Miss Malpas had a small list of last-minute requirements, and she herself had another. There were, besides, Gavin's prescriptions to take to the chemist. In the middle of her shopping it occurred to her with a violent shock that adults were as liable to the contagion of pink-eye as children were, and she began with feverish anxiety to consider what precautions she ought to take for Evelyn's protection. Gavin had been told by the doctor that he must keep to his own towel, but what confidence had she that he would remember to do it? She would put all his washing apparatus in his own bedroom, give him paper handkerchiefs to throw away immediately after use and put a pile of clean towels in the bathroom for Evelyn so that he should never use one of Gavin's by mistake. The implications of Evelyn's having to appear in court with an inflamed and running eye were so obvious and so frightful that Imogen knew it ought not to be beyond her to gain Gavin's eager co-operation in saving his father from such a risk. At lunchtime she tried to impress on him the extreme seriousness of the matter, but between anxiety to bring home to him the importance of taking care, and the fear of antagonizing him by being too dictatorial or too emotional, she was harassed and distraught. Gavin ate steadily and in silence, looking at his plate. She thought he had understood the position, and that was no doubt enough; but an insane longing for a word, a look of sympathy or response made her dig her nails into her palms. 'It's idiotic of me,' she told herself angrily. 'A boy of his age – I don't *want* him to be any different. All I want is to be sure he knows what he's got to do.' It was not so much Gavin's unresponsiveness, his latent hostility, that horrified her; it was the picture of herself as the cause of all this.

After lunch she put drops in his eye, scrubbed the bathroom basin with disinfectant and laid the pile of clean towels full in view. When she came downstairs Tim had already returned from his own lunch and was back in the play-room again. Imogen went to the door to ask if his parents had said anything about pink-eye, but at that moment Tim shouted: 'Look out, you silly mucker!'

'All right, all right!' said Gavin. 'If you're so jolly scared of catching it you'd better go home.'

'I'm not scared.'

'What's all the row, then?'

'Well, if you want to know, I said I wouldn't.'

'Oh, all right, all right,' muttered Gavin under his breath. At that moment the air was filled with a low, soft but powerful vibration. Imogen hurried into the hall in time to hear the delicate crunching of gravel as a large car drew to a standstill. It was the Rolls. Blanche Silcox sat at the wheel, and Evelyn, moving more slowly than usual, was getting out and reaching into the back of the car for suitcase, briefcase, a pile of books with paper markers jutting from them and a carrier containing two bottles of Bristol Milk. He turned slowly and faced the front door, stooping slightly, his face heated and tired, with an absent smile. While he maintained this pose, the car drove off.

Imogen came and kissed him with an impulsive clasp which she immediately released, stooping to collect some of the luggage.

'Well!' he said, and came in. The drawing-room, protected by the verandah roof, was always cool. In contrast to the dry heat and glare in front of the house, its atmosphere had a zest like that of a chilled drink. Its long windows were filled with translucent emerald. He sat down, saying nothing, staring at the floor. She wondered whether to speak, or to leave him alone. At that moment however he raised his head.

'You look nice and cool,' he said.

'It's deliciously cool on this side of the house.'

'Where's Gavin?'

'Oh!' she exclaimed, then sat down opposite him because it annoyed him when people stood about, and told him calmly about the pink-eye, the doctor's advice, the precautions she had taken, and her failure to keep Tim out. Evelyn listened without much interest.

'It's a nuisance,' he said, 'but it's not serious. He mustn't give it to me, though.' He settled his head more comfortably against the back of the chair and crossed his legs.

'I mustn't ask anything, must I?'

He smiled, though in a tight-lipped manner. 'You mustn't even say that you mustn't ask! By the way, I wanted Blanche to come here to dinner—'

'Oh, yes. Can she?'

'I should have thought she could, but it seems that half-sister of hers is there – I may go up there after dinner.'

'It will be nice going through the woods.'

'Yes. She's been extremely kind in driving me so much. It's very convenient for me to have someone like that. She's going to drive me back to-morrow night.'

'Would she come here for a meal to-morrow?'

'It would mean having the sister as well. I don't think we want that.'

'I could talk to Mrs. Plender—'

'No. We won't do that.' Imogen was silent, and in a few moments he got up and went out to the play-room. The light out of doors was too strong for Gavin's eyes, and he and Tim were sitting at opposite ends of the table playing paper cricket. Gavin said:

'Hullo, Daddy. I've got a foul eye to give you.'

'Thanks, my boy,' said Evelyn. 'You keep it to yourself.'

'Yes, I'm going to,' said Gavin seriously.

'I should jolly well think you are,' said Tim. Evelyn sat down in a creaking basket chair on the other side of the room and began to talk to them about fishing. He promised them each a rod and said he would take them out when he came down from Scotland. The boys were enchanted by the prospect, and the fact of Evelyn's introducing this delightful subject was a relief to them both, for the sense of the ordeal that awaited Evelyn on the Monday was present in different degrees with everyone. The only member of the household who expressed her concern boldly was Miss Malpas.

'Think you'll get a verdict for 'im?' she asked, putting down the tea-tray with a thud. Imogen who was just coming in from the verandah with a handful of white clematis, stood still, horrified, but Evelyn answered with perfect unconcern:

'Too soon to say.'

'Worst of those cases where you got no jury to swing it over,' continued Miss Malpas with genial sympathy.

'I've no wish to swing anything,' said Evelyn in mild reproof.

'Ah!' said Miss Malpas. 'I dare say. Still, when you got the judge deciding, that's not so funny, is it?'

'*Funny*, Malpas? No one suggests it's funny. People don't go to law for fun, my good woman. Cress sandwiches, are they? Good '

'I see by the papers,' continued Miss Malpas in remorseless flow, 'that old lady is to give evidence. We was all thinking, according to what they said before, that she'd be too screwy by this time. Still I suppose you all know what you're about.'

'I hope we do.'

'Bit of a knock if she was to come unstuck before the end, eh?' Miss Malpas left the room, chuckling at the idea of anything so exquisitely ludicrous.

'Really,' Imogen thought, observing the calmness with which Evelyn helped himself to cress sandwiches, 'I think anybody is allowed to say or do anything except me.' But the relief of seeing that he was unruffled outweighed everything else, just as his coming back towards eleven that evening, serene, cool with the night air and declaring himself thoroughly sleepy, reconciled her to the fact of his having chosen to spend all the time since dinner with Miss Silcox.

The next day brought Monday so very near that it created a condition of forced calmness, like that of a top spinning so furiously that it appears to be standing still. Imogen made herself busy so that she should not seem to be watching Evelyn's movements. She went to church and seeing the lawn empty on her return, made up her mind that he must be over at the house behind the trees. As she was walking upstairs however, the door of the study, ajar for coolness, showed him inside, sitting absolutely still, his forehead bent over one of the books he had brought down with him.

Immediately after lunch the telephone rang and he went into the study and shut the door to answer it. A few minutes later he walked out of the house, across the lawn and down the river bank in the direction of the bridge. He returned however in not much more than an hour and spent the rest of the afternoon on the shady turf by the stone urn. They had tea here by themselves. Gavin had carried out his sanitary obligations nobly, removing his towel from the bathroom whenever he had used it, burning his paper handkerchiefs, and Imogen blamed herself for her lack of confidence in him; but she was still nervous of the idea of his skirmishing about in his father's neighbourhood as he was apt to do at their garden teas. Miss Malpas agreed as to the danger and undertook to give both the boys tea in the play-room. The threat of quarantine had alarmed Tim so much that he was now spending his whole day with Gavin instead of only the greater part of it.

Evelyn said very little as he drank his tea but the painful nervous tension in which he had arrived the day before was loosened. In the gold light of the garden, the freshness of the water, the stillness of the wooded shore, they seemed to be returning, like two ghosts, to a scene of former happiness. The silence was like some enclosing, preserving element, in which their two selves, freed from anxiety and pain, rested on the grass in the immortal light of a landscape by Claude.

At last Evelyn raised himself on one elbow and said gently: 'I must think of the time, my dear.' He drew the flat gold watch from his waistcoat pocket, looked at it in the palm of his hand and put it back, gazing at the woods again, pensive, unwilling to break the quiet. She had seen that the hands said twenty minutes to six; he had spoken of six as the time for going, and as his suitcase and briefcase were ready in the hall, she thought with a luxurious sigh of another quarter of an hour of this soothing, exquisite tranquillity. He smiled up at her and she returned his look with a serene tenderness in which joy touched the eyes and lips but did not disturb them by a smile.

For the hideous onslaught of sound she was so unprepared, she thought for a second she must be dreaming, then eye and ear assured her she was only too well awake. Blanche Silcox's car drew up at the front door and Imogen found herself following Evelyn's tall, majestic figure across the lawn, and forcing back the stinging tears of anger and disappointment.

Blanche Silcox did not leave her seat, she leaned across the wheel to say good evening to Imogen. She was pale and tense, with an air of dedication. It was clear that she regarded her self-appointed task of driving Evelyn back to town on the evening before the day on which the hearing of Mountjoy *v.* Mountjoy was to be resumed as a sacred trust that wound up her faculties to the utmost.

'Don't let me hurry you,' she called to Evelyn, in a voice husky with emotion. 'I'm early! I wanted to be safe.' Even Imogen, usually anxious in excess of what any occasion required, could not but remember that with five trains at least between this and nightfall, there could hardly be any question of Evelyn's getting back to town. She had neither the power nor the wish to make pleasant conversation with Blanche Silcox, and with a brief word and smile followed Evelyn into the house. She followed him out again but came no further than the threshold. As he was putting his cases into the back of the car he answered casually some question of Blanche Silcox's. She said in important, intense tones: 'I don't want you to get up there and find you've left anything.' The proprietary tone was unmistakable.

Evelyn turned and kissed Imogen goodbye. She clung to him a moment and in the smallest whisper wished him good luck, her lips against his ear. He pressed her to him and, as he often did, lifted her for a second right off her feet. Even as his head was bowed over hers in a final kiss, she thought hysterically: 'Blanche Silcox will be sounding her horn in another minute!' This, however, did less than justice to Miss Silcox's sense of the occasion. With Evelyn beside her, she drove off, head forward, lips pursed, with an air of almost sacerdotal dignity.

TWELVE

Evelyn telephoned on Monday evening. The evening papers that reached Chalk were the mid-afternoon editions and these of course contained only a brief reference to the morning's hearing of Mountjoy v. Mountjoy. Imogen dared only to ask him in very general terms how the case was going. Their conversation was brief, for in her anxiety not to be a nuisance to him, she ended it herself, and it was filled only with murmurs of sympathy, praise and affection on her part and a few remarks on his about the heat, the noise of aircraft and the utter impossibility of getting anything fit to drink under the most exorbitant price, all of which were uttered in the measured tones of great fatigue.

The papers on Tuesday morning carried only a paragraph or two though one of these bore the significant heading: 'Recollection perfectly clear.' Imogen dived into the matter beneath and saw that this statement had been made on behalf of the aged Marchioness, but as the paper had omitted for the time being to say who had made it, she could not understand how decisive it might be. Nor was there any indication that she could see of how long the case might be going to last.

The heat continued, but the house and garden were cool and

quiet. Gavin was obliged to miss the last two days of the school term; he was sitting in the window of the play-room, absorbed, in spite of the difficulty of reading with one eye, in *The Memoirs of Sherlock Holmes*. Miss Malpas had gone out early on some mission connected with the bottling of fruit, which she thought it better to see to herself than to trust to Imogen. The latter was examining one of the store cupboards in the kitchen when Tim glided noiselessly in on his way to the play-room. It was ten o'clock.

'Tim!' she exclaimed. 'Aren't you going to school either?' Tim said nothing but paused, rocking backwards and forwards on his heels.

'Do your people know you haven't gone?' she asked. Tim still said nothing. His lowered eyelids gave his face a look of great purity and remoteness.

'Well,' said Imogen weakly, 'I think you ought to have asked them.' She felt incapable of any further gesture. Gavin's resistances were almost too much for her – Tim's as well were more than she could contemplate. She sighed and turned to put back a half-full tin of baking powder. When she turned again, the kitchen was empty.

There was very much to engage her mind, a letter from Paul being among her painful preoccupations. Paul seldom wrote to her but when he did it was always at considerable length, in a reflective, intimate and yet impersonal vein. His letter, she had thought, was one of the usual kind. He described how he had made use of their readings of Charlotte Yonge in a paper on literary evidences of the incidence of tuberculosis in the eighteenth and nineteenth centuries. He made some remarks about the value set on human life being influenced a good deal by belief or disbelief in survival after death, and copied down some sayings of Marcus Aurelius, which Imogen felt she would like to think about at some time but was not enough at leisure from herself to consider now. Then he said something about ill health – a condition of the heart, and that he could not expect many more years of active work in front of him, though he hoped never to get to the state of being a burden to other people. Imogen laid down the letter in impatient dismay, feeling that this was too much, on top of everything else. And what did it mean? She consulted the letter again but its studied inexpressiveness told no more on a second reading. It did not say he might die at any moment, or that he would probably die in a few years' time – why then did she immediately suppose that one or other of these fates was now his prospect? She knew it, she realized, not from the letter but from the whole of her experience of the man. He must have received very serious warning of the condition of his heart before he said as much as this to her, and have spoken now only because not doing so might be to expose her to a terrible shock. There was more overleaf, of his saying very little to Primrose, not wanting her to be weighed down by the idea of living with an invalid, of his determination never to live as one while he could avoid it, and his begging Imogen not to talk about this to anyone except Evelyn.

The chill misery of this news invaded the background of her thoughts, making her feel that when she could detach her mind from her jealousy and distress, there was nothing anywhere to turn to that would give relief. Her opinion of herself was mortified as she recognized that her strongest feeling at the moment was resentment that Paul, Paul of all people, should be adding to her unhappiness instead of alleviating it. The image of herself as she wished to appear, aided by her real affection and the awakening sense of what his loss would mean, presently banished the base emotion from her mind and she sat down to answer his letter. She spent the best part of the morning writing and re-writing and sitting for long minutes with her pen in her hand and eyes too full of tears to be able to see.

At lunchtime she came downstairs gloomy, languid and with traces of weeping. She glanced at Gavin to see whether he showed any latent amiability to which she ought to respond but as he appeared not only self-contained but sullen she made no effort. At the sight of the fish salad however, beautifully arranged with pimentos, cucumber and piles of shredded lettuce, she suddenly remembered Tim and asked if he had gone home?

'No,' said Gavin, kicking the table leg. 'He's having his in the play-room.'

'What*ever* for?'

Gavin muttered: 'He thought you thought he ought to muck off, or something.'

'*I* thought so? I never—' Imogen was out of the room by this time. In the play-room she found Tim eating a salad a replica of their own but arranged on an individual plate, and reading *The Memoirs*. He seemed surprised but pleased to be summoned to the dining-room, closing his book with quiet alacrity and following her with his plate. Imogen was struck, not for the first time, by the completeness of the arrangements that could exist in the house unknown to herself.

'How far have you got?' asked Gavin in an interested voice as they appeared.

'To where they said there were some sheep that had gone lame.'

'Oh. I bet you don't know what that means.'

'Of course I don't – not yet. I don't want to till it comes out.' The meal took on a more cheerful aspect at once, and while the boys chattered, Imogen gradually revived from the wretchedness of the morning and began to look forward, anxiously but hopefully, to their hearing the result of Mountjoy *v.* Mountjoy. Evelyn's clerk would telephone her, she knew, as soon as the judgment was known.

Some time towards three o'clock she went down to the village to collect a small suitcase that Evelyn would want on his Scottish holiday. It was being repaired by the local ironmonger, who did saddle-stitching for the farmers. Imogen was glad of her large, shady hat; as she came out of the shop, the suitcase in her hand, the road was a blinding white. She paused, seeing everything quiver in the vitreous brightness of the afternoon, when suddenly a wave of languorous but powerful scent engulfed her, a heady, synthetic perfume utterly inappropriate to a village street. It exuded from Mrs. Plender, whose roadster stood glittering at the curb.

'Oh, Mrs. Gresham!' she exclaimed. 'Isn't it grand? Perhaps you haven't heard yet? Blanchie phoned just before I came out. I've come down now to see if they've got any raspberries.'

'What—?'

'Evelyn's client has won his case. Blanchie says Evelyn was marvellous. But of course we all expect that, don't we? And the old lady gave her evidence without a hitch. Blanchie had been awfully worried about her. I know it had been on her mind ever so.'

'How nice of her to take so much interest.'

'Oh well, of course she was so much in on this, wasn't she? Driving Evelyn so much, and seeing to those late meals as he hates restaurants so of course she naturally heard a great deal about it all. I know they had a number of pow-wows about the case – I think she feels she helped him quite a lot.'

'*Helped* him? In what way?'

'Oh, you mustn't attach too much importance to anything I say, Mrs. Gresham. I know I let my tongue run away with me. My husband often laughs at me for never being able to keep a thing to myself; but there you are, I always say, that's the feminine type, isn't it? If you didn't like it you shouldn't have married it, I always tell him.' Mrs. Plender seemed to sense some lack of enthusiasm in her listener for she repeated in slightly huffed tones: 'You mustn't take offence at anything I say, Mrs. Gresham.'

'I won't, Mrs. Plender.'

'But of course,' Mrs. Plender continued more comfortably: 'he found it a help to have someone as practical as Blanchie to discuss the case with. Of course we know you're very clever, Mrs. Gresham—'

'No, I am not.'

'Oh yes, *I* should be quite afraid of you, I know. But Blanchie is very practical, you know. We often used to say, at home, she ought to have been a boy, and I think she's a great help to Evelyn because of that.'

'How nice. But if you'll excuse me, Mrs. Plender, I must go home at once. My husband's clerk will have telephoned now that the case is finished, and I must hear the message.' She turned and walked swiftly down the pavement, disregarding Mrs. Plender's calling out an offer to drive her back to her own house with the suitcase. Pretending deafness was the only resource; she could not reasonably refuse a lift or endure to accept one.

She could only think that this preposterous time-lag was owing to Blanche's having telephoned her half-sister the moment the case was finished – she must, then, have been in court – had she been there all the time? – while the clerk would have to wait for the news till Evelyn telephoned him or returned to his chambers. Sure enough, she found that the call had come while she was out. Gavin and Tim were hanging about the hall, inarticulate but joyous, while Miss Malpas met her in sober triumph. The clerk had promised to telephone again, to speak to Imogen personally, but she did not wait for this. She put through a call herself and heard that the decision had been given immediately after the luncheon interval. Mr. Mortimer Mountjoy had been successful in his claim, the Marchioness had sustained the ordeal of the witness-box to admiration.

'And Mr. Gresham?' said Imogen, wanting to hear something of him but hardly knowing what to ask.

The clerk answered solemnly: 'I have been talking to one of our gentlemen who was in court, and I understand that we were very great.'

Imogen turned to the boys as she rang off. 'Isn't that splendid?' she asked.

'Yes,' they said, and disappeared again.

The brief answer was so full of feeling, it was all she wanted to hear; the moment was one of perfect satisfaction. Then its glow faded. In the cool, stone-floored hall the shadows were deep. Outside the open front door, a small bright vista of foliage and light gave the impression of being far off. Her head had begun to ache from the tears of the morning and the glare of the village street. She went upstairs, bumping the suitcase at each step, the hat in her other hand brushing the wrought-iron balustrade, but she was oblivious of what she was doing. The revelation of the degree of Blanche Silcox's intimacy with Evelyn – 'all those late meals, as he hates restaurants' – yet did it tell her anything she did not know? Did it not merely fill in the details of a picture she had unconsciously drawn for herself? But she had never known until this moment that in a state of jealous agitation each separate detail is as painful as the whole: The comings and goings, the telephone calls, the brief visits paid by car between the two houses, the evenings in London, the constant, close intimacy filling every hour that she herself was not there, and now this monstrous arrangement of the holiday in Scotland: it was like some closed book she was wild with curiosity to read, although the meaning was known to her already. For a moment she bitterly regretted that in turning her back on Marcia Plender she had shut off a source of plentiful information on what she now wanted to know more than anything in the world, but even in the moment of regret she knew she could never bring herself to seek information from such a source. Mrs. Plender was abominable. Besides – the remembrance came to her with a moment's cool relief – she had no need to ask information from anyone but Evelyn. In the last resort, she would have only to apply to him. But it would be a last resort.

She was usually restless and alert for the possibility of Evelyn's ringing, but with so much in her mind of which she could not speak on the telephone, she was for once reluctant to hear the sound. When it summoned her that evening the effort she was obliged to make put spirit into her tones. She gave him all her congratulations and added the boys', which pleased Evelyn particularly. He was going to a public dinner that evening; the next day he was to lunch with the Cochranes, and make the final arrangements for going north on Thursday. He would come home on Wednesday afternoon, and pack. Had Imogen remembered to collect the suitcase? When he rang off she was in a much calmer frame of mind. The knowledge that he had a dinner this evening and a lunch to-morrow neither of which could include Blanche Silcox was, for the time being at least, a consolation.

His arrival the following afternoon in a taxi from Chalk Station was a pleasure without drawback. Though much worn, and stooping more than she had seen him do before, he was in calm and zestful spirits. He said he had something to show her, so she begged to see it; partly to tease her curiosity and partly to show that he disapproved of any uncontrolled eagerness, he first went into the study and opened his letters and then went upstairs and unpacked. When he came down again she was sitting at the little desk in the drawing-room, her graceful head bent over Paul's letter. He stood in the doorway but she did not look up.

'Well,' he said, 'don't you want to see it?' The look of returning delight in her face as she raised it and came towards him both touched and irritated him. He made her sit down in a chair by the window, then laid on her lap a small object wrapped in an old, soft Indian silk handkerchief.

'The old lady gave it to me,' he said. 'I was seeing her into her motor and she took it out of her bag, wrapped up like this, and gave it to me. Mountjoy told me afterwards it had been lying about in a work-box ever since he could remember.'

Imogen had now unwrapped the treasure. A small gold image of Hercules with a gold orb on his bowed shoulders formed the handle of a stiletto whose rock crystal blade, eight-sided, tapered to a point, emerged from the round gold plinth on which the statue was standing. The rich tint of the gold and the crystal's purity made the perfect complement, while the modelling of the image, bowed but of tremendous strength, and its shape, conforming to the design of a haft without departing from vigorous realism, impressed even the uninstructed eye as a work of genius. The metal needed cleaning and the world's orb and the god's head and shoulders showed the unmistakable small dents of children's teeth.

'It's simply wonderful!' cried Imogen softly.

Evelyn took it from her and began gently polishing the haft on the silk handkerchief. 'I took it in to the Museum this morning,' he said. 'They asked me to leave it with them while they considered it. I didn't want to part with it just yet, so I promised to take it in later.'

'Could it – I wonder if it could possibly be by Cellini?'

'Well, well, that's flying rather high, isn't it? What makes you think it might be?'

'Something about the design reminded me of his descriptions of how he made designs and settings.'

'As a matter of fact, that's what I asked them this morning. They wouldn't say anything except that it was sixteenth-century Italian; they just asked me to leave it with them.'

'It's ravishingly beautiful, anyhow.'

'It was nice of her to give it to me, wasn't it? It touched me very much.'

Imogen smiled. 'It was very—' She paused.

'Well, what?'

'Very *suitable* in every way. Because it is not only so beautiful, it is very masculine too; and very – how can one say it – very natural. If you had it in a cornfield, or on the shore, it would look perfectly in keeping.'

'I'm glad you appreciate it,' he said. 'Fancy letting those little brutes cut their teeth on it! It might be possible to hammer out those dents.' He took it into his own hand once more. The image was less than the length of his middle finger; his palm was spanned by the transparent blade through which the flesh showed radiant and warm.

Presently the boys came in to tea. Evelyn took Gavin's head in his hands, bent it backwards towards the light and examined his eye closely. He seemed satisfied. 'Now we'll have to wait for Tim to come out with it,' he said.

Tim smiled cunningly.

'What'll your parents say if you take a bad eye home, eh?'

Tim appeared to consider.

'What'll your mother do?' asked Evelyn, this time with genuine curiosity.

'She won't mind,' said Tim. 'She is busy with her ballet-work.'

Evelyn put down his tea-cup. 'Her *what?*' he asked. His face looked as if he had received a personal insult.

'Her ballet-work,' repeated Tim, almost in a whisper. 'With the gramophone.' He sat in silence, looking at the carpet.

Evelyn recollected himself. 'Well, well,' he said, clearing his throat, 'it's a good thing she doesn't worry. But if you do get it, don't give it to your sisters. In fact, if you develop it, I should think you'd better come here and stay till it's better.'

Imogen who could see at once how Tim's mind would react to this proposal, said: 'Couldn't he stay here anyhow, while you're away? It would be so nice for Gavin, wouldn't it?'

'Jolly good show,' said Gavin.

'Gavin,' said Evelyn, 'don't talk with your mouth full. I wish you would, Tim, unless your family has arranged anything else for you to do?'

Tim made a sliding movement of his legs. His face was alight with anticipation. He did not think it worth while to answer the question of whether his family had made any plans for his amusement.

'You won't mind, my dear?' Evelyn turned to her kindly. 'Make them work for you. They can do all the errands in the village and weed the beds in their spare time.'

After tea when they had the drawing-room to themselves she offered him Paul's letter.

'Oh, oh yes,' said Evelyn. 'This is a letter about himself, is it? He told me he should write to you. No, I won't read it, my dear. Keep it.' He held it out to her. She was much surprised, for though he would often impatiently reject things that interested her, as trifling or dull, he liked to be told things about people he knew; he had in fact a lively degree of curiosity. She supposed this must be one of those instances in which men's delicacy is much more sensitive than women's. A little abashed, she took the letter and allowed it to lie on her lap while she remained in an uncertain silence. Evelyn said with a tender and yet impersonal concern: 'You must feel this very much. I thought of you immediately he told me how serious his condition was.'

'I do feel it dreadfully. But it is worse for you. You knew him long before I did.'

'Still, he is very fond of you, my dear. You and he have always been—' He paused and walked to the french window, standing there with his hands in his pockets.

'Been what?' she asked in a strangled voice.

'Been very close friends, of course,' he replied firmly. 'Why shouldn't you be? It is a close friendship with a romantic tinge. At least, it is on his part. I don't think it's possible for a man to have a great regard for a woman without some slight romantic element in it. In a marriage, one has to be tolerant about these things.'

'Yes, but Paul and I – we hardly ever see each other—'

'You need not explain the relationship to me at this time of day!'

'No, naturally; but it is not like – you speak of being tolerant but our friendship is not the same as—'

'As what?' He turned round. Brilliant anger illuminated his face; she had an instant's impression of seeing it by a flash of lightning. Then he moved his head, and there was nothing but a handsome, elderly, tired man, standing in a drawing-room made gloomy by the foliage outside.

'Well, as what?' he said coldly. 'Finish what you were going to say.'

'I mean, it has not been the same as yours with Blanche Silcox.' She continued hurriedly: 'Paul and I almost never see each other, but I think Blanche Silcox really has more of your company than I do.'

'Imogen,' he said with forced patience, 'you have plenty of occupations of your own, and you don't care to do the things that give a great deal of pleasure to me – when I have time to do them. You don't want to fish or shoot and you can't drive my car, which would be a help to me sometimes. Am I to understand that you object to my having the companionship of another woman who can do these things? My life is a fairly hard one, as you know. Do you want me to give up these relaxations because you don't enjoy them yourself?'

'No! God forbid.'

'Then what are we arguing about?'

'We are not arguing.'

'You're not going to say we're quarrelling, I hope?'

'No! No!'

He sighed shortly and walked towards the door. Frightened as she now was and unequal at the best of times to opposing him, the experience of twelve years of marriage with Evelyn which had contained innumerable occasions when he was at her feet, had given her a sort of mechanical confidence that sometimes came to her aid without her seeking it. She got up out of her chair and said in tones that were appealing but a command also: 'Wait a moment, dearest.' He came back again and she thought she could just make the effort required to say her piece with affection and calmness: 'Don't misunderstand me. Of course I don't want – I wouldn't dream of trying to stop your pleasures. It *does* upset me a little that she can do so much for you when I can do so little, but I will try hard not to let it.'

'So little!' he exclaimed. Her hand was on his arm. He picked it up and kissed it, then tucked it into his elbow again and pressed it against his heart. They started to walk upstairs together, for he meant to pack. In the delightful ease and naturalness of their reconciliation, she found it a simple matter to ask whether Blanche Silcox were going to drive up with him to-morrow?

'Good Lord, no,' he said, throwing clean shirts on to her bed. 'She and her sister's family are going to Whitby first. Then the children will go somewhere else and Blanche and the Plenders will come up to Scotland. After that they'll go to Skye, when we come home.'

As he collected his belongings the constriction of the past few days was loosened and he began to talk to her about the case: what he had feared, what had encouraged him. He described the scarecrow-like, indomitable figure of the Marchioness in the witness-box. 'Everything she had on was perfectly good – quite sumptuous, some of it, yet somehow she looked as if she were in rags. She wore a great flapping felt hat with a diamond brooch pinned into it that flashed like a lighthouse all the time. I suppose her head was shaking a little. She said just what we wanted her to say, without a tremor, in a hoarse, rough voice that carried like anything – though *I* kept thinking each word would be the last. Caxton behaved like a thorough gentleman – just asked her one simple question in a very courteous way, and let her go. It was all rather superb – when it was over.' He took out the stiletto and laid it on the dressing table. 'That must go to the bank while I'm away,' he said.

A little later when he was in the garden talking to the boys the telephone rang and Imogen approached it, prepared to be cordiality itself to Miss Silcox; it was not Miss Silcox however, but Evelyn's clerk. He asked if Evelyn had seen the evening papers?

'No,' said Imogen. 'I don't think he can. He didn't bring any with him.'

The clerk said that they had just read the announcement in the stop-press column that the Marchioness had died of a cerebral haemorrhage at one o'clock.

THIRTEEN

Tim moved into the house with silent speed. He came up next morning carrying a small cardboard attaché-case tied round with string. He appeared on the drive as Evelyn was seeing to the disposal of his luggage in the car. When Imogen, having received Evelyn's parting kiss and watched him drive out of the gate, returned to the house, Tim was already in it, lying on the playroom floor deeply absorbed in *The Hound of the Baskervilles*.

His presence in the household was a great asset, for it made Gavin entirely easy to deal with. The boys were happy all day long and Gavin made none of his usual protests about household routine. As for Tim, he seemed to relish having regular hours imposed on him, and would be heard saying mildly: 'It's time for our milk and biscuits, isn't it?' or: 'We'd better not start that now; it's nearly time to go to bed.'

The household seemed in such good order that Imogen thought this would be an excellent time to do what she both wanted and felt she ought to do, to spend a few days in Welbeck Street. She suggested herself to the Nugents for three nights and received a civil reply from Primrose, saying they would be glad to see her if she came before Mum's visit. From Paul she had a note saying merely: 'Thank you. Please come.' She wrote to tell Evelyn that she meant to leave the boys under Miss Malpas' care and go to Welbeck Street and had in reply a photographic postcard showing a beautiful stretch of river-bank. The card said: 'Don't worry about the boys. Very glad you should see something of poor P. Hereabouts is where B. caught her first salmon.'

'Good God!' thought Imogen. 'What do I care if it is?' and she tore the picture into minute fragments. Gavin had seen the post-card lying on the hall table and had obviously read the back. 'Was that a picture of where Daddy is fishing?' he asked later in the day.

'Yes.'

'Can I see it?'

'I've torn it up now.' He looked at her but said nothing.

Her first few hours in Paul's company were reassuring, for, ignorant as she was, she expected to see him looking much more ill, and did not recognize the significance of the change she actually saw. Paul looked paler but he also looked younger, for the outline of his face was a little fuller and the lines considerably smoothed. He was so alert and willing to talk, that the fact of his moving more slowly than usual made him seem only a little more impressive than he appeared as a rule. Hitherto, Imogen had always slept upstairs in the part of the upper flat Evelyn retained. Now she found herself in the Nugents' spare bedroom, an arrangement which meant that many an odd ten minutes' conversation was added to the day. For the first time she gained a clear impression of Primrose as a poised, mature young matron. Nor was the impression in itself disagreeable: it was dismaying only in relation to the man she had married. Primrose was in perfect command of her situation, from the simple fact of not understanding what it was. Her appearance had not much altered since her marriage but had gained a great deal of assurance. Her lovely, youthful slenderness was now a little angular but with her white skin and hazel eyes, the straight, silken brown hair that had an almost greenish tint, and her agile movements, she still retained her nymph-like charm. Her clothes were not elegant, but they were chosen with some care. The garnet ornaments, the jet, that Paul had once hoped to see on her white neck and arms, were never taken out of their boxes. 'Fancy anybody wearing *them*!' she had said. 'They look as if they came out of the Ark.' She did sometimes wear the string of pearls he had given her; left to herself, she preferred pink- and blue-enamelled flowers on a bright gold chain. Her manner had a lightness and decision like her movements. As Paul had long ceased to exacerbate her by demands she could not meet, as he was tolerant of any failures in the practical sphere and appreciative of her successes, responsive to any efforts she made towards pleasing him and always mindful of her pleasure and comfort, there was nothing to interfere with her self-possession and self-confidence. She would set him right without hesitation on any point under discussion except a professional one, and even in a matter of medical opinion, she would sometimes say that she did not see how that could be right, or that her friend's brother-in-law, a doctor at Wimbledon, had said something quite different.

To Imogen she was pleasantly condescending. The latter watched her with an anxious, wondering, sympathetic attention; it was clear that Paul, as he himself had said, had made no serious disclosure to her.

Paul had arranged his engagements for the three days of Imogen's visit so that he had one entire morning and two afternoons at her disposal. He wished to spend these times making expeditions in her company. A harmonious element in these schemes was the fact that Primrose had, in all sincerity, no wish to join them. She had no fears now of Imogen's influence over her husband and she did not take much interest in what she called seeing the sights. A journey by water to the Tower or a walk in Westminster Abbey held no attraction for her since she had 'done' both in expeditions while she was at school. As for walking round the Nash terraces of Regent's Park, what was the point of that? She could not think why those houses should not be pulled down, anyhow. They all had basement kitchens.

Paul and Imogen were therefore completely free to enjoy the outings by themselves. The weather was warm, bright and still, and London was steeped in that gracious quietness that descends for a brief time in late summer; it cannot show itself over the city as a whole, which is covered with a mesh of screaming traffic at every season of the year, but it is felt in strange midday pauses and early morning quietness, in a blessedly empty space of pavement here and there, an unexpected calmness at a street crossing. Every moment of such relief, every charm of sound and sight, added to their happiness. In Imogen's case the happiness was that of an enclosure, outside whose walls pain is kept back for the time being. As she willed herself into a state of calmness and receptivity in which Paul should be able to find response, she found herself preternaturally aware of his frame of mind. She realized with a sense of awe that for the present tranquillized grief, that he not only thought that he would not live, but that he no longer wanted to. He would continue to work as unremittingly as his powers allowed; he would do nothing to husband them.

On the second evening of her visit they all three sat in the drawing-room whose three splendid sash windows, their panes filled with the clear, delicately coloured evening sky, made a decoration with which the room needed no other. Primrose sat cutting flowers out of a piece of patterned stuff and stitching them on to a plain piece. Paul half lay in a wing chair; the blue smoke of his pipe hung about his head in wreaths that seemed as if they would not dissolve.

'*Time doth transfix the flourish set on youth,*' he said. Did Imogen know that sonnet? It was one of his favourites, he scarcely knew why. That line seemed to him one of the most magical in the whole of Shakespeare's poetry. Imogen did not remember it, and having seen his copy of the *Sonnets* on one of the shelves, got up at once and brought it to him. As she returned to her seat she saw Primrose pause in the snipping of her bright scissors and look at them before she bent her head over her work again. Imogen would not willingly now have caused any hostility between them, but it was too late to deflect Paul's interest from the book, even if she were right in thinking that Primrose resented it. He began to read aloud, sonnets of which he was particularly fond himself, and ones she asked him to find, and most of the evening till they went to bed was spent in this way.

Imogen got to bed in a strange state of heaviness and suppressed dread of which she did not try to examine the cause. She had brought the *Sonnets* with her and began to read them as she lay in bed. With the fatal pull of a lodestone, her attention was drawn to the one poem that could wreck her uneasy peace:

When to the sessions of sweet silent thought
I summon up remembrance of things past

and its catalogue of woes: disappointment, emptiness, losses by death: that was Blanche Silcox's life up till very lately, unprotestingly, bravely borne.

But if the while I think on thee, dear Friend!
All losses are restored and sorrows end.

That was Blanche Silcox now. That these exquisite words should describe Blanche and her relations with Evelyn, gave Imogen a deadly pang. She turned out the lamp and allowed the book to fall on to the floor. Burying her face in the pillow, she felt that she would never sleep, but she had misunderstood the exact nature of the night's ordeal. She slept fairly soon, and it was not till half-past one that she started up, broad awake and fully conscious.

Without a second's warning images began to stream through her mind as if she had wakened up suddenly to find herself in the middle of the showing of a film. They were of Blanche Silcox, under all the aspects in which she had ever seen her, the brooding, intense, suffering look, the restrained watchfulness, the heavy, humourless expression, the frumpish appearance – the tremendous vigour, the throaty voice, the vehemence, the paleness, the heat.

'It's an art, some people have it,' Evelyn had said. I must be dreaming! she thought wildly. It *could* not be! A woman without looks, without – but Paul had said: 'Are you sure you know what men fall in love with?'

She sat up, pushing the hair out of her eyes with palms that were wringing wet. The pain was like a knife with a searing edge. In the absolute stillness she closed her eyes, picturing the hundreds of miles' length that lay between her and Scotland: the long land that loomed up in darkness, while all round its shores the sea, faintly visible in starlight, slipped in and out with foamy edge. The sense of helplessness in the face of frightful calamity, the longing to project herself through the dark air, filled her heart to bursting. An insane chatter reached her ear: she opened her eyes; it was the light, rapid tick of her travelling clock. She moaned as she saw by the luminous face how early in the night it was, and wondered how she was to bear the time till half-past seven. A sickening answer told her that she was going to find out.

The next morning was not one which Paul had to spare, though he would be free after lunch. Imogen, pale and with heavy eyes, was glad to see very little of him except at breakfast. She spent part of the morning sitting with Primrose, and now that they were alone together she wondered very much if the latter would speak about Paul's condition. While they drank their coffee, Primrose said abruptly: 'You've heard, I expect, that Paul is rather worried about his heart.'

'Yes,' said Imogen softly, wanting to show the sympathy she felt but afraid of seeming to know more grounds for it than Primrose knew herself.

'He told Evelyn, I suppose.'

'He did, and we do both feel so sorry – for him and you.'

'Oh,' said Primrose, 'I don't let it worry me too much. That condition may go on for years and years without its becoming much worse.'

'I'm sure you're right not to worry more than you can help.'

'Of course it would be very sad if it stopped him from working – he's so wrapped up in his work.'

'Yes, he would feel that dreadfully.'

'Of course he's had the very best advice.'

'Yes, that must be some comfort.'

'So I don't feel there is very much to be done about it. One has to realize it, but it would depress him very much if I started to take a gloomy view of it.' She rose and carried away the tray, neat, sensible, light-footed. Imogen felt that she was looking at a child. It was eerie, uncanny, to sit so close to that bright, practical unconscious creature, with the burden of her own knowledge. She longed for Primrose to be given a serious warning, so that some wretchedness endured now might lessen the impact of what was to come; she felt that Primrose had a right to such a warning, but Paul had judged otherwise for her and no one was in a position to overrule him.

Primrose and she were not very good company for each other and she would have much enjoyed being able to see Cecil; but Cecil was taking a holiday in Yorkshire before joining Hunter's party for the Doncaster races. Imogen's satisfaction at this arrangement did away with the disappointment of not being able to see Cecil now, though there had never been a time since their being known to each other when she had wanted Cecil's company so much.

That afternoon Paul had decided they should go by water to the

Tower and nothing could have been more soothing. The sky was a soft, deep blue, and though in the streets it was a hot afternoon, a delicious breeze met them at the water's edge. As Paul handed her into the boat he regretted that she could not be said to be, like Belinda, launched on the bosom of the silver Thames, for the water was opaque and of a dark, brownish grey. But as they began to move, the sunbeams trembled on the floating tides as they had on Belinda's voyage, and strewed the ripples with flakes of burning silver. The fresh, bright day, the dazzling expanse of water were a source of joy in themselves, and as the boat worked its way onwards, the buildings on either side, though deadening reminders of all that had been lost in grace and beauty in the past hundred and fifty years, yet stood back far enough on either hand to adopt some kind of dignity. By looking very hard at the waterfront of Somerset House as they passed it and half-closing their eyes against everything else except the small wharf over which Wren had lodged during the building of St. Paul's they got on happily enough until they met the beautiful sight of the Tower, lying low on the pebbled shore, with its solid grey walls and bastions, and its group of airy turrets paler than the brilliant sky. The outside view was to be all they gained for Paul was in no mood to be impinged on by the reminders of blood and darkness that haunted the precincts inside its walls. They disembarked on the little gravel strand, and waited idly for a boat to take them back, while the distant shouts of boys playing mingled with the raucous cry of gulls. Imogen had determined not to cloud the happiness of the moment by speaking of her own miseries, and sorely as she had wanted to confide in Paul, she now felt the benefit of not having done so, for the resolute putting away of the preoccupation had made her able to gain the relief of complete distraction. She stood on the strand facing the river, the great, air-drawn structure of Tower Bridge rising on her left, and for the moment she felt nothing but a release of spirit in keeping with the warmth, light and air around her. Paul was beside her but turned towards the walls and towers inside which he had refused to go with her. He said something but in her careless ease she did not grasp its sense, until the word, endurance, caught her ear. 'A very great quality,' he was saying. 'One wishes that soft and gentle creatures weren't called on to show it as well as the tougher ones. But they are.' She found herself standing arm in arm with him on the edge of the landing stage, while a boat came towards them buoyantly over the small, sparkling waves. At some time on their return journey though she had no recollection of just when or where, he had thanked her from the bottom of his heart for giving him so much happiness and had said that this was not goodbye: it was something stored up against the time when good-bye must be said.

She came back to Chalk a good deal saddened but much calmer. When she was not thinking of Paul himself and the loss with which she was threatened, she would re-live again and again that strange moment on the pale, bright strand before the Tower when she had heard him say: 'Endurance.' The word had come to her without context, as if it were a message from another sphere, and she remembered the scene as if it had been a vision rather than an actual happening. She had received, too, the impression, unde-fined but very strong, that though she had not spoken about it, Paul knew of her troubled mind and had given her all that advice and support she so badly wanted. Yet what did this amount to? 'Endurance,' he had said, as the Tower loomed behind them, a mute, awful reminder of what this word could mean.

The day after her return came a letter that abruptly changed their plans. The husband of the lodging-housekeeper in Dorset where they had engaged rooms for three weeks wrote to say that his wife had met with an accident and had had to cancel all book-ings for the rest of the season. Imogen wrote at once to tell Evelyn, and wondered in desperation how she was to set about finding accommodation at a week's notice in the middle of August. But Evelyn's reply, much to her relief, accepted the impossibility of this. He said he himself would be perfectly happy at home, and so long as he had Tim's company, he had no doubt Gavin would. It was hard on Imogen not to have a change, the letter went on, in affectionate, considerate vein, but she must see about taking a holiday in the autumn. He would use this time to see Gavin started on his riding lessons; if he were to ride at Brackley Hill, it would be as well to have made a start before he got there; and he looked forward to taking the boys fishing.

Imogen was greatly contented by this reply; to have Evelyn at home, while Blanche Silcox went on to Skye with her relations, seemed to her a prospect of almost perfect satisfaction. The time in London though very brief and though it had meant repressing her own thoughts continually to be at the service of somebody else, had yet been such a thorough change that it had been of great benefit to her. She felt a new hopefulness about the future and was the more glad that she had not opened her troubles to Paul's gaze.

Gavin was beginning to make plans with reference to his autumn term. He was going to give Tim his rabbits to look after while he was away, and would resume a share of them in the holidays. At first he had thought of taking the hutches down to the Leepers' house, but a total want of confidence in the Leeper ménage deterred him from this. He decided Tim could keep the rabbits in the Greshams' garden just as well. Tim agreed. He said he'd probably be about the place a good bit anyhow.

The riding stables where Gavin was to have lessons were attached to a farm some three miles away over the chalk down that rose behind the hanging woods. Imogen told Gavin what his father had said about beginning to ride as soon as Evelyn got back and Gavin seemed considerably interested. She suggested that they should all walk to the stables next day, look at the horses and have a picnic lunch on the downs. Gavin agreed to this, though briefly. She suspected from his manner that he was unwilling to have her company at the stables, where he hoped to enjoy himself with only his father. She ought perhaps to have foreseen this; but since he had acquiesced, however guardedly, in the arrangement, she decided in her new-found confidence, to keep to it. Tim at least would have no nervous fears as to her deportment; fond as he was of being alone with Gavin, he always greeted her appearance with warm, untroubled pleasure. Miss Malpas packed one of her famous picnic lunches, and they set out on a clear, colourless morning to walk three miles before lunchtime. Since Imogen was walking and carrying the basket, the boys could hardly go on bicycles; they compromised by taking one bicycle between them and using it on the ride and tye principle. Once they had scaled the steep path through the hanger, an unbounded stretch of down was all around them.

They were walking in the direction of the sea, and though this was separated from them by the whole width of the intervening county, it was possible to imagine a salt freshness in the air and that the glisten on straw-stacks and small ponds was a part of that peculiar brightness that comes as a reflection from the sliding flashing masses of the waves. The boys were usually about a hundred yards ahead of her, dwarfed by the wide landscape. One hopped along with a foot on one pedal of the bicycle, the other ran tirelessly beside. From time to time they changed places. They came to a short rise of turf, and from its summit looked down to the left into a long valley whose bare, chalky sides were patched with yews, growing in thickets that wore a sombre, frightening look even in the bright day. Beyond this valley, in the centre of a wide, shallow dip, stood the farm, surrounded with low, flint-studded walls, its barn roofs bright orange-red with lichen. As Imogen came down the gradual descent she made out several horses tossing their heads in a stone-walled paddock. As the party drew near the horses lifted their heads high and ran swiftly across the field in different directions. They all appeared highly strung and exceedingly energetic. The retired Major who owned the stables and the farm came out to meet her and she explained who she was, for Evelyn had already been in touch with him. She looked round for Gavin, to introduce him to Major Craike but he was nowhere about; then she caught sight of him on the far side of the paddock, leaning over the wall with Tim, not even looking at the horses who, by this time had crowded together at the far end.

'Which is yours?' asked Major Craike. 'The black? I thought so; he's like your husband. Well, he has the right build. We must see how he takes to it.'

Imogen wanted to say that the horses seemed very fresh, but loyalty to Gavin restrained her. She made a few careless remarks to the Major from which no one would have supposed that she was already in a cold sweat of fear for her child's limbs. Major Craike walked with her across the yard to the gate that gave on the downs. He was a man of few words, but he ran his eye over her bosom, waist and legs in as thorough and practised a manner as if she had been a mare. He gave a slight nod and small smile as if to himself, then raised his stitched tweed hat and turned back to the yard again. Imogen walked straight on over the rutted, stony track, feeling pleased with herself that she had not called to Gavin or in any way compromised him in the Major's eyes, but had in fact neglected his presence so entirely that to the riding-master the visit must have appeared almost pointless. She supposed that the boys would have seen her set off; she walked on as if they had, and sure enough, within a few minutes, Tim swept into view on the bicycle, making a wide detour, while Gavin ran at his back wheel, with a light-footed, leaping gait like an animal's. There was a grove of beeches within view, standing like a temple on the bare turf, and Imogen called out that this would be a good place to stop for lunch. The boys at once increased their pace towards it, Tim bending low over the handle bars and Gavin tearing after him. Imogen came on slowly with the basket, which she now looked forward to putting down. She dropped once more into her former uneasy musings and began to lose the sense of how long she had been walking. For some time the object in her eye had been a single beech tree detached from the grove; unlike its neighbours, which were of greenish bronze foliage, this one was of deep, sultry purple, so dense a hue as to be almost black. As she slowly drew near it, however, the leaves became purged of their violent darkness, until, when she stood underneath them, looking up, they were translucent and of a greenish brown like seaweed.

'Perhaps that is like one's troubles,' she thought, standing still with head tilted back, the basket, held in front of her with both hands, dragging her shoulders forward. She was roused by Gavin's voice, harsh with annoyance, shouting:

'Oh, come on, Mum!' He stood a few yards away, scowling with impatience. She was for the instant almost as much afraid of his displeasure as if it had been Evelyn's. She realized that the mild, genial climate of Paul's adoration had unfitted her for the time being for the rigours of home life.

Gavin said nothing about the horses, nor spoke of the visit at all in her hearing. He submitted good-humouredly however to being measured for a pair of jodhpurs. The firm of outfitters whose name Blanche Silcox had given her sent down a form on which to enter the particulars of his size, and undertook to supply a pair within a few days of its being sent to them.

All the household doings were now seen in the light of Evelyn's return. When he came into the house Imogen thought she had never seen him look better; he was not only hale and strong, in the full lustre of his formidable handsomeness, but there was an embattled, impregnable good humour about him. His mood was set fair and it was clear that he would allow nothing to alter it.

Imogen had had his bed made up in their room again and he accepted this without comment, strewing his possessions about as he unpacked, telling her of the glorious weather they had had, and of how, when poor Bannister had crocked his ankle, he and Cochrane had left him to sit about all day in the garden, heartless as it was, for they could not endure to sacrifice their walking.

'I don't suppose he would have let you!' said Imogen.

'He didn't get the chance, poor old chap. One doesn't go away for a walking holiday to spend it sitting in a garden the size of a pocket handkerchief.'

Imogen was about to ask whether Mr. Justice Bannister had been able to hobble down to the river bank to watch the fishing, but at this moment the gong rang for dinner and she was on second thoughts thankful not to enter on those troubled waters. There was a great deal to talk about: of the boys' doings, of the riding stables, and of Evelyn's presents for them, two fishing rods which he had ordered while he was away and which might arrive by any parcel post. Blanche Silcox's name was mentioned once or twice but only in passing. When the boys had gone to bed, it was no different. They talked now of Paul, and then Evelyn branched off into details of his holiday once again: the excellent lunches he and Cochrane had carried in their pockets, the walks they had made, the stories Cochrane had told him. Sometimes he led her to the river bank, through the delicate, tilted birch trees with white-spotted pink toadstools growing among them, down, down to the very edge of the water, deep, clouded, hurrying over rounded stones, and making its own low, echoing sound. 'All rivers have their own noise,' he said; 'so different from this clucking warbling creature here—' There was the scene of the river, there was the sound – but what else was there was not shown her.

Partly from cowardice, partly from a true wish to please, she kept resolutely from asking any questions about Blanche Silcox and her party. Every hour that went by untroubled increased their mutual happiness and the companionship of the night was all that she had hoped and longed to regain.

Next morning the telephone rang soon after breakfast. Imogen was in the garden cutting off rose heads; she did not come in, knowing Evelyn was at hand to answer it. She did not suppose that Miss Silcox was making a call from the island of Skye but she was prepared to view the matter with equanimity even if she were. She finished her work on the rose bushes and made her morning journey into the village. As she approached the post office a figure in tweed, the jacket jutting out in a familiar fashion, crossed her vision: how strange, she thought, to see someone with a jacket so like—

'Good morning,' said Blanche Silcox.

Imogen was so stunned that she did not attempt any courtesies. She said stupidly:

'I thought you were going to Skye.'

'Oh no,' said Blanche. She added nothing. She might be awkward, deficient in grace; but she had the obverse quality of being unruffled. That social dictum, Never explain, so difficult for the sensitive to obey, was performed by her with as much thoroughness as if she had learned the lesson through centuries of high breeding. Imogen was silent. The obvious truth, that Blanche had changed her plans and come home when she heard that Evelyn was not going to Dorset, filled her mind to the exclusion of everything, and it afforded no grounds for conversation. Blanche stood looking at her. Her figure was bold-fronted, firmly planted and still. It was as uncomely as ever, but her face, as Imogen saw with a shock, was improved almost out of recognition. Some vitalizing emotion had done what all the expensive beauty treatments in the world could never do; the sagging facial muscles were tautened and the skin, slightly powdered like a daring schoolgirl's, had an inspired clearness; it was white as vellum and the cheeks a perceptible, charming pink. The eyes were candid and soft, and it struck Imogen for the very first time that Blanche Silcox might have been a pretty girl.

'Hasn't the weather been *mar*vellous?' said Blanche at last. 'I've just come in to send off some papers to my broker. Things pile up so while one is away.' She walked to the counter where registered letters were received. Imogen watched her leaning on the counter, and heard her speak in her low, determined, authoritative tones. There were now several people in the small office and it was easy enough to walk out without saying anything further.

Imogen put down her basket on the hall table. While she was out, the fishing rods had arrived from town, and the two boys were with Evelyn in his study, collecting scattered wrappings, examining the rods and listening eagerly to Evelyn's primary instructions on how to use them. Imogen was glad of their presence; she said somewhat breathlessly:

'I've just seen Blanche in the village.'

'Oh really? She's usually down there about this time of the morning.'

'But I thought she was going to Skye?'

To her own dismay, she sounded injured, resentful, querulous.

'Well, my dear, if you feel she owes you an explanation of all her arrangements you should ask her for one.' His tone was humorous. Tim laughed as children do when one adult is pleasantly making fun of another. Imogen longed to say: 'I don't think she would want to give *me* an explanation of her arrangements.' But she shrank from the ordeal of provoking his hostility and was glad that the boys' presence withheld her from it. She walked slowly from the room without saying anything. Silence was becoming a shield, a cloak of invisibility. 'If I have not said anything, he can't be angry.'

She found however that once she had lost the initial opportunity of making an issue of Blanche Silcox's unexpected return, the chance to assert herself slipped rapidly farther and farther out of reach. Evelyn's intimidating good humour was one of the chief causes of her defeat. It seemed to encase him like a brilliant armour of glass, through which his limbs could be seen but receive no touch. Debonair, energetic, unusually talkative even, he played and fished with the boys, gardened by Imogen's side with driving vigour, and set her to paste up his scrapbooks, for which newspaper cuttings under various headings had been accumulating since the last vacation. Imogen was often sitting at work with scissors and paste when he returned from one of his several daily calls at the house behind the trees; but when his majestic tread was heard on the hall flags she never plucked up spirits to say, 'And how did you find Blanche this morning?' Not to comment upon, not to seem aware of his absences gained such a noticeable reward in his kindness, his continued benignity, the effort was immediately worth while though a faint chill of dread, intermittently felt, warned her that the longer this state continued the more fixed and immovable it would become.

For the encroachment of Blanche Silcox upon their family life: the degrees by which her intimacy with Evelyn was being enforced as an accepted fact, were increasing almost daily. A good deal of this was due to her very successful relation with Gavin. Blanche drove him over to the stables for his first lesson; she waited while this was carried out in the paddock and on the downs outside it and then drove him back at lunchtime. She stayed to lunch at the Greshams' house and returned to her own immediately the coffee had been drunk. In fact, her form on the occasion was irreproachable. During lunch the conversation was almost all on the subject of riding and Gavin's lesson in particular. Blanche briefly but impressively stated that he had done well and would be a very good horseman, and no one doubted the intrinsic value of her opinion. Imogen was secretly much irritated that Blanche should be allowed to spend this lavish amount of interest, time and trouble on the lessons, for it was clear that she was going to repeat the morning's performance as a regular thing. It laid them under an obligation to her which Imogen was highly unwilling to see and it established her in one of their most intimate coñcεɾnɕ on the footing of a member of the family. It was however useless to indulge this disapproval. Gavin's going over on his bicycle, adding six miles of cycling to the unaccustomed exercise of riding was not desirable as a regular thing, though he would be able to do it at a pinch. His father would sometimes drive him, but Evelyn himself would not be so suitable a companion as Blanche Silcox for he did not ride and though he had any race-goer's interest in horses and was anxious to see Gavin on horseback, his combined interest in boy and mount would be apt to flag during a couple of hours, whereas Blanche Silcox did not care how long she spent watching the performance, Gavin himself would tire sooner than she; and as soon as he was off the leading rein and riding about the downs, she would ride with him. Evelyn was plainly enchanted at the prospect of her doing so. From the fact that he had not thanked her in Imogen's presence for her kindness and trouble, the latter deduced how much he must have said in private.

Imogen said: 'How did you like it?' each time Gavin came back in Blanche's company, and each time he answered: 'Jolly fine,' in a tone which made it obvious there had been no drawback of any kind to his enjoyment.

During the last fortnight of the summer holidays Gavin rode every day, usually in the mornings, though occasionally the time was changed to afternoon or evening. The hour of the lesson was arranged between Major Craike and Miss Silcox with regard to when the former could mount him and the latter bring him, without reference to anybody else. This was perfectly natural, it was not even inconvenient, for Gavin had no other fixed engagements; and as Evelyn said, they were exceedingly lucky to have Blanche to be so kind to the boy. Imogen accepted this statement in silence, but silence was all that Evelyn required.

It was assumed without words that Tim would stay with them till the end of the holidays. During Gavin's lessons he seemed to occupy himself quite placidly. Imogen, seeing his brow propped on his two hands above the play-room windowsill as he read Gavin's copy of *The Lost World*, said to Evelyn regretfully that perhaps it was as well that he should be getting accustomed to Gavin's absence.

'Well, possibly,' said Evelyn, 'but he ought to be riding himself. I don't think I can very well pay for lessons for him – it's a big item, and after all—'

'Yes, why should you? I really think it would be unreasonable. They have plenty of money themselves, I should think.'

'They spend plenty. But why don't you suggest to them that Tim might join Gavin? Say we find Craike very satisfactory, and we'll undertake to see him out there and back with Gavin. Go and see them about it, why don't you?'

Imogen ventured into the Leepers' house that afternoon. She found Mrs. Leeper in the atelier, and at once raised the question of Tim's riding lessons A wild, vague look came into Mrs. Leeper's eyes. 'Oh, my dear,' she said. 'I should have to consult Foss. We couldn't take a step of that kind except in direct consultation with Foss.'

'Foss?' repeated Imogen.

'Oh my dear,' exclaimed Mrs. Leeper, 'Kelvin Foss? He's simply one of the most brilliant alienists now practising anywhere. He is the only alienist in the country at present who employs Schenk's approach.'

'And is he treating Tim?' asked Imogen, astonished.

'Not as yet,' replied Mrs. Leeper, 'but Cliff and I have agreed that Tim can't go to anybody else.'

'Then you don't feel he can have riding lessons?' She got up.

'Heaven knows we've never grudged him anything!' cried Mrs. Leeper. 'It's simply that we can *not* act in the matter without Foss's sanction. It's a matter in which we can't *move* without Foss.'

Imogen realized as she made her way home that if the

consultant's view were to be favourable to the riding lessons, Mrs. Leeper would never say so. Riding lessons would be expensive and so would treatments from Foss; but it would amuse Mrs. Leeper to be liable for the latter; in the former she would take no interest whatever. But alarmed as she was on Tim's account, Imogen did not feel positive that Mrs. Leeper intended to do more than talk about the stupendous Foss, whose fees would undoubtedly be on a scale suitable to his distinction. If she looked like going any further in the matter, Imogen determined that Evelyn should step in and save Tim. She never doubted that he would be able to do so. She thought of all the people who had tried at different times to stand in Evelyn's way. She thought of the Marchioness who had died of a cerebral haemorrhage, properly enough, since she was eighty-five, but she had stood to that great ordeal, with her head shaking so that her diamonds flashed like a lighthouse, because Evelyn had summoned her to it from a bourne where most people could not have reached her. Then she thought of herself. She had no doubt that he would be able, if he liked, to overcrow Mrs. Leeper.

FOURTEEN

Gavin's boxes were packed. Imogen thought that the coming departure had made him a little nervous, but he showed no outward sign of this, and gave Tim last instructions about the rabbits and put away his possessions in private places with calm efficiency. Evelyn was going to motor him to Paddington, where he would join the school party. Imogen took it for granted she was not to go herself: knowing how unsuitable her presence would be on the occasion, she did not even want to go; therefore it was somewhat outfacing to discover that Blanche Silcox was to accompany them. Her look of startled annoyance when she heard it made Evelyn say testily:

'Why shouldn't she, my dear girl? She's going up to town anyway and she'll drive me back.' He added a moment afterwards: 'She won't come on to the platform with us.' Imogen had to admit to herself that it really wouldn't matter to Gavin if Blanche did. He would be shy and wrought up at the first meeting with boys and masters, and whereas Evelyn's presence would be an asset to him, her own would make him apprehensive. Blanche Silcox's, on the other hand, would worry him no more than if she were one of the porters.

It turned out that they were to go up to town in Blanche's car. The Rolls came round after breakfast; Gavin in his new clothes, a little pale, said: 'Goodbye, Mum,' and got into the back seat while Evelyn lifted his boxes into place. Imogen would not come out. She knew she did not look entirely calm and she was unwilling to appear in Blanche Silcox's eyes as the tiresome, emotional mother who embarrasses her son. Besides, who cared whether she came out or not? They drove off, without calling out any further word to her, but it was some satisfaction to see that Evelyn was sitting next to Gavin in the back seat.

When he came back in time for dinner that evening, Evelyn was as kind and attentive as possible. He spoke a great deal about Gavin, said what a nice-looking crowd of boys had been at the station and that the master in charge had been one of the young men he and Imogen had liked when they saw him at Brackley Hill. He himself had spent most of the day in chambers. Michaelmas Term opened in less than a fortnight.

Gavin's absence was unexpectedly painful to Imogen. Seeing that they had never been companions to each other, she missed him with surprising acuteness. Some of the pain came from the inescapable knowledge that he would not be missing her. This however she tried to conquer or disregard. Did she want her child to be miserable, as a tribute to herself? She knew she would have strongly disapproved of the sentiment in another woman.

She realized now how much pleasure, support even, Tim gave her by his affection, and by his silent admiration of her as a charming person who did everything right. Tim came up every morning at their breakfast-time, to feed the rabbits, and every afternoon after school to bed them down. On the second visit he naturally had some tea himself in the kitchen, or in the drawing-room if Imogen happened to see and ask him in. Then Miss Malpas took to giving him a mug of coffee in the mornings, and before many days were out, Tim was sitting down regularly in the kitchen to porridge, eggs, bacon, toast, butter and marmalade as well. He came in so silently, and sat down to work with such intense concentration, to see him wielding a large silver spoon over his brown porridge bowl was like getting a glimpse of Lob-lie-by-the-Fire. He was now using the play-room after school and at week-ends almost as much as he had when Gavin was at home.

He showed however a delicate tact. He did not obtrude himself, and never came into the dining-room or drawing-room unless directly invited. When he was in one of these rooms with her, Imogen noticed a surprising habit he had developed of putting things away. She found him quietly restoring her scissors and thimble to their drawer in the work-table, or slipping a copy of Country Life which he had found on the sofa into its place in the paper-rack. He regularly helped Miss Malpas with the washing up and as he passed to and fro the kitchen, if he noticed any crockery piled on the draining board, he washed and put it away. Neatness and domestic order seemed to be a passion with him.

Imogen now looked forward eagerly to a visit from Cecil, who was to come for the first week-end in October, arriving on a Saturday morning in time for lunch. As the time approached, Evelyn produced an invitation from Blanche Silcox for them all to dine with her on the Saturday evening. Whatever might have been Imogen's feelings in other circumstances, she was glad of this. She longed for Cecil to see Blanche again, and in Evelyn's company, so that she herself might have the benefit of Cecil's observation. That Imogen should want this assistance was, on the face of it, surprising. She had had a good deal of experience with men and had been married for twelve years and more. Though Cecil's professional contacts were chiefly with men, she had no experience of men in an amorous or even an intimate relationship. Imogen was well fitted to learn a thing by the feel of it, as the saying is, and she had had plenty of opportunity in emotional relationships of perfecting this skill. Merely to be in the same room with a man and another woman would usually tell her more about their relations with each other than their friends could learn over weeks. Cecil on the other hand had none of this apparatus of intuitive perception, but the thing she had, she possessed to an unusual degree. She had very acute vision combined with the power of holding the mirror quite still so that the reflection did not waver. Her face, calm-eyed and close-lipped, never suggested that her powers, whatever they were, made up into happiness; Imogen's expression, pensive and even wistful as it often was, had that dawning luminosity that is on the verge of delight.

Nevertheless on her arrival, Cecil looked better than she had ever looked in her life, tranquil rather than repressed, and beautifully dressed in tweeds the colour of tow and ashes, with rows of smoked pearls round her neck. Imogen was delighted by her appearance but Cecil was unable to return the compliment. In the spare room, Imogen kissed her and for a moment clung to her, trembling and sobbing in a way that all but unnerved Cecil, who was not easily dismayed. The next minute Imogen released her, laughed and wiped her eyes. Like many women who cry easily, she was not much disfigured by tears. When they went downstairs, she was only flushed; Cecil was some degrees paler than before.

At lunch Evelyn was charming. He always liked Cecil and now he seemed to go out of his way to entertain, almost to propitiate her. They discussed the stock market: company meetings and reports, oils losing ground, textiles supported, improvement at Paris, easier tendencies on Wall Street, Funds irregular, a steadier tone perceptible in Mines. Evelyn was highly pleased. 'You seem to know as much about it as Blanche,' he said. Imogen watched him as he examined Cecil and waited for her considered replies. As always, his intent expression showed no trace of even a subconscious recognition of his extreme handsomeness. The holiday had left his face the colour of tawny marble; the sea-bright eyes with their dark framing of brows and lashes had a look of indulgent interest; the short nose with its springing arch of nostril suggested, it was true, a less benevolent temper. In the heavy lower part of the face, the lips were shut like the edges of an iron box.

Immediately after lunch Evelyn disappeared on what Imogen now accepted as his daily visit to the other house. For once she was glad of it, she wanted Cecil to herself. She meant to confide to Cecil all her misgivings and miseries, but with as much of her mind as she could detach from her own concerns she wanted to hear of Cecil's. She was now confident of an interest in Cecil on Hunter's part. She could imagine that the unusual qualities of each might suit the other very well but she was cautious of approaching the matter. The absence of romantic interest in Cecil's life up till now had had the effect of increasing her shyness, her hesitation, her scepticism. Imogen, in her anxiety to influence Cecil towards giving Hunter encouragement and her fear of alienating her by any intrusion on her feelings, felt herself in the predicament of someone trying against time to induce a hunter to enter a horse-box.

The mere pleasure of each other's society however was enough for such an early part of the visit. They went into the drawing-room and Imogen lit the wood fire. The heaped twigs burst into crackling flame, sending out an instantaneous glow of warmth and pink gold light which bathed their wrists as they quickly laid on the fuel.

'I used to think,' said Imogen, sitting back on her heels, 'that a fire was one of the most potent snares for making you lose yourself. The water in the river was another. I seemed to spend so much time being lost, it used to alarm me, almost, how one half of my mind always seemed to be mislaying the other half. Sometimes at the end of the day, if I'd been more or less by myself, I simply couldn't account for how the time had gone. Have you ever felt like that?'

'No.'

'I don't now, either. But I find it's very uncomfortable not to. Being – conscious, I suppose you'd call it – *all* the time – it makes anything which is the matter, worse and worse, like an uncomfortable pillow that you want someone to turn for you when you're ill.'

Cecil looked at her with an unusual darkness welling up in her glass-clear eyes.

'How is the thing that is the matter?' she asked gently.

'I do so long to tell you. But we've got to go to dinner there tonight. And I think we'd better not talk much first. I'd feel so self-conscious when we got there.'

'Yes, I see that.'

'Now tell me all about the Doncaster races.'

Cecil smiled and began her story, which Imogen found very satisfactory.

When they walked into Blanche Silcox's dining-room that evening Imogen saw with a shock how much it now showed the influence of Evelyn's taste. The flocks of Edwardian water-colours in ornate gilt frames had disappeared; the walls were now bare except for a circular looking-glass surmounted by an eagle, and a colour print of Nelson engraved by Valentine Green, both of them bought under Evelyn's tutelage. The dining table and chairs were of Hepplewhite design, and as the room had been cleared of numerous pieces of unnecessary furniture, the good shape of what remained was strikingly seen. Combined with these elements, those supplied by Blanche Silcox herself, the warmth of central heating and the beauty of open fires, the luxurious softness of the carpets, the rich dinner served on Goode's china, the enormous array of bottles and decanters ranged in shining rows three and four deep, and the low but silvery light from powerful lamps in white parchment shades made up a domestic interior of some importance.

Cecil's watchfulness though unremitting was as impartial as a looking-glass. She showed none of that sharp scrutiny, the narrow observation that had been so noticeable in Blanche's manner towards herself. This trait in Blanche's behaviour, however, was now much diminished; she showed a new feature, an ebullience so striking as almost to alarm. A stranger such as Cecil could hardly say with entire assurance what had caused this, but it was consistent with that peculiar buoyancy of a woman who has a lover for the first time, in an elderly woman an almost overpowering exhilaration. Blanche Silcox had no idiom of gaiety, her manner was abrupt, uncouth as ever, and she was, at the same time, attempting a severe self-control, but even so the surging tide of triumphant happiness would not be concealed. Seeing her in these surroundings, and in this state, it was at last possible to understand where her attraction for Evelyn might lie. Cecil saw, moving about in this scene of rich comfort, a woman of vitality so intense that her outward form was for the time being of no more importance than the shape that encloses a bright light. But her actual appearance had altered immeasurably for the better. The pale skin glowed, fine and translucent; the greying hair which Cecil remembered as waved in such harsh corrugations, it was a puzzle to think how an expensive hairdresser could have achieved them, now wore a different air altogether. Nothing had been altered, the same operations had been performed by the same hand; but now, great, creating Nature had co-operated in the work. The result was a small head, with classically parted hair drawn down each side of a high, clear forehead and neatly undulating over the ears, like a sitter of Leonardo's. As she stood looking at Evelyn, smiling, rapt, speechless, attentive to his every word and look, agog to promote his comfort and happiness, it was the moment of revelation: of an equipoise between the two. Their weights balanced. There appeared to Cecil in a naked flash, a vision of that chemical sexual affinity which can exist without any of the outward attractions or graces, and where it does so exist, makes such attractions irrelevant.

Evelyn moved without invitation to the head of the table, where he carved a pair of ducklings. It was evident to the two female guests that all the hospitable and festive preparations had been made to do honour to him. The dinner was a celebration, in whose honour was plain enough. Imogen for the first time in her married life found herself at a gathering where she was of less importance than anybody else. She was not Blanche's chief woman guest, for Cecil was that, and she was anything but Evelyn's first interest; but there were other painful impressions to occupy her, and she soon lost sight of the disagreeable novelty of her insignificance.

Evelyn talked most, in a genial, unforced manner. He was so full of well-being, so thoroughly at ease, he had leisure to spare for both courtesy and caution. He made a point of drawing out Cecil, who, civil and unsmiling, answered with remarks that he appeared to find uncommonly pertinent.

Blanche Silcox was somewhat silent as usual; when she spoke it was in an exclamatory, vehement way. Cecil had not had an opportunity before of noticing how very dogmatic her utterances were. The topic of the free Health Service had come up and Miss Silcox unhesitatingly accounted for the crowded condition of doctors' waiting-rooms by the fact that the lower orders could now do their malingering for nothing.

'If they're slightly hoarse or have the slightest twinge of rheumatism, in they go!' she stated.

'Up to a point,' said Cecil. 'But don't you think that—?'

'There's nothing else in it. It flatters their self-importance. And we pay for it.'

'That accounts for some of the crowding, but isn't some of it due to—?'

'It's due to nothing but their determination to get something for nothing.'

'But I really think that one reason—'

'My dear, there *is* no other reason, none at all.' Cecil gave up the attempt to suggest that previously, many housewives and bread-winners had not dared to admit themselves ill, because it would mean expense. She felt no urge to make the point against such odds, and had she been allowed to bring it out, Miss Silcox might have denied it any validity. Nor would Cecil have quarrelled with her for her opinion. What struck her was the persistent refusal even to hear the opinion of somebody else. She glanced at Imogen and saw her looking at the table cloth with an expression of shrink-ing despair.

Evelyn did not in so many words dissent from Blanche's view but he led the conversation away from it and by easy stages, through State education and journalism, arrived at the sales of popular novelists. Like many men who command large incomes in their own profession, he was always interested to hear of the large incomes to be made in other professions, and his pertinacious enquiries about advances down, royalty scales, serialization, play and film rights and fees for broadcasting, made him so exclusively occupied with Cecil that the climax of the meal, a ham mousse iced, had to be praised by Imogen. Evelyn paid it only one 'Most delicious,' before he was back again among the intricacies of copy-right like a terrier after a rat. Blanche Silcox did not show any mortification at his cavalier reception of a dish which, on another occasion, he would have enthusiastically welcomed. But nor had she shown any obvious gratification when he praised the duck and the mulberry pudding. In their deep domestic intimacy silence before other people was the appropriate thing. When however after coffee in the drawing-room, Evelyn seemed about to return to the question of Messrs. Cotman and Blewett's financial dealings with their authors, Miss Silcox rose in a decided manner and opening an escritoire, brought out a brooch. It was the represen-tation of a flower and two leaves, set in platinum, which, together with the several hundred pounds' worth of diamonds of which it was composed, might as well have been nickel and paste for any life the designer and jeweller had been able to evoke from their materials. She handed this to Evelyn, saying she had just had it sent from the bank, and inviting him to separate it into its three component parts, for the flower and its two leaves could be made to form a brooch and earrings. Evelyn at once settled himself in a chair under the standard lamp and set to work. He was impressed by the value of the stones but said the setting was in shocking taste. He spoke with the complete frankness of a brother, or a husband. Blanche Silcox stood at his shoulder. They all three watched him while he screwed up one eye and directed the piercing gaze of the other to the minute catches which secured the parts each to each. When he had separated them he put them together again to make sure he had mastered the process. Then he undid them and handed the three parts to Blanche.

'You should have them re-set,' he said, 'or else sell them and buy something more elegant.'

'I am no good at choosing anything of that kind,' she said gruffly. 'I never have been. I shall have to get you to advise me.'

'My dear girl,' he said absently, 'I don't know that I could advise on such an expensive thing as that. Still, we could find somebody who would.'

The two female guests were completely silent. Imogen was incapable of saying anything and Cecil was not disposed to take the trouble. The long pause made itself uncomfortably felt by the other two. Evelyn began to speak of Gavin's first letters home, and the conversation became general. At a noticeably early hour Evelyn said they must go. He said in a careless, random, facetious manner that Cecil burned the candle at both ends in London and that when she came into the country it would do her good to get a long night. The shameless falsity of the excuse he gave for breaking up the party, and the impossibility of calling him to any account for it, impressed Cecil uncomfortably. The sight of Imogen's downcast face made it plain that to her the sensation was already a familiar one.

They all exerted themselves to be civil in the hall, and when Imogen thanked Blanche for such a delicious dinner and a pleasant evening, Blanche thanked her for coming with a good show of having really wanted to see her.

The front door was composed of two leaves, one of which was opened for them. Imogen walked out first into the autumn night, fragrant and chill. She made her way with bent head across the gravel to where the car stood. Cecil followed her but on the doorstep some instinct made her turn round. Though Evelyn and Blanche Silcox had been just behind her, neither was there. Cecil hurriedly walked on and a second later Evelyn came out from behind the left-hand half of the door. Blanche followed him on to the drive and called out that they would be washing her car tomorrow. He'd better bring his and let it be done at the same time. Evelyn was climbing into the driving seat and made some answer not quite audible. Blanche Silcox repeated her commands in an absolute halloo.

'Don't forget,' she shouted in authoritative tones; 'it's much better to do two at the same time.' Imogen and Cecil who were sitting together in the back seat stared through the window speechlessly. Evelyn called out that he'd be along some time, and they drove off.

The next morning Imogen and Cecil went to church. The former never asked anyone to come with her but she was always much pleased when anyone offered to do so. Cecil never went of her own accord; she had no religious instinct, only an ethical one; but the beauty of the service impressed her and she was always ready enough to go when Imogen went.

At lunchtime it was explained to Evelyn that Cecil must go back by an early train; he deplored the shortness of her visit and said he would drive her to the station for the five o'clock. 'You'd better give her a cup of tea early,' he said to Imogen. The latter understood this as meaning that he would not be having tea with them. Immediately after lunch Evelyn repeated his promise of being ready to take Cecil to the station at twenty minutes to five, and a few minutes later he drove away.

Imogen and Cecil went upstairs to the sewing-room where they could not be disturbed. Cecil sat in a cane-backed chair but Imogen took a low stool on the hearth. Cecil had wondered how they would begin this subject but Imogen startled her by saying with unusual directness: 'What did you think?'

Cecil's own opinion amounting to a certainty was that Blanche Silcox, however unexpected, and hard to credit the fact might be, was now Evelyn's mistress. She paused in considerable distress. If Imogen did not think this Cecil did not want to encourage her to think it. She kept silent, fearing to do harm if she said anything. But Imogen was not after all waiting to be told what to think. She went on:

'It's got quite beyond me and it's getting worse every day. You see, quite apart from what there is down here – Evelyn is so much in London during terms, and she is too. They would not be in the Welbeck Street flat, I know, because of Paul. But I suppose hotels are quite easy to find—' Cecil said gently:

'She has a flat of her own in Halkin Street, you know.'

After a moment or two Imogen realized that Cecil was standing over her, forcing her head forward over her knees, down and down till her forehead touched the floor. The sensation this produced reminded her of being on a giant switchback. The walls and floor raced round and round and over and over but gradually they came to a stop. The door was open and Cecil was bringing a drink of water. When Imogen had drunk some she said:

'I don't know when I knew. But I did. I have for a long time. Only I wouldn't let myself. When you said that, about a flat, I had to admit it. That's why it made me – for the moment—' her voice died.

'It was too sudden. I am so sorry.'

'No,' said Imogen. 'It was too silly of me, really!' She dipped her handkerchief into the glass of water. Cecil took it from her hand, pressed out the drops, and began wiping her temples with it, saying softly:

'When did you know, do you think?'

'Some – some long time now.'

'When they went to Scotland?'

'When they came back. But one part of my mind was always saying it was impossible.'

'Yes.'

'But once you've admitted it's true, everything tells you how true it is.'

'Yes.'

'You don't feel any doubt, do you?'

Cecil paused. 'I don't feel any,' she said, 'but that's not the same thing as knowing. It wouldn't count as proof.'

Imogen agreed carelessly but brushed the consideration aside and went on: 'It's such a defeat – to see her, and realize what I've lost to– –'

Cecil said hurriedly: 'I don't think – it doesn't seem to me that one can argue like that—' She stopped, in despair. The subtle distinctions she attempted to grasp and to draw, eluded her.

Imogen gave a half-sobbing laugh. 'It's absurdly vain and trivial of me, in any case. And I do see – most terribly clearly – the attraction of another sort she has for Evelyn, and it's all a sort of thing I haven't got. He was romantic and emotional once, but of course he isn't now. How should he be? And he wants something different from what he wanted when we were married. He wants solid, worldly, satisfying pleasures: and she does all the things he wants now, that I can't do. And' – her voice became thickened with tears – 'I have a most dreadful feeling – certainty, in fact – that she's so much more satisfying as a lover than I am. It does seem extraordinary that she should get the chance to show she is, but now she has got it, I am sure she is most tremendous. I feel it in my bones.'

'Yes. One does.'

Imogen wiped her eyes and blew her nose several times. In an extinguished voice she said:

'Evelyn's always saying she's such a thoroughly *nice* woman.'

'If hypocrisy and adultery are no drawbacks to being a nice woman, I'm sure she's as nice as can be.'

The mordant edge on Cecil's tones roused Imogen from herself. 'I must be honest,' she said earnestly. 'I cannot honestly blame her for doing what she's done – I'd like to, but I can't. She's done what almost anybody would do if they had the chance; I'm only staggered, and shocked, and – and appalled that she's *had* the chance.'

'But surely you don't *condone* – you wouldn't, even in some case where the people had no connection with you – you wouldn't condone—?'

'But Cecil – you and I didn't grow up together. And I – we – the people I knew, we always took a worldly point of view about affairs with married people. We used to say, if people behaved sensibly, it needn't break up the marriage – the marriage was something separate.'

'But if you did think that – can't you think it now? After all, there can be no question of a break, unless *you* wanted it.' Imogen was silent, and for so long that Cecil grew alarmed.

'At least,' she said urgently, 'promise you won't take any rash step?'

'No, no, I won't. But I have a dreadful feeling – all those solid qualities – the money and the comfort and the devotion to his wishes – I don't mean that Evelyn is mercenary, for he is not, he married me without a penny – even the money I have got now was all left to me years after we married, we never knew I'd have it; but he does enjoy things so, and he needs to enjoy himself, the terrific rate he works. And I believe that she'll get more and more an essential part of his life, and I'll get less and less – my failings – I shall become just a neurotic bore.'

Cecil was at all times unable to say what she did not think, and Imogen's vision of the future appeared to her to be of deadly accuracy. Imogen's attractions, more even than most women's, depended on her feeling successful and secure. Unhappiness and lack of self-confidence would reduce her charms to the condition of some fragile garland, meant to float in mid-air over a festive scene, blown down and lying rain-soaked on the pavement. The position as Cecil saw it was acutely disquieting, and she suffered in every nerve from longing to give comfort and encouragement and seeing none to give. While she paused, enduring the sensation of being brought completely to a standstill, Imogen said:

'She's even better with Gavin than I am. He doesn't mind what *she* does with him.' Then she began to cry unrestrainedly. It came upon Cecil with an inescapable thrust: 'I can't fetch anybody, there's nobody who can help. I would avoid it if I could, but I can't. This has got to be done by me.' Yet there was nothing to be done, except to show affection in silence. Happily, to someone of Imogen's receptiveness, the desire to comfort made itself felt even when comfort could not be given. After a time, she stopped crying and was contending only with the backwash of her sobs. It was now getting late, too late for Cecil to have any tea and in any case Imogen's coming downstairs was out of the question. Cecil ran to her room and packed her suitcase rapidly. Then she came back to the sewing-room. Imogen's head was aching now, but she preferred to sit in a chair where she was rather than lie down in another part of the house where Evelyn might see her. Cecil made her as comfortable as she could and took an almost speechless farewell of her. Then she walked downstairs with that composure which had been very useful to her in her lonely and somewhat arduous existence.

When Evelyn met her in the hall, she realized what a blessing

Imogen's headache was. No one who is upstairs with a racking headache can be accused or even suspected of being unco-operative or unreasonable, or wanting to make mountains out of molehills. Evelyn said: 'Oh, poor dear. Well, we must start, I think, if you're quite ready?' The road to the station led past the gates of Miss Silcox's house and Cecil prepared to look out at a building that was now invested for her with a morbid interest. Before they reached the frontage however Evelyn gave an exclamation and pulled up. Blanche Silcox was standing under the hedge, waiting, and hailed him. She opened the car door with her usual calmness. 'Can you give me a lift in to the village?' she said. 'I want to tell my old gardener not to come to-morrow.'

'Certainly we can,' said Evelyn. 'You'd better come and see this young woman off, then I'll take you to Saul's cottage.' Miss Silcox settled herself in the back seat. Cecil thought she would have made a very good policewoman; imperturbable, mild, adamant, she was a loss to the force.

The run to the station was so brief that there was no need for conversation before they drew up in the station yard; this was fortunate for Cecil could not have made any. She realized that Blanche had discovered from Evelyn the train to which he would be taking her and had lain in wait for the car, and that so far from resenting this surveillance of his dealings with another woman, Evelyn was unfeignedly glad of the meeting. There was no mistaking the complacency on his face, his air of genial well-being. That was plain enough to Cecil's sidelong glance. The mystery was, what should cause it. Cecil would not turn round and speak, even for the opportunity of looking curiously at the occupant of the back seat. She was hostile on Imogen's account, and on her own she felt the irritation of one woman who must put up with impertinent intrusion from another. It was fortunate for her that her silence was habitual; on occasions such as this it was not noticed. She meant to get rid of both her companions as soon as she alighted, but she found this was not to be. Evelyn with expansive kindness changed her third-class ticket for a first and carried her suitcase to the right part of the platform. They were in excellent time and Cecil attempted to loiter by herself, studying the posters at the front of the closed bookstall. She found to her surprise that Blanche Silcox was beside her, and that she was not only being polite but showing a warm friendliness. Evelyn had walked to the edge of the platform, scanning the line. In the solitude of their two selves, Blanche said, in the private, intimate tone that is never achieved in the presence of any third person.

'Two railway journeys in such a short week-end are awfully tiresome, aren't they?'

'You don't often go by train, I suppose?'

'I like to drive when I can. One's car lets one down sometimes.' The strained look which Blanche's face often wore, making it disagreeable and harsh, was now quite gone; a gentle smile was there instead. There were no strong, repressed emotions to thicken her voice; she spoke with complete ease and simplicity. This naturalness allowed a touching vestige of her young self to appear, an almost girlish unselfconsciousness. She went on:

'Do you cook yourself a meal when you get back? Or do you go out for something?'

'I cook something for myself.'

'I wish we had thought of it before. You could have taken some cold duck back with you.' Her unassuming tone was full of regret for a kindness missed. Cecil had great reasons for disliking Blanche and she was one to whom dislike came easy, but she could not resist the influence of the warm kindness, and the quick, practical expression of it, which Blanche Silcox showed. She began to understand how comfortable, how pleasant, to say nothing of how useful, it might be for someone who stood in great need of sympathy and efficient service, to have this powerful emotion, combined with such resources, devoted to his concerns. Blanche now moved towards Evelyn to suggest a position further down the platform as more likely to command the first-class carriages when the train drew up. As she stood beside him, ungainly, solid and dignified, she looked, as Cecil could not but see, perfectly appropriate as the elderly wife of a distinguished man: one of those ladies whose past charms are taken for granted, who now, calm and trustworthy, stand as the bulwarks of society against the insidious tides of frivolity and vice. As Cecil joined them, Blanche said that she herself was often in town, and it would be so nice if Cecil would lunch with her one day. Cecil replied with cautious civility and Blanche promised to telephone her at her office. Had the delay been longer it would scarcely have been possible to avoid some mention of Imogen, who, ignored in a mutual conspiracy of silence, was the cause of this strange rapprochement. Cecil endured a pang as she thought of her friend as she had last seen her; but the noise and commotion of the approaching train drowned the possibility of anything but brief goodbyes, though Evelyn found time to say heartily what a good idea it was that Blanche and Cecil should lunch together.

FIFTEEN

Michaelmas Term opened and Evelyn was so much occupied and absorbed, the idea Imogen had begun to entertain of forcing a crisis she abandoned, almost with relief. She did not know what to do, scarcely even what she wanted to do. Apart from Evelyn himself there was no one in her life to whom she could turn for authoritative advice, no one from whom she would have consented to take it. She had no brothers or sisters, but up till now she had never felt the want of any, and the deaths of her parents which had happened, one shortly after the other, within the first few years of her marriage, though they had meant a great personal loss, had not brought upon her any sense of isolation. Evelyn, then, had stood in the place of everyone who had ever given her protection and support.

Now for the first time she felt the lack of someone to advise and help her. Paul was the obvious choice and she foresaw that sooner or later she would undoubtedly appeal to him. At present a mixture of feelings restrained her. The fear of giving him anxiety and trouble in his illness was not so immediately effective as her wounded vanity. In all her resentment and unhappiness she never, except in a perfunctory way, thought of Blanche Silcox as a woman who was doing wrong. She thought of her as of someone whom she had despised by feminine standards, who was now enjoying a triumph that brought her own head down into the dust. She was reluctant to confess the extent of this humiliation to Paul. Sense told her that his love and admiration of herself would not be diminished because she had lost her ascendancy over Evelyn. Instinct told her to be afraid of seeming less desirable to one man because she had become so to another. She turned the matter over in her mind continually, wondering what to do, but returning always to the conclusion that the time had not yet come to do anything. She had sometimes thought of braving Blanche Silcox, brushing aside all those awkward, troubled pretences of good nature, and forcing from her the admission that she was Evelyn's mistress. But unless she herself had the courage to show an implacable front, and she had no such courage, the situation would result only in a triumph for Blanche Silcox. The mere admission would be a triumph. Less often she had thought of braving Evelyn. He would not lie to her, she was sure; but what would happen then? Could she force him to give up something on which his mind was so much set? Or if she could, what would it be like to live with him when she had done it? She almost shuddered and put the idea away, glad to take refuge in the reasonable and proper alternative: to bear anything as well as she could and hope that matters would improve or that she would acquire some sort of fortitude or even indifference, that would do instead.

Fortitude or indifference were at present equally out of reach. It was a source of exasperation to Imogen that Evelyn should feel such gratitude to Blanche Silcox for the services she performed: her help with Gavin's riding lessons, her acting as chauffeur to himself, the errands she did for him, her unbounded obligingness. They were all spoken of with a kind of awed thankfulness by Evelyn as if he could scarcely credit his good fortune. In Imogen's view the astonishing good fortune was Blanche's, that she had been able to establish a relationship with a man of Evelyn's calibre, in which she was free to offer these attentions. In the general estimation, of the female sex at least, Blanche Silcox would have been lucky in having an intimate connection with any man reasonably pleasant and presentable. That she should be on terms of affection, of passion, with Evelyn of all men, was a fact that made Cinderella's story tame and negligible. Cinderella had been a young and pretty girl. It had never before occurred to Imogen to question Evelyn's knowledge of the world, or his acute perception of other people's motives and character. Now, as she listened to him explaining that Blanche had ordered the village cobbler to deliver his shoes to her house instead of his own, so that the shoes would be all ready to take up to town the next morning, and had cancelled his standing order for *Country Life*, as they might just as well have her copy – she never did more than glance through it – adding solemnly, 'It's very good of her!' Imogen began to feel that though Evelyn must undoubtedly know a very great deal about men, it was perhaps open to question whether he did, after all, know very much about women.

In this perplexity and suspense, one of her keenest hardships was the ambivalence of Evelyn's feelings towards herself. Though most of the time the very imagination of a complete break and parting made her shrink with dread, there were moments when she would have welcomed a severance as a relief from the pain of those short spells of happiness when they reverted to their past ways again: when his brief kiss turned to a long embrace as she clung to him, when a meal-time was a space of intimate, delightful conversation, when some incident recalled a shared experience which they discussed with the interest that lovers feel in their mutual past: all of which as like as not would be interrupted by the stabbing ring of the telephone, at which she would be left to feel that the renewed misery was sharper than the previous hopeless, continuing one.

She had not seen Paul since her visit in August, though he now wrote to her very often, as he had never done before. He said next to nothing of his condition in these letters but she guessed that it was worsening from the increasingly intimate and yet still impersonal tone of them. They showed, more and more a tenderness and anxiety for her happiness; they discussed Gavin at length as a boy of difficult nature but one who would become more open and amenable as he grew up; and the latest one had said: 'There is something to be said for a world which has such a person as yourself in it.'

She was now to spend a night in Welbeck Street, for she and Evelyn were invited to a dinner given by one of the City companies. Evelyn was in the middle of an important case, and he would have cancelled the dinner engagement if it had not happened to be a sort of thing he particularly enjoyed. The food and wine of this company were famously good, and he loved to sit at his dinner in their dark-panelled hall, with the light of silver-gilt candelabra awakening gleams from Grinling Gibbons' looped and gilded garlands of flowers and fruit.

'Mind you look very nice, eh?' he had said to Imogen.

'Oh yes, I shall,' she answered, somewhat loftily. He pinched the lobe of her ear and said he would take her diamond earrings out of his safe before he left. He had an impression of how he wished to see her against the dark wood, fair-haired and pale with diamonds trembling in the candlelight.

Evelyn returned to town on Sunday evening and Imogen timed her arrival in Welbeck Street for the middle of Tuesday morning. She did not expect to see anything of Paul till lunchtime and had in fact decided to go out again as soon as she had unpacked her evening clothes, but she had hardly done this when a message that Dr. Nugent wanted to see her at once brought her downstairs.

Paul was standing behind his desk. There was a subdued urgency in his manner, yet it was calm and reassuring. He held out a piece of paper to her.

'Sorry to present you with this so abruptly,' he said. 'Your invaluable Malpas telephoned it here to await your arrival. It seems to have been sent off at half-past eight this morning.' The message was a copy of a telegram. It said: Dear Daddy I bust a boy's arm from Gavin.

'Oh *Heavens!*' exclaimed Imogen. She sat down at once. Gavin's predicament weighed less with her than the utter impossibility of disturbing Evelyn in court.

'We can't possibly get hold of Evelyn!' she said.

'We may have to.'

'But, but surely – can't I ring up the Headmaster and find out what's the matter?'

'He mightn't be able to tell you. But we'll ring him by all means. I think perhaps I'd better go up myself as it would be so difficult for Evelyn. I think Gavin might accept me as a substitute. Anyway, we can try that first.'

'But, Paul! I couldn't think of allowing you – at a moment's notice! – I'm sure there can't be any need for such a—'

'My dear, we can't ignore this. It wouldn't be safe. His father or I must go. Do you trust me with the business?'

'Yes, yes, of course, I'm only too thankful—'

'Very well. Then we'll speak to the school.' He drew the telephone towards him. 'Number?' It was gently asked, but in a tone she had never heard him use to her before. Fortunately she could repeat the number without hesitation. Paul made the connection and explained who he was. Imogen gathered from this one-sided conversation that he was speaking to Mrs. Maude.

'What is the injury? . . . I see . . . Yes, at that age they break more easily but they join quicker . . . Mr. Gresham of course will be writing to his people . . . No, I'm sure you didn't . . . not harsh at all; I'm sure it's his own view of what he's done that's worrying him . . . Quite. And with such a self-contained boy as that one doesn't like to pass over any appeal for help . . . Of course his father will come if it's necessary but meantime, I'll telegraph to let him know I'm coming. That will be better than a message, I expect. You'll look out and see he gets the wire as soon as it's delivered, won't you! . . . By the way: I suppose he hasn't vanished, has he? . . . Good. Good. About trains . . . Oh, is there? I can get that then; arrive at three? and will you have something to meet me at the station? . . .' As Paul put down the receiver he rang his bell. Imogen was collecting herself to give her thanks, but the secretary's instant appearance at the door stopped her. She realized that she must leave him immediately and with a murmured 'Thank you' she left the room as the first of the messages: 'Dr. Nugent is extremely sorry but he must postpone your appointment,' was being dictated.

Imogen was not obliged to see Primrose, who was out playing squash; she was to lunch with Cecil, a brief office-day lunch to which she none the less greatly looked forward. When she called for Cecil at her office in Garrick Street, she found that they were to meet Hunter at Simpson's. Imogen felt contrite that she should intrude on a *tête-à-tête* lunch between them but a glance at Cecil sitting beside her in the taxi, so composed and capable, and so anxious about Imogen herself, made the latter realize that it would be unnecessary, even foolish, to make any sort of apology. Hunter met them in the foyer with his air of feckless gaiety that suggested a changeling or elemental rather than a highly placed and responsible civil servant. When they were sitting at the table however, and Imogen related what had happened with Gavin, while Cecil exclaimed and wondered and thanked providence for Paul Nugent, Hunter looked at his plate, thoughtful and silent. He roused himself to take charge of the ordering and in the efforts of both of them to console Imogen and divert her from her cares, the lunch passed very agreeably, but the cheerfulness with which Hunter had met them was not recaptured, even while he was describing the good win he had had on the Cambridgeshire. When the meal was over, Cecil had to return at once to Garrick Street and Hunter proposed to take her there in a taxi. As he had to return to Whitehall himself, Imogen said goodbye to them both and refused offers of further escort. In the taxi Cecil took out a ten-shilling note and handed it to Hunter, saying: 'Thank you very much.'

'What is this in aid of?' he exclaimed in dismay. He was afraid that she was attempting to pay for her lunch.

'You lent it to me last Friday when I wanted to shop.'

'But, God help us—'

'I would have returned it by post,' continued Cecil determinedly, 'but I never like sending money except in a registered envelope, and I knew I should be seeing you to-day.' Hunter felt himself silenced. He took the note from her hand and put it in his wallet without a word. His feelings for Cecil were in that state of rapidly-growing enthusiasm when almost any marked trait in the object becomes another attraction. He recognized that this was so, but he fancied that scrupulous honesty in a woman was rather charming in itself.

'You seemed worried at lunch!' she continued.

'I didn't like that story, I must say.'

'Does it sound as if Gavin had done something serious?'

'He may have, at that. But I meant about Imogen. She ought to have hauled Evelyn out of court. He'd have respected her for it.'

'Well, even if he would, how *could* she?'

'I don't mean she should have walked into court and tapped him on the shoulder. But she could have telephoned his clerk and told *him* to get hold of him as soon as possible.'

'I do not think she *could*.'

'No. That's the trouble.'

The taxi drew up at the doorway of Messrs. Cotman and Blewett, but Hunter made no move to open the door till he had arranged a dinner date for the next evening but one.

Paul's journey to Shropshire would take over three hours each way. Allowing for his spending some time at the school, he could not be back until long after dinner. Imogen wondered whether Evelyn would cancel their engagement and wait in for Paul's return; but when she got back to the flat about five o'clock she found that Paul had just telephoned and left a message for her with Primrose, that Gavin was well and gave no cause for alarm and that he himself would take a five-thirty train that would get him in to London at somewhere after nine. She and Evelyn had no need to put off the dinner. Imogen attempted to convey to Primrose, who had met her in the hall, her deep sense of gratitude to Paul and her concern that he should have undertaken such an expedition on their behalf. Primrose said: 'Fancy breaking a boy's arm. I should think they must be pretty wild with him. Paul never minds what he does for people. Of course it's a pity he had to go just now when he needs all the strength he's got. I should think the school must have thought it rather funny Evelyn didn't come himself.'

She retired into the drawing-room and Imogen went upstairs with bent head and dragging step.

Evelyn came in as she was preparing to dress. She felt all the comfort of dealing with a highly trained mind when having to impart such information. Evelyn listened intently, did not interrupt and then asked questions on the few details she had left unexplained. He was profoundly grateful to Paul for his unselfish kindness, above all for the promptness with which he had acted, and he was especially touched by Paul's having sent Gavin a telegram. In the light of his telephone message, there was no reason to put off the dinner. They would go and enjoy it as best they could.

Imogen hoped that enjoyment would be within their reach. Evelyn was pleased with her looks. He stood off from her, scanned her up and down and then said: 'Very good.' But from the moment of their getting into the car together it was clear that her companion was not a devoted husband but a tired professional man who was also an anxious parent. Anxious herself, she found no fault with this but as the evening wore on, she wished that they might have been anxious in the comfort and privacy of Welbeck Street instead of sitting upright for what seemed a very long time, before a parade of dishes which she could scarcely touch, while her jaw ached with forced smiles and her head swam in rich fumes and the shivering radiance of candlelight. On their way home Evelyn, with the masculine ability to sort out his impressions and enjoy those that were enjoyable, said that though he hadn't been much in the mood for dining out, some of the food had been very good, especially the game pie. 'I believe you didn't eat it?' he said in an accusing tone. Then he commented on one or two of the speeches. Imogen heard him with wonder. She herself had no recollection of anything that had been said, and remembered only that there had been a great deal of speech-making. As they came in at the front door whose fanlight showed a pale glow, Evelyn said abruptly: 'I hope to God he's back.'

They found Paul already in bed, propped bolt upright with a great many pillows. He apologized to Imogen for such indolence. She could not speak. Evelyn sat down near the head of the bed and she sat on its foot. Primrose, whom both of them regarded with humbleness and contrition, now came in with a tray of tea. Paul himself was the most composed and cheerful of the party; nor did he look ill, unless that smooth, waxen look meant illness.

Gavin had been extremely pleased to see him; the Headmaster's wife had sent him down in the taxi to meet the train. Paul had found him pale and strained, but as soon as he had told what was the matter, his looks began to mend, and at the end of an hour and a half Paul had left him looking perfectly recovered. Some boys had been on the roof of the pavilion, looking for any balls that might be lodged in the gutter, and an argument was begun, during which Gavin had exclaimed: Say that again and I'll chuck you off the roof. Topliss Minor repeated the remark and Gavin instantly made good his threat. The pavilion roof was some nine feet from the ground, and when it was discovered in the Sanatorium that Topliss Minor had broken only the bone of his left forearm, the first feeling was one of relief that he had done nothing worse. Since Gavin had gone down to the village before breakfast to send his telegram, Paul asked him when the accident had happened?

'On Saturday,' said Gavin.

'Two days before?'

'Two and a half. It was just after lunch.'

Paul silently acknowledged the force of the correction. 'But did you really mean to chuck him off, or were you just assing about?'

'I did mean to, but I didn't think.'

'And did you apply your famous first aid to him?'

'No,' said Gavin sombrely. Then he went on: 'The other boys kept saying I'd bust his arm. Besides, I *had*.'

'It gave you a bad time, didn't it? But you *will* be careful how you go for anybody again, won't you? A fair fight on the ground is one thing but even then, it's much better not to fight people if you can avoid it.'

'You have to sometimes, or people would think you were a funk.'

'Well, yes; and you do need to be very brave not to mind that.' Gavin looked at him sideways.

'Shall we go and see your friend in the San?' Paul suggested, and Gavin had pattered down a long corridor in front of him with such eagerness that Paul was outstripped and came into the room in the Matron's convoy to hear in a voice made sharp by pain and apprehension: 'I don't want your whiffling ass of a godfather messing about with it.'

Paul was very soon on excellent terms with the patient and the apology he made on behalf of Gavin's family was received with gracious magnanimity:

'It's all right, sir; he can't help being a whiffling ass.'

'He must learn to help it,' said Paul. He wrote down at Topliss's dictation the titles of all the books about aeroplanes, space-ships and life on other planets which Topliss had a curiosity to read. He enlisted the Matron's help in getting the current issue of *The Aeroplane World* from the local shop that same afternoon and undertook that the books should be sent from town the following day. An interview with the Headmaster was of the briefest to allow of his catching the train, and when he left, his last sight of Gavin showed him playing chess with Topliss by the sickroom fire, and raising a preoccupied face to say goodbye.

Evelyn got to his feet. 'We are most deeply grateful,' he said.

Paul said carelessly: 'I love the boy and I'm glad I was able to do anything for him. These, by the way, are the books you'll have to send off to Master Topliss tomorrow.' He held out a leaf torn from a memorandum book.

Evelyn took it and handed it to Imogen, who wished that the shops were open at that hour that she might set about the ordering at once. They prepared to leave the room, wishing him, with great anxiety, a good night.

At the door Primrose said: 'I don't think he ought to go down there again. It's such a long way, isn't it? And it isn't as if he hadn't a lot of work of his own to do.'

Evelyn walked upstairs without reply. Imogen murmured something apologetic. She could not blame Primrose even to herself.

She returned home the next day after despatching five books of quasi-scientific, quasi-popular and horrific nature to Topliss Minor. She did not write to Gavin herself upon the matter but she knew Evelyn was doing so. Evelyn came home on Friday evening. When she asked him anxiously whether Paul seemed any the worse he would only say that he did not know that he was. The answer was not reassuring. Evelyn then told her that he had written a letter to Gavin serious though not, he hoped, prosy. He had also spoken on the telephone to the Headmaster, and Mr. Maude had told him that he did not think a visit from himself was necessary; indeed, it would be better not to have the episode marked any further. Gavin did not write except on Sundays and they both awaited a letter from him on Monday morning with some anxiety. Imogen had been afraid he might not write at all, but an envelope in the half-formed, sharp, interesting hand was lying on Evelyn's plate at breakfast. He tore it open, read it, then laid it before her. It said:

Dear Daddy, – Can I have a rugger pill to practise with in the holidays. If you buy one now I can start as soon as I come home.

From
Gavin.

'Well!' said Evelyn, spooning porridge into his plate, 'I think that's all right.' He wore the shocked yet invigorated expression of someone who has plunged into a cold bath.

'Yes. He wouldn't be wrapped up in football if he were upset still.'

'I must get that ball. Plenty of time but I mustn't overlook it. We must begin thinking about Christmas soon. I expect Blanche will begin to ride with him these holidays.'

SIXTEEN

The Christmas holidays were not favourable to riding. For a week before Christmas there were heavy falls of snow. This froze at night and was renewed the next day for several days, and though when Gavin came home, the weather had become milder, the depths of frozen and fresh snow would lie for some time. The trees in the hanging woods were like the breasts of swans, the banks under them silent in snow. The edges of the river on each side had frozen and the ledges bore weights of snow, here and there encroached over by a greenish film of ice; between them ran a narrow stream of still uncovered water dark like agate.

The morning after Gavin's arrival was one of bright, watery sunshine. The snow on the shaded banks had a solemn purity; on the open lawn it was dazzling. Here the snow and ice, frozen in layers, was hard as marble and slippery as glass. When Imogen came down to breakfast, Evelyn was already standing at the open french window of the dining-room; on the lawn Gavin was dribbling his football. As the ground was too slippery to afford a foothold to shoes, he was doing it in his stockinged feet.

She was about to exclaim but Evelyn checked her, and stood a few moments longer, admiring the sight of such enthusiasm; then he walked out and asked Gavin if he didn't want his breakfast? Gavin followed his father back into the dining-room, retrieving the shoes he had left on the verandah. Imogen decided not to urge him to change his stockings; she would offer him a dry pair after breakfast. She poured out the coffee, which smelt delicious in the fresh, snowy air, for the morning was so bright they made no move to shut the french window. Miss Malpas by saving the top of each bottle of milk for some time, had produced a jug of cream so rich that when the jug was tipped up the cream wrinkled like a blanket. Gavin poured a good deal of this on to his porridge and added dark-brown sugar. Evelyn meantime was reading his school report. It said: Number in form, 16. Place in form: Mathematics, first, Science, first, Biology, first, History, fourth, Geography, third, English, fourth, French, fifth, Latin, tenth. Evelyn, making an effort to sound serious, said:

'What do you mean by being tenth in Latin, eh?'

'I don't know.'

'Don't know? I shouldn't think you did! What do they say your conduct is? Monstrous, I suppose. Very fair! Great Scott, they must be thinking of somebody else.' He handed the report to Imogen, and took out two pound notes, which he put beside Gavin's plate. 'There's some pocket-money for you,' he said.

'Thanks, Daddy. How super.' Imogen saw from the corner of her eye a slight figure hovering on the edge of the verandah. She was wondering whether to call Tim in, afraid of his being unwanted in this delightful moment between Evelyn and Gavin; but to her relief, Gavin, although sitting with his back to the window, was aware immediately of Tim's presence and, cramming the notes into his pocket, rushed out.

The holidays went by very fast, with the two boys as the centrepiece of the household. The Greshams had now dropped any pretence of consulting the Leepers with regard to arrangements for Tim. They merely told Tim what time he must be ready to be motored up to town to the pantomime, to the skating rink, when the picnic would be held. Evelyn had kept from his boyhood the custom of picnics in the snow. On a bright, still morning, the party under his guidance walked over the downs to the edge of the valley of yew trees. Blanche Silcox came with them; what could be pleasanter? Evelyn, as an old hand at snow picnics, found, at a suitable time, a five-barred gate between two trackless white fields. He cleared the top bar of its ridge of opaque ice, and announced that the ladies should sit there. Imogen climbed on to the perch, wrapping her coat about her. Across the middle distance a rank of some tall weeds marched, bent all one way by the wind's onslaught and now cased in ice that sparkled and sent out prismatic colours. When she withdrew her eyes from this entrancing sight she found that Blanche Silcox had declined a seat on the rail and preferred to stand and lean. Blanche had provided the chief part of the lunch and Evelyn was now extracting it from his various pockets. It proved to be liberal portions of cold goose neatly wrapped in grease-proof paper. 'Perfect,' said Evelyn. He offered to clear a seat for Blanche on the low stone wall but she said, no, she would stand. Evelyn stood leaning on the gate between them. His impact made it sway and Imogen put her arm over his shoulder to steady herself, while she ate the goose's wing in her other hand. She saw Blanche Silcox, looking, not at her face, but somewhere about her waist, with a set countenance and slight frown. After a moment, Evelyn detached himself from Imogen's hold and with a feint of wrapping up a bone in paper, took up his station on the other side of Blanche. Presently he said: 'We ought to have some coffee. Why didn't you see to that?'

'I?' said Imogen, withdrawing her gaze from the glittering file. 'I am afraid I thought Blanche was seeing to everything.'

'I would have done if I'd known,' said Blanche Silcox.

'Never mind,' said Evelyn.

'You'd better all call in at home on the way back; we can have it there,' said Blanche.

'That'll be rather late in the afternoon, won't it?' he said.

'Oh no,' said Miss Silcox with great finality. 'We might start back now, unless you want to go any further.' There was a pause, and then Imogen found to her great surprise that Blanche was addressing her.

'*I?*' she repeated.

Evelyn said: 'There's no need to sound so astonished at somebody's asking what you'd like to do.'

'I am astonished,' Imogen said. She slipped down from the gate. The boys were at a little distance, snowballing each other; one wore a crimson muffler, one a sapphire blue. Both scarves belonged to Gavin, but she had given one to Tim, who had arrived with a checked duster round his neck. She approached them. 'I'm going home now,' she told them. 'Daddy is going home with Miss Silcox. You can do whatever you like.' She then walked on, without waiting or looking back. At the turn of the track above the yews she did look round. The white path was empty, and though it was little past midday the sky was already slightly overcast. She was relieved to be solitary. As she walked on, the landscape about her wild with snowy light, she was frightened but exhilarated too, almost as if some release of spirit had come to her from looking at the rainbow-coloured sparkles in the ice.

Evelyn came back to the house in time for tea. The boys were having theirs in the kitchen and she was sitting with a tray by the drawing-room fire, reading *Revelations*, which she had taken up to find the verse about the rainbow that was like an emerald. He walked straight up to the hearth saying: 'What possessed you to walk away like that?'

She laid down the book and said: 'I'll tell you if you'll let me get it out. But if you're going to destroy me as soon as I open my lips—'

'Destroy you! What on earth are you talking about?'

She was silent.

He said: 'I've asked you once to tell me what was the matter. If you don't choose to, I will drop the subject.' He poured out some tea. There came into her mind the picture of the room he had just left, warm, firelit, luxurious, and filled with the ease and pleasantness of a thoroughly comfortable, amorous relationship. What a change to come to this! He had made a severe sacrifice to propriety in coming home at all. She said:

'I don't want to spoil your happiness and be a drag on you.' Uncontrollable sobs rose in her throat, and the next instant he had pulled her to her feet and was holding her in his arms, saying gently:

'Things wouldn't be difficult if you didn't make them difficult.'

Sniffing and gasping she managed to say: 'When it comes to her resenting my even leaning against you on top of a gate—'

'Oh, come, come,' he said soothingly.

She leapt like a fish. 'She did!' she cried vehemently. 'That's why you left me and went over to her.'

He tightened his hold and after a brief silence he said: 'You mustn't make too much of little things. I *have* a very close friendship with her, but it needn't disturb you if you don't allow it to. After all, there's room for more than one good thing in life, isn't there?'

Had Imogen heard such a thing related of somebody else, she would have found it difficult to believe that a woman would allow to let slip such an opportunity of bringing matters into the open, demanding explanations and laying down conditions. In her own case, she was content to stand within the circle of Evelyn's arms while he allowed his tea to get cold. When at half-past six, the telephone rang as it always did unless Evelyn were already at the other house, he answered it so briefly that he appeared almost to have hung up on the fair subscriber, and it was plain to Imogen in the next day or two that he had given Blanche Silcox some warning, for Blanche was not only unusually pleasant when they met in the village, smiling at her with calm goodwill, but the telephone calls were reduced in number for the time being. Imogen however, even in her grateful relief, never supposed that this meant any weakening of Blanche Silcox's position or any strengthening of her own. It meant only that Miss Silcox's campaign was to be carried on with more discretion. What was the campaign's object? she asked herself. As far as wishes went, Blanche Silcox's must be to find herself, at some foreseeable future, married to Evelyn. Could such an idea be entertained by her as anything but a fantasy? And yet, if it were an actual object, would it be one altogether unreasonable and beyond the bounds of probability? True, the breaking up of a marriage between a man of Evelyn's professional position and a woman who, so far as she knew her own mind, had no intention of giving a divorce, must seem an impossible feat; but in Imogen's own view, what Blanche Silcox had accomplished already was something even more remarkable: the gaining of Evelyn as a lover. There was, so far as she could determine, no course open to her except the onerous one of waiting to see. The present position could not remain exactly as it was; first, because no situation can do so within the laws of nature, and secondly, because she herself would not be able to endure it and would precipitate a crisis of one kind or another. She knew her own shortcomings, her tendency to unreasonable despair, and she reminded herself of all the strong and sound elements in her relationship with Evelyn, which in her moments of exaggerated feeling she was too apt to overlook. She willed herself from day to day into a state of tranquillity and quite often spoke and laughed with spontaneous light-heartedness; but she began to be troubled by a tiresomely recurring nightmare, based on the childish game of Steps. She stood with her back to someone whose face she could not see even when she turned round, which she was repeatedly doing, in an attempt to catch the person in the act of moving. She never succeeded in this, but each time she turned round, the faceless figure had come nearer.

During the days after Christmas Evelyn went about the village, where he was very much liked, paying calls and wishing people the compliments of the season. The postman's wife showed him pieces in the papers about him which she had cut out, and Mrs. Mounsey of the Fisherman's Rest gave him a half-bottle of gin. Fortified by so many pleasant encounters, he told Imogen they should perhaps look in on the Leepers for a few minutes, and they went down soon after lunch the following day.

The Christmas preparations in the Leeper household were of an ambitious nature but they did not seem to have been made with any view to children's amusement. The walls of the atelier were studded with greeting cards, both dashing and sophisticated, and there was a Christmas tree at the back of the room, but its ornaments were wire mobiles and tiny bottles of liqueurs, and little boxes containing objects that suggested a horrible adult parody of a schoolboy's vulgar joke. There was, strewn about, a wealth of foreign confectionery in elaborate, sticky boxes and the company had the air of having drunk a good deal at lunch. Mrs. Leeper, reclining by the fire, seemed altogether too flushed, confused and inarticulate to get up. There were three men about her, at her side and on the floor, but from the loud pitch of their voices they gave the impression at the first moment of being several more. Mr. Leeper was nowhere to be seen. The room struck the newcomers as overheated, disorderly and garish, but suddenly from the shadows at the far end, Zenobia appeared, walking in beauty, a little wreath of gold and silver fir cones on her head. Ludmilla, dirty as ever but now decorated with green bows and some of Zenobia's jewellery, clung to her hand and looked at her with adoration and at the visitors with hostility and reserve. Varvara seemed not to share her sister's enthusiasm for their fabulous aunt, for she hung back, looking cross and dispirited, and frequently kicked the base of the Christmas tree so that the objects on it swayed and jingled.

As one of them seemed about to fly off, Evelyn put out a hand to it, glanced at it and let it go.

'Tony brought all those things,' said Zenobia in the voice that had been compared with the music of the spheres. 'I'm afraid he's rather badly behaved.' She indicated one of the men with fair, greying hair hanging round his hollow temples and a jaw that receded so sharply, his face looked like a skull without its lower teeth.

Evelyn said as a way of escape: 'I really looked in hoping to see Leeper, but if he's out—'

Zenobia raised her head towards the upper flights of the copper staircase while Ludmilla clung with both arms about her waist. 'I think he's taking a nap,' Zenobia said. 'But you can go upstairs if you like—'

Imogen looked with interest at the girls, this being only the third time she had laid eyes on them. She wished she could ask them to the house but she knew that Tim and Gavin would think them in the way, even if the girls themselves wanted to come. Evelyn had made it plain that he didn't want to go upstairs, and that he would look in some other time. As Mrs. Leeper was too tipsy to be spoken to with any advantage, they prepared to take leave without more ado. Zenobia seemed displeased, her face, usually luminous like alabaster took on an opaque and stony look. As she walked with them towards the door, she said: 'I hear Hunter is very much *affairé* with his little typist.' Imogen gave a great start. For a wild moment she feared that Hunter had begun some intrigue which was going to interfere with Cecil's happiness. Then she realized that the person so spoken of was Cecil herself. Zenobia continued: 'She works in a publisher's office, I believe? Cotman and Blewett's?'

'I do not think she would be described as a typist,' said Evelyn with judicial calm.

'Oh really! I quite thought that was what she was. I must have been misinformed.'

'It scarcely matters, does it,' said Evelyn, 'as you aren't likely to meet?'

'No,' said Zenobia pensively. 'I hardly think he could expect *that*.' She smiled, once more bewitching. 'I do so want him to be happy,' she said. 'One must *hope* he may be making a fortunate choice. Poor Hunter! I have always felt he was his own worst enemy.' There were actually tears in her eyes, giving the smile a tremulous, starry brilliance. 'I certainly bear him no ill-will. In fact, our marriage was such a vital part of my experience, I even feel I owe him something.'

Evelyn heroically bit back a reference to the spoons and forks. They left with brief goodbyes and Evelyn then asked Imogen if she would like to walk up to Blanche Silcox's. She answered amiably, 'I don't think I will. You're the one she wants to see, after all.' He accepted the answer with some relief, she could see, but as far as their way lay together, he talked to her about Blanche.

'You've never done her justice,' he said gently. 'You think she's dull, but she's not. She's a most absorbing companion and friend. She is not an *intellectual* woman, but —'

'She doesn't need to be,' said Imogen. She felt the tide of bitterness rising in her and determined to be silent. When Evelyn parted from her outside the village and she went on alone, she found herself wishing that they had not seen Zenobia. The latter was no longer even an object of interest to her; she was an exaggeration, a parody, of the values Imogen had once thought all-important. Zenobia had beauty, fascination, elegance, and even of a kind, intellectual distinction; and where had these qualities brought her? She was a symbol of failure and mischance: to meet her was to encounter an ill-omen.

SEVENTEEN

The Hilary Term opened and Gavin went back to school in the same week. Imogen found that both these events weakened her position. While Gavin was at home his parents had at least a strong mutual interest, and during the vacation Evelyn was naturally a good deal about the house. Now she was unavoidably left very much to herself – and Blanche Silcox was with Evelyn continually. His comings and goings were all made by car and always with her beside him. In the affairs of both houses, the order for a load of gravel, for clearing out gutters, for a load of logs, was given in the village by Miss Silcox, or by Evelyn, irrespective of which house it was for, as they stopped the car on the way up to town. Evelyn would have felt that this sort of behaviour in another man, a friend or a client, was indiscreet and if called upon to do so, would have put the matter before him in a strong light; but he himself had a majestic unconcern for opinion when he had decided to ignore it. As for Miss Silcox, the set and suffering expression she was sometimes seen to wear seemed to suggest that she was conscious of a certain observation focused on her; but the status that wealth, quiet conduct and personal dignity confers shielded her from any near approach of impertinent comment.

Imogen hoped and indeed took for granted that the villagers would never suspect Blanche Silcox of any intrigue. It seemed however that the villagers were sharper than she had been. She was standing by the play-room window one morning, about to mend some of Tim's stockings. Evelyn was at that moment being driven from the door in Blanche Silcox's Rolls, and the men to whom he had just given instructions about laying gravel were standing on the path with their backs to the window. One said something she did not catch. The other said: 'When the heart is young, Bert!'

It was not only necessary to find something to do because of her state of mind; it was desirable to use some of the leisure created by Gavin's being away, a leisure she had never had since the beginning of the war. Once she would have been at no loss to fill it with longer spells of her usual pastimes, but now she determined for the first time in her life to give time to voluntary work. An afternoon a week in the hospital library was arranged for her almost before the offer was out of her mouth, and the W.V.S. were very ready to consider her services. She felt ashamed that she had never offered them before, but the pleasant, capable woman to whom she was speaking seemed to find it perfectly natural that she had not been able to do anything of the kind until her boy had gone to boarding school.

In spite of her efforts to be active and useful, her nights became more and more disturbed by dreams. Wild, low-lit landscapes and ruined towers merged into realistic scenes. Once she saw herself late at night in a closed-off part of a street, lit by lanterns, where road-menders were digging fast in the bottom of a pit. She stood looking down at them, till they laid aside their picks. One of them said: 'Now it's ready,' and they held up their arms to help her down into it.

Blanche did not very often come to the house, but Evelyn had brought her in for a drink one evening when she had, as usual, driven him down. The sherry was in the dining-room, and on the sideboard were standing the pair of Sheffield plate dishes, newly polished, in all the beauty of their lustre and design.

'Those are nice,' said Blanche Silcox.

Evelyn turned one round by a handle, then pushed it away impatiently. 'They were,' he said. 'But in that condition—'

'They could be re-silvered, surely?' said Blanche. 'That's all they want.'

'Imogen prefers them as they are.'

'Oh, I see,' said Miss Silcox.

Imogen said: 'I don't want to stop their being re-silvered if—'

'You don't want to stop it?' said Evelyn with an emphatic incredulity that, pitched to the scale of a court, almost stunned in an ordinary room. He said no more and Blanche Silcox took her leave a few moments after. As they went through the hall after Blanche had said goodbye to her, Imogen heard Evelyn giving his explanation of the state of the dishes.

'*Such* a pity,' said Blanche in a voice in which deep sympathy was restrained by discretion.

Evelyn was now exceedingly busy and sometimes he did not come home till late on Saturday evening. In the first week of February he said however that he need not go back to town till Monday morning. Imogen had looked forward to this extension of time when she heard of it, but unhappily she was now apt to find that even when she had some uninterrupted hours with him she could not make the most of them. The sense of grievance would rise in her breast, making her neglect those small opportunities to be magnanimous and endearing. Her mind, once so sensitive and alert to what was likely to please or annoy him, now seemed hardly to function in that direction. She made mistakes in tact and sense that would once have horrified her, and she did not care. The Sunday had passed wretchedly, even though Evelyn had spent most of it at home. She had felt weary and discouraged and unable to respond when he introduced topics that should have interested any rational person: Land Development Charges, Conrad's novels, the abolition of capital punishment and the pros and cons of bringing the English coinage into line with the Continental system. In face of all her silence, lack of interest and monosyllabic replies, Evelyn maintained a civil, reasonable and fluent conversation. Any stranger who had overheard them would have pitied him. Towards evening, the evening she had been so glad to think she would spend with him, he said quite pleasantly: 'You don't seem to have much use for my company, do you? Perhaps you won't mind if I go out.'

'No,' she said. 'I shan't mind.'

He was obliged to make an early start the following morning and breakfast was ordered for eight instead of the usual half-past. Imogen usually woke early and liked early rising. This night however was an unusually exhausting one with a prolonged series of dreadful dreams, after which she fell into a deep, unconscious sleep. She did not wake until long after her usual time, and when she got downstairs she found that Evelyn's breakfast was nearly finished. He not unnaturally supposed that this late appearance was owing to a disinclination for his society, and that her pale and heavy looks and her speechlessness were other symptoms of their extremely disagreeable situation. She was still sitting at the table when he came down into the hall with his luggage. At the same moment the Rolls drew up at the gate. It was Blanche Silcox's habit now to pause there instead of driving up to the door. As Evelyn was taking a last look inside his despatch-case Imogen appeared in the doorway. He gave her a hasty kiss and said: 'The post hasn't come yet. If a big registered envelope comes for me, will you forward it by the twelve o'clock? Then I'll get it first thing to-morrow. It's important. Will you see to that, my dear?'

'Yes,' she said.

'Goodbye. I'll telephone this evening.' He hurried out and she went back to the breakfast table. She had not been sitting there long when the post arrived and with it a large registered packet addressed to Evelyn. She left this on the hall table for the time being and carried her own letters, among which was one from Paul, upstairs to the sewing-room. On the table were various objects that she cleaned and polished with particular care: a pair of branched candelabra, the tortoiseshell and ormolu furniture of the writing desk, and the pair of Sheffield plate dishes. She moved them to a side table and sat down to read Paul's letter. It was short and contained very little beyond expressions of calm, deep affection for herself. It was the more difficult to answer. With slowness and many pauses she gradually composed a reply, in which she said nothing of her trouble but tried to make a collection of ideas of happiness. They had to be of an impersonal nature; she could not write about Evelyn, barely of Gavin; she told him that she had been reading the sonnets that he liked best, of the different birds who came to the dish of breadcrumbs she put out every morning, some of whom she had taught herself to identify from the coloured plates in a Victorian child's book, of how instantly and vividly she felt her emotions respond to colours, that she was longing for the appearance of her gentians, longing with almost a physical appetite to see that darkest of brilliant sapphire blues. As she finished these words she raised her head and the dishes caught her eye, their insides burning like the heart of a rose in the morning light. The pleasure turned at once to pain. She remembered in misery how she had ruined Evelyn's pleasure in them by not allowing them to be re-dipped. 'How could I, for one moment, have been so selfish? Or so stupid? What did anything matter, compared with his being able to enjoy them?' The penalty for such selfishness and stupidity had been paid in hearing Evelyn's grievance related to Blanche Silcox and the latter's tender but tactfully restrained reply: 'Such a pity.' She remembered how he had said once of her defence of Gavin: 'Your usual thing, of going against me instead of backing me up.' 'Is it true?' she thought. She had disregarded it as one of those hasty, unjust imputations that no one is expected to take seriously. The re-dipping of the dishes was a small matter, but the emotional texture of married life is made up of small matters. This one had become invested with a fatal quality. When she had suggested to Evelyn after Blanche's visit that the dishes should be taken to a gold- and silversmith, he had brushed the idea aside as one that no longer interested him.

She sat for a time, she could not have told whether it were long or short, remembering innumerable impressions of Evelyn's character which she had formed in the course of years, without being aware of doing so, and dwelling on small episodes as if she now saw their significance for the first time. Her recollection was filled with the sense of his great power, of which, in their happy days, the current passed into her own being, making her feel that she lived to her full capacity only in her connection with him. The mental image of him was inseparable from that of his beauty, his austere but solid handsomeness, the decisive cast of his features which yet held the airy, springing quality of an impetuous nature. The unselfconscious character of his good looks was as striking as their perfection. He had never wanted to make himself attractive to women. He enjoyed their company often, and if he had shown a disposition to be seriously attracted, they would have passed beyond that state of alarmed attention and restless consciousness that his appearance and his masculine personality aroused, into actual passion, but his innate reserve had always made itself felt, a subtle, deadly discouragement, till now. Now it was not so much a woman to whom he was responding but a whole way of life, a gratification of needs which he would no more readily give up than a famished man will forgo food and warmth. What have I done, or failed to do, that he feels such needs? she asked herself. The dreaded answer came to her, not that she *did* wrong, but that she *was* wrong. She remembered a sentence of Evelyn's in a lunchtime conversation during which he was explaining to Mr. Ames his reasons for disliking a junior. 'I don't want somebody who's afraid of me,' he had said. She had thought at the time that in anyone as formidable as Evelyn this was almost unreasonable and had felt sorry for the young man. How condescending such pity seemed now! 'I never was afraid of him, never, until I realized I'd lost my power to someone else. Now, I am. And how it's altered me! I am like a different person – valueless, useless.'

She raised herself stiffly and came out to the head of the staircase. The hall clock was on the verge of one. The registered letter was still lying on the table. The village post office could not despatch it in time for the morning delivery in London. The only thing she could think of was that she should take it up to town by train that afternoon and leave it at Evelyn's chambers. She had half decided to do this when just at lunchtime the telephone rang. It was the clerk, asking for Evelyn whether the packet had been delivered. Imogen explained the matter and offered her solution. The clerk consulted Evelyn and returned with the answer that Mr. Gresham did not want her to bring it to town but would be very glad if she would post it immediately. When Evelyn telephoned to her that evening, he cut short her apologies by saying: 'Never mind now, my dear. Look here, you know this flat that Blanche has in Halkin Street?'

'I knew she had it. I've never seen it.'

'I'm sure she'd be very glad for you to see it, but you've not been very approachable lately, have you?'

'No, I suppose not.'

'No. Well I dare say I've been as much to blame as anybody. But what I am ringing up about is a suggestion of hers that I should become a paying guest there for the nights in the week that I have to be in town – transfer myself from the Nugents there. It would be to their advantage because they could then let the whole of those upper floors if Paul – if they would like to. I must say I think it's a good time for me to make a change there, and this arrangement would suit me very well. Blanche wouldn't be there all the time herself but it's a service flat, and of course when you wanted to be in town for a night you could fit in too. It strikes me as a very convenient suggestion, but of course I am mentioning it to you before we settle anything.'

'Yes.'

'Yes what? Do explain yourself, my dear. I'm trying to make a practical arrangement.'

'Yes, of course you mentioned it to me first and of course I can't make any objection.'

'What do you mean, you can't make any? You can make any that occurs to you.'

'Very well. I mean I don't make any.'

'That is what I have been trying to find out. Very well, then. I'll get down to details. It won't be just yet, of course.'

No, thought Imogen as she rang off, not just yet, but when the formal occupation takes place doesn't matter. The essential part of the arrangement had been in force this long while, she knew well enough.

After her visit to the Greshams in October Cecil had at first daily expected to hear from Blanche Silcox about the proposed lunch, and had wondered a good deal as time went by without her doing so. She came to the conclusion that Blanche did not find social contacts easy, and that in spite of her capacity for the absorbing of one individual she was somewhat shy of people in general. Probably the slight effort needed to open communications with Cecil was enough to put her off. Besides, she had, beyond a doubt, plenty to occupy her, and of the most engrossing kind. As Cecil was considerably occupied herself, she gradually ceased to think of the possibility of a meeting, though she had long and frequent letters from Imogen, which reflected the position of affairs, and gave her great disquiet. She sometimes discussed these with Hunter, though she never gave him the letters to read, for she had scrupulous notions about private correspondence. Hunter thought this admirable in itself but unnecessary in regard to him. He was fond of reading other people's letters. He would have begun a correspondence with Imogen himself on the subject: it would have given her some relief and him much interest, if of a painful kind, but his loyalty to Evelyn prevented this. He saw a good deal of the latter now that Hilary term had begun; there were of course no race meetings open but Evelyn asked him to small dinners with others of his male friends and Hunter asked Evelyn to dine at the Beef Steak Club and the Junior Carlton. Evelyn's unvarying kindness to him, no less than the pleasure he took in an evening in Hunter's company, endeared him to Hunter very deeply. The latter's affection for Imogen made no difference to this. He took no side and viewed the matter, with distress and apprehension certainly, but with a tolerance and a power of suspending judgment that was extraordinary to Cecil.

One afternoon late in January, when the whole question was for the moment quite out of her thoughts, Cecil came down from Mr. Blewett's room and found on her desk a telephone message asking if she would meet Miss Silcox for lunch the next day but one. The place chosen was Boulestin's, which showed that Blanche Silcox either knew or had taken pains to study the neighbourhood of Garrick Street. Cecil, innately punctual, was there a few minutes before one, prepared to wait, but Blanche Silcox was already sitting at a table and got up to greet her. She made friendly, attentive enquiries as to what Cecil would like and the effect of her friendliness was enhanced by the soft, rich lighting of the restaurant, the devotion of the waiters and the delicious dishes which they brought. All this surrounded the guest like an emanation of Blanche Silcox's anxious attention to her comfort. As Blanche sat opposite to her, upright and solid and commanding the deference of the establishment for a wealthy client, yet simple and unassuming in her own demeanour, Cecil could see that her appearance was strikingly improved even since the autumn. The parchment-coloured skin with its pink colour in the cheeks had the clearness and brilliance that comes from the effect of radiant happiness on the circulation of the blood, and the eyes had the rapt, soft look of a woman in love, particularly touching in one of elderly and homely appearance. The influence had extended to her clothes also. She wore a good fur coat and the suit under it was one to whose cut her figure had been adapted, unlike those she usually wore whose cut had been adapted to her figure. Her pearls, naturally, were very good, and in her choice of gloves and bag she could hardly make a mistake, since she liked things to be plain and did not mind their being expensive. The triumph, however, was her hat. It was merely a hard, unbecoming felt. No one would have looked twice at it.

Cecil was never hurried into speaking from any fear of silence; she had had a hard morning, and she now found herself painfully aware of the charm of Blanche Silcox's company – quiet, ladylike, dependable, and alight with the warmest care for her. This, violently conflicting with her anxiety for Imogen, made Cecil so uneasy and uncomfortable that even her composure was not maintained without a little effort. She made monosyllabic replies to Blanche's conversational openings. This obliged the latter to be more direct than she might otherwise have been in bringing out the topic uppermost in her thoughts.

'Have you seen Imogen lately?' she said, her voice weighty but toneless.

'No,' said Cecil.

'I don't see much of her,' continued Blanche. She paused, but Cecil remaining silent, she went on with a slight heaving and swallowing: 'I think she *is* very self-absorbed. I mean, she doesn't go about in the neighbourhood, or take part in any of the local activities. It's rather hard on Evelyn, I think, because he's such a social person.'

'She always entertained people when Evelyn wanted her to.'

'Oh, I don't *know*.' Blanche Silcox spoke meditatively with a slight, dubious shake of the head. 'I don't think her entertaining amounted to much. People always *know* when you don't like them, don't they?'

'Perhaps. But people *do* like Imogen. I don't know, myself, any other woman who has so many people that are fond of her.'

'Oh, my dear!' said Blanche Silcox. 'I feel that's taking rather a rosy view of her. Of course as a friend of hers you naturally stick up for her. But one can't help seeing Evelyn's point of view. I think he feels there's a great want of sympathy between them. If he hadn't felt that, he'd never have made a friend of me.' Cecil gathered herself for an effort.

'I'm sure he would,' she said. 'You live near each other in the country and have similar tastes. There's every reason why you should be friends. He's a sociable man, as you say, in the small amount of time he has for society. And after all, you gave him every encouragement.'

'I gave him encouragement, as you call it—'

'Well, what do *you* call it?' asked Cecil reasonably.

'Yes, it was encouragement, certainly, because I could *see* how deep the incompatibility went between them, and how much he needed someone to be a friend to him. I know I have rather taken her place in some ways, but *what* else could I do? She's useless to him. The other day he asked her to forward a most important letter by the midday post and she didn't do it! Think of that! After all,' said Miss Silcox, speaking quietly with a reversion to well-bred moderation and restraint, 'with a man in Evelyn's position, that sort of thing is so important, isn't it?'

'Yes, but your having so much influence with him destroys her self-confidence, and the more scared she is the stupider she gets. She's run ragged by this time.'

For an instant Blanche Silcox's face wore a distorted expression of pain and fury like that of an animal in a trap. 'But don't you see,' she said, almost hissing, 'that the position would never have arisen if there hadn't been this lack in the first place? He *turned* to me. I know how much he needs what I can do for him. That's what makes me able to put up with things. Because of course he can't leave her.'

'Of course he can't.'

'No, I don't see how he can. But it seems peculiar that people should have to drag on, in a relationship that doesn't mean anything – just in the name of virtue. It makes one wonder what virtue is, after all.'

It occurred to Cecil that had the question been one of embezzlement, theft or poaching, passing a worthless cheque or doping a racehorse, Miss Silcox would have found no difficulty in deciding what virtue was. She merely said: 'As she is my friend, I naturally feel more anxious about her happiness than about anything else.'

'Naturally. Of course you do. But *is* it for her happiness, for them to go on like this? She certainly doesn't make *him* happy. One wouldn't think in that case she could be happy herself.'

'Of course she is not happy as things are at present.'

'I can't see how they are to improve,' Blanche said.

'Perhaps not.' Cecil didn't add: 'You'll see to that.'

Her replies had been far from encouraging, but the tone in which she uttered them was so civil and unimpassioned that Blanche, eager as she was for Cecil's opinion, found it easy to continue the conversation on a basis of assumed co-operation. She now said with her voice in its deepest register: 'Do you think she would agree to a separation if he asked her for one?'

'A separation? You mean a divorce?'

Blanche nodded. She said: 'Yeh—' as if her powers had given out before she could finish the word. Having got out the momentous question, she seemed afraid of giving Cecil time to answer it and went on hurriedly: 'Of course one knows that for a man in Evelyn's position such a thing would be very serious, very serious indeed.'

Cecil's secret agitation showed itself in the asperity with which she now said: 'That is not a question for anybody except Evelyn himself, is it? And any other men in the same profession with whom he might advise. The opinion of anybody else would be quite irrelevant, wouldn't it? If you are talking about his asking for a divorce you must assume that he has come to all the important decisions about it already.'

Blanche Silcox looked momentarily surprised but she showed no annoyance. She merely said: 'Well, supposing he had. Is it your opinion that she would consent?'

Cecil was now in a quandary. It was her opinion that Imogen would consent to anything that Evelyn asked of her, but she felt she must on no account say so to Blanche Silcox. She said: 'I'm afraid I simply don't know. I've never heard her speak of such a thing.'

Blanche seemed to recollect herself. 'Perhaps one shouldn't discuss it,' she said. She went on to say how awfully interesting Cecil's work must be, *quite* fascinating.

Cecil's allegiance to Imogen never faltered but she saw with increasing clearness that the whole situation was at once more understandable and more formidable than she had at first believed. Blanche Silcox's vehement desire to give everything she had in this unique, amazing opportunity for such giving, Cecil had realized soon enough. What she now saw, was that there was much more to give than a superficial view of Miss Silcox would have in any way suggested. She was glad that the shortness of the lunch hour obliged her to put an end to these distracting sensations. Blanche, rising, said:

236

'I am glad we have had this talk.'

'I'm afraid I've not been able to say much.'

'You know them both so well, I feel it's cleared the air.'

So far from having cleared it, Cecil felt that this exchange had thickened the air like an imminent snowstorm.

Hunter came to dinner at her flat that evening bearing several tins and jars from Fortnum's (not, he said, that he expected to eat the contents now, but they were comfortable things to have about.) When they had finished their meal, Cecil repeated to him what had been said at lunch. The gaiety went from his face. He rolled an unlighted cigarette in his lips, staring at the ground. At last Cecil said: 'I cannot see what she is to do.'

'There are two things that somebody else in that state could do. She could have a showdown with Evelyn and insist on his either giving the thing up or else reducing it to reasonable proportions. Or,' he continued, disregarding the incredulous exclamation she was about to make, 'she could settle for it and simply come to some sort of *modus*. In a way, the second would be better because it would keep Evelyn in a good temper and she'd find it an asset to have such a claim on his gratitude. Unfortunately, as I see it, she's absolutely incapable of doing either.'

'Yes, absolutely.'

'So the only prospect now is that sooner or later, something or other will tip her up and she'll break up the marriage herself.'

'You don't think Evelyn will ask her for a divorce?'

'Most unlikely, I should say. For one thing, he'd feel he ought not to. And then, though it's wretched for a good deal of time, he probably manages to keep the thing on a fairly even keel, and I feel pretty sure – though naturally it's a thing she won't see her-self – that this thing he's got for Blanche Silcox – though I dare say it's stronger than his feeling for Imogen now, it doesn't mean he doesn't care about *her* any more.'

'Blanche Silcox wants him to ask for a divorce.'

'She won't be able to make him do that if he doesn't mean to. I doubt if she'll try to, in so many words. It wouldn't be like her, to attempt something she couldn't pull off.'

'She has been able to do so much one wouldn't have thought she could.'

'Yes.'

'Though I must admit, now, that though I should never have foreseen that she would be able to, I am not astounded as I was at first.'

'I never foresaw it,' said Hunter, 'but I don't think I ever was astonished once I saw how it was going. You see, from a man's point of view, she's got no intolerable faults, and she has a very warm, magnetic nature.'

'And a great deal of money,' Cecil added.

'Always a point,' Hunter agreed dispassionately.

Cecil was silent, for she was reflecting in haughty self-criticism that she herself was neither warm nor magnetic, that her faults were no doubt intolerable and that she had no money. For the last few weeks Hunter's manner towards her had been one of such close attention that, though she had tried hard not to attach any importance to it, she had not been able to prevent herself from expecting him to make a proposal to her, though of what sort she did not know. Her self-confidence in such matters was so easily deflated, that the most oblique reference to her disadvantages was enough to make her withdraw into herself, assuring herself steadily that she neither expected to excite affection, nor even wished to. So although she had been almost expecting Hunter to declare himself at any moment, it was with a second's genuine surprise that she found him leaning forward to take both her hands and saying that they'd talked enough about other people for that evening. He wanted to know if she would marry him and if so, when?

EIGHTEEN

The arrangement concerning the flat was nothing much to regret once the shock of hearing it was over; it made the situation no worse and in some respects it even made it better, for having broached the matter, Evelyn now seemed to feel himself generally at ease. He spent more time in the house at week-ends, and took trouble to maintain those parts of their relationship that could still be enjoyable. One Saturday he drove her to see a great house that had been opened; but the expedition was not what it would once have been. Evelyn, indeed, enjoyed the spectacle himself, walking through lofty, beautifully proportioned rooms under moulded ceilings, admiring gilded looking-glasses and views of the park through great sash windows, whose panes were erratically tinted with heliotrope and amber. Imogen followed, where once she would have had to be pulled back, and it was he who now pointed out to her the various beauties, and called on her to admire a chandelier or a marble chimney-piece. The surface of their relations was courteous and pleasant, and whenever she could bring herself to respond to his overtures by effort, or did so involuntarily in a moment of blessed forgetfulness, the embers of their affection glowed again. But she was increasingly oppressed by the sense of

Blanche Silcox's being there all the time, present in every part of Evelyn's life. When in her days of carefree ignorance, she had been accustomed to say that an affair, properly conducted, need not interfere with a marriage, she had had in mind some sort of arrangement in which the mistress, established in retirement in some charming early Victorian villa in St. John's Wood, was visited only on certain recognized nights during the week. Her theory that the dual arrangement could be made to work rested on the watertight nature of its two parts. Whether such segregation of emotions were at all possible in human life or belonged only to novels, she would not now have undertaken to say. She knew only that in her own case almost every impulse of affection for Evelyn was choked at the source by the vision of Blanche Silcox, with him, beside him, sharing not only his interests, his confidence, but every sort of domestic intimacy.

Imogen had been afraid that Evelyn would remove permanently to his dressing-room, but though he slept there more often than before he had not altogether made it his bedroom. She did not know whether his continuing presence in hers was owing to the fondness for her society of which he still sometimes gave a sign, or to that extraordinary capacity for being remote and self-contained which enabled him to be private even when within a few feet of someone else. They were both in their bedroom on the Sunday after Blanche's brief call. Imogen had come back from church and Evelyn was putting iodine on a grazed knuckle. The telephone rang and he picked up the receiver of the instrument that stood on the table between their beds. By some freak of transmission the caller's voice was audible in the room, and Imogen heard Blanche Silcox say:

'What about lunch? Can you?'

'Better not,' Evelyn said.

'My dear man, you might just as well. *She* doesn't want you.'

'And you do, eh? But I won't, thank you very much.' Imogen

walked out of the room. As she went downstairs she realized that what Blanche had said was now very nearly true.

Some weeks later she was sitting at breakfast with Tim opposite to her. When Evelyn was away, he came in to breakfast with her every morning. He said very little but she was growing nearly as silent as he. On this morning she looked through a small pile of letters; not seeing one from Paul as she had hoped she might, she put them aside while she poured out the coffee. Tim had finished and left the table by the time she came to the bottom of the pile, and saw an envelope in an unknown hand, which she assumed must be from a member of the W.V.S. She opened it and caught the words: 'Girlie of course is heart-broken' – what in the world could this be? and the signature: K. F. Waddy? The letter must have been sent to her by mistake. She turned it over again and saw 'our poor little Primrose,' 'such a fine man.' The truth could not be held off any longer. Paul was dead, and Primrose's mother was writing to tell her so.

It was not so much pain that she felt as a chill premonition of what the pain would be. She got up, feeling a heaviness in her limbs and all day, she was alternately forgetting the calamity and remembering it, each time with worse alarm as the delayed impact of full realization came hourly nearer.

Evelyn came into the house at lunchtime next day with a face of concern. He was relieved that she had already heard the news. He had many details to tell her, for he had been in Welbeck Street the evening of the day on which Paul had collapsed at the foot of the staircase, a minute after leaving his consulting-room. Imogen had not yet reached the stage of weeping, though she felt it would come upon her at any moment and rather wondered not to find herself in tears when she cried so readily as a rule.

She and Evelyn were in the drawing-room after lunch and Evelyn had spoken to her with great gentleness. Outside the grass was grey with rime; in the veiled sky the sun was like a ball of pink glass. Tim crossed the lawn, carrying a basin of bran and tea leaves to the rabbits. The clock ticked sedately between two alabaster columns, beneath an alabaster urn, reflected in the looking-glass. Nothing suggested the imminence of a cataclysm.

Imogen, continuing their conversation in a desultory way, said: 'I feel so guilty when I think of his going to Brackley Hill that day. There and back straight away. I knew it was too much and that he ought not to do it. But I simply didn't know what to do. He said himself someone must go to Gavin and I knew it would be worse than useless for me to. And I felt I *couldn't* send for you, in the middle of that hearing. I was in an absolute impasse. I didn't know *what* to do.' Evelyn said:

'You could have got into touch with Blanche. She'd have gone like a shot.'

'What?' said Imogen, doubting her senses.

'She would have gone up in the car, and found out what was the matter. Gavin would have told her; she gets on so well with him.'

'How *dare* you!' said Imogen. Her voice, low and threatening, rose to a scream. 'How *dare* you!' she shouted. 'How dare you!' In that second the consciousness of her failure, her helplessness, her hopelessness, rushed on her with inescapable force. The boat which had been carried nearer and nearer to the weir was now over it in a thunderous, stunning roar. The broken sentences and ejaculations of passionate abuse in which she tried to pour out her sense of injury died away, for her heaving chest and swollen throat were unable to produce coherent sounds. The physical exertion, though involuntary, of the great racking sobs which her rage and grief tore from her, so occupied her senses that she barely realized that Evelyn was helping her upstairs, that she was lying on her bed, that Miss Malpas with compressed lips was in and out again. After a long time the depth of quietness in which she was lying, that surrounded her bed, the house, the lawn, the woods, stole upon her senses, calming and restoring. The windows were now filled with dusk, but somewhere the February moon had risen for sharp daggers of moonlight lay on the floor. Miss Malpas came into the room with a tray of tea and Evelyn followed her. He put on the lamp, propped up her pillows and poured out the tea as if nothing but illness were the matter. She said, and the soreness and huskiness of her throat surprised herself: 'Is the bag you brought from town still in the hall?'

'Yes, my dear.'

'Then if you could go to Blanche Silcox's house for the night, it would be ready?'

'It would. I can do that if you would like me to.'

'I would like it, really.' She lay motionless, longing to see him go, willing him to leave her before she should break into crying once more.

In the calmness that succeeded his departure and the last, attentive cares of Miss Malpas, she slept for a time and woke to see the round, brilliant moon staring through one of the pointed upper panes of the Gothic window.

'Gavin,' she said aloud in the empty room. The statement that Blanche Silcox could have gone to Gavin in the crisis, because Blanche, unlike herself, had got his confidence, was an intolerable affront. It was also the truth.

Imogen lay, living with laborious effort from one minute to the next as if she were the victim of some horrible accident. Image after image succeeded each other in the brain, of Gavin in Blanche Silcox's company, unembarrassed, contented, intensely concentrated upon what they were doing: riding, fishing, learning to drive the car. ('Most improper at his age,' Evelyn had said. 'I shouldn't like him to be doing it with anyone except her.') Blanche Silcox's deep emotional interest in him as his father's son, plain as it was to an adult eye, was kept under such strict control that to a boy nothing was apparent but good humour, reliability and an inexhaustible sympathy in practical affairs.

The killing pain, the wound that was fatal, was the loss of the first place in Evelyn's affections. In Gavin's she had never had it. Her position as Gavin's mother might have made it allowable, right, even, that she should determine to retain her position as Evelyn's wife. As it was, Gavin provided neither an obligation nor an excuse.

The torrent of tears that she poured out made it for a while impossible to think, to be conscious of anything but the act of weeping and the blind compulsion to it; when the tears subsided, she knew that at some point in time, passed before she recognized it, the certainty of parting with Evelyn had been reached. She lay in deathly stillness like a wounded man who is afraid of pain if he moves, and accepted, imprinting deeply on her mind, that there would be no question ever of separating Gavin from his father. Everything that made Gavin's home life precious to him, would remain here. When she removed herself, she would take nothing with her that would draw him to her. There would be in this case none of those distracting divisions of sympathy from which children suffer so much in broken homes. Gavin's home would not be broken.

The bitterness of this thought dried up her inclination to weep, and left her instead with a slowly mounting, spreading, consuming passion of hatred. She got up at the usual time and though it cost her an extraordinary effort to remember what day of the week it was, once she had discovered that it was Sunday, she found herself in a state of high capability. She telephoned to Blanche Silcox's house, not caring who might answer. Evelyn did so and with such promptness that he must have been waiting for the call. She asked him to come and talk to her and within ten minutes they were engaged in the most momentous conversation of their lives.

There was no leading in to the matter, no discussion of for and against, no demands for explanation; not even hesitation or uncertainty.

'Of course I have known for a long time,' she said.

'You have no evidence,' he answered instinctively. 'But,' he added, 'I do not deny it. Nor would she wish to. And of course I take the responsibility for that part of our relationship entirely on myself. She was not to blame.'

Imogen could not tell whether he felt himself bound by chivalry to make this assertion, or whether it were another instance of the astonishing myopia which affected his vision of Blanche Silcox. When he had felt and responded to the force of that demand, made with all the stored-up energy and passion of a lifetime, did he really believe that the demand had not been made because it had not been made in words? Could he genuinely think that because the words of invitation had been his, the initiative had come from him? She felt suddenly weak and sick from the long hours of crying. Turning her neck languidly, she said with closed eyes:

'Don't be idiotic.'

'You have never appreciated her,' he answered. 'I think you never did her justice from the beginning.'

'Well, from her point of view, it scarcely matters, my not appreciating her, if you do, does it?'

'I don't mean to talk about her at present. I want to talk about ourselves and Gavin. He is the chief—'

She opened her eyes and sat bolt upright. 'Don't talk about Gavin. He – he would not mind losing me. He is not – not part of the argument.' The weapon that should have been her keen defence, she stripped from herself with nervous haste and threw down in front of him, but her air of desperation prevented him from using it himself.

'You mustn't think,' he said, 'that I defend myself, or that I have lost my affection for you. We are in a bad way, and I take the blame entirely to myself. I suppose I thought, once I was in up to the neck, that everything could be managed. I was a fool, no doubt. But you did use to have very liberal ideas about these matters, once.'

'Yes.' She paused. 'But I did not ever imagine quite this sort of thing. Not gay, like an ornament, an addition, but so domestic, like a wife already. And so solemn and intense – that dreadful face – such power, such will. And suffering, too. Such deep emotions, naturally! Going about quite pale and stern with love!' She seemed occupied with spreading and examining the handkerchief on her lap. As if to herself she murmured: 'Driving me silly.'

A deep silence followed. At last he said: 'We must face the fact that we've got a frightful problem on our hands.'

Her head came up. She looked at him with surprise. 'A problem!' she exclaimed. 'Do you mean because of your reputation? In your profession?'

'No, no,' he said brusquely. 'That is a problem of another sort. I am talking now about ourselves.'

'I do not see any problem,' she answered coldly. 'Our parting isn't problematical. It's just something to endure.'

'It is much too early to decide,' he said with awful mildness.

'I do not see why,' she answered, her teeth chattering. 'In fact you have allowed Blanche Silcox to make the decision already.'

'That is not true. You yourself are the only person who can make a decision for us to part. I am in your hands.' He looked at her face but for an instant it was not she who looked back; it was not someone else, even, but some thing. Then with a sudden turn of her head, the inhuman appearance vanished. She sat with downcast features, swollen and heavy with the remains of weeping. Sighing she said: 'Nothing has been in my hands ever since she – I have been defeated by degrees, until—'

'Imogen,' he said, getting to his feet and leaning a little towards her: 'I must make this offer to you. I don't make it heartily, but I am sincere. If your happiness demands it, I will give up Blanche and she and I won't live near each other. She is everything to me

246

and I am everything to her. I adore her. If I were free, I'd marry her to-morrow. But my duty is to you. And if you decide that we must go on, we will.'

In spite of the night hours, some invisible wraith of hope must have remained with her, because at the sickening sound of the words 'I adore her,' she felt it die. She got up herself and moved about the room without any clear idea of what she did. At last she turned towards him but without looking at him and said:

'I should not dream, naturally – I should not even wish, to continue in such a state of things. Naturally.'

He restrained his anxiety to hear her commit herself, for she looked in no condition to make so important a decision.

'I keep telling you,' he said, 'that I don't expect a definite answer now. You must take all the time you need – weeks, months, a year if necessary. Of course, as soon as you *can* decide – I know you won't keep me waiting beyond what you must.'

'No,' she said, with a sideways smile that had no sooner alarmed than it was gone. 'It would be so tiresome for Miss Silcox to be in suspense about her housekeeping arrangements. But she will stand by you never fear. *Steadfast* is what she is.' The smile returned and stayed. It was like a rictus. He came up and took her by the elbow.

'Don't say any more now,' he said in an authoritative voice. She stood quite still with his grasp on her arm, then her face softened into its own aspect and she sighed again. He led her to a chair. 'Just tell me if you'd rather I stayed with you for now, or left you alone?'

She gave the question honest thought, then answered: 'I would like to be by myself.'

NINETEEN

The day and the night and the following day ran into each other confusedly in her recollection. Evelyn was sometimes beside her making suggestions, plans, for practical arrangements. To everything she answered: 'Yes, certainly. Yes, by all means.' Once she had accepted the crushing and final defeat of her existence, she thought herself indifferent to all the minor circumstances connected with it. This frame of mind was based in part on an unthinking, complete reliance upon Evelyn's generosity and his high standard of conduct in all matters of business. At least, this dire event would be free of the petty meannesses, the sordid and indecorous wrangling that aggravate the misery which brings them out. She meant to be equally well conducted and though she could not attempt anything like friendly co-operation or cheerful and sympathetic discussion of their affairs, she determined that she would not take any step that was wantonly hostile.

Such a state of feeling was very good while it lasted, but it was easier to preserve it in the daytime than during the night. Then, in darkness of mind and darkness of the sight, she would feel the renewing impulses of hatred, at first small and intermittent like the sparks of phosphorescent wood on a dark path, increasing until her whole being was burning. With a morbid energy of imagination, she planned the various means of suicide, so as to inflict the greatest degree of discredit and dismay on Evelyn and Blanche; but before she had regained the power of rejecting this idea on moral grounds, she was convinced of its uselessness as a method of revenge. Such a trial would only bind them more closely in mutual sympathy and support. Paul had said: 'Endurance'; but he had not known what he was telling her to endure. Paul would have wanted her, while making every effort at tolerance and conciliation, to take advantage of Evelyn's offer to maintain the marriage – to lay herself open either to the sufferings of watching Evelyn and Blanche Silcox in the free enjoyment of their liaison, or to the almost unimaginable severity of living with Evelyn when she had deprived him of Blanche's society. And for what was all this to be endured? So that she might continue to live with Gavin, who did not want her, and who, in all sincerity and innocence, was utterly incapable of response to any appeal of hers. Paul had by implication enjoined all this on her as plainly as if he had put it into words. That was his idea of love! Obstinate, callous and completely mistaken as to matters of fact, he had forced this intolerable conception upon her so that her shrinking from it would be a standing reproach to her; then he had died, leaving her without his comfort and advice. Impotent anger passed into passionate grief and she cried again with frantic abandonment. Between bursts of sobbing she heard Miss Malpas give some dubious raps on the door but she buried her head beneath the clothes and to her relief the door did not open.

When she opened her eyes she saw first the window, filled with a light which told her it was later than she usually awoke; then, standing at the foot of her bed, she saw Tim. His round face was a deep pink, his neck milk white, from his run through the morning air; the eyelashes were lowered on his cheeks, and his expression had the calmness of a sculptured Buddha.

'Aren't you coming down to breakfast?' he asked with gentle reproof.

She sat up. 'Yes, I am. I'll be down in a few minutes.'

Tim walked out of the room and she hastily washed, combed and put on a few clothes, meaning to go down in her dressing-gown. She threw it off again however. Tim would be astonished and disappointed to see her at the breakfast table not properly dressed; it was better to be a little later and appear as he expected her to. At the meal they were both almost silent. Tim ate indus-triously with his eyes on his plate. Imogen drank cup after cup of tea and watched him. The strong temptation seized her to do the thing which above all she would have disapproved in somebody else – to make a bid for his sympathy, to exploit his affection for her. He would be on her side in any event; why should she not tell him the position, frankly – no child of the Leeper household would be at any loss to understand it – and console herself with his indignation? While she thought of this, Tim finished his last piece of toast, and got up, as she thought, to go to school. She was relieved in spite of herself. He went however to the sideboard where the unopened letters were lying and came back with a letter, opened and creased, which he held out to her. 'I found this in the corner of the drawing-room sofa,' he said. 'You must have left it there.' It was the letter she had had from Paul, saying that there was something to be said for a world that had her in it. She had taken it out on hearing of his death, and thought in her contrition and grief: 'The world is no better for having me in it.' She remem-bered her re-reading of it now.

She said to Tim: 'It was from our great friend Dr. Nugent. He's dead.'

'What a pity.'

'I wanted to tell you: I shall be going away soon.'

'When will you come back?'

'I am afraid I shan't come back to this house. But Mr. Gresham

250

and Gavin will be here, and Malpas. You'll be all right with them, won't you?'

'Yes. But I would rather you stayed.'

'Darling boy, I don't think I can. But we shall all go on being friends with each other. And somebody will come here instead of me who will be very nice to you and Gavin. So you mustn't mind or think everything is going to alter.'

'But I want you to be here as well.'

'Tim, let us make a plan. As soon as I'm living in a new place you shall come and see me.' She saw for the first time turned upon herself the remote, unmoved gaze of the child who no longer trusts a promise. She said earnestly: 'Look: have you got some very secret place, where you could keep something?' He nodded. 'Then suppose I give you five pounds. You could put them there, and then you'd know that you could always get to me, if you felt you really had to?'

'That's super. But where will you be?'

She went into the drawing-room and he followed at her heels. Evelyn had left the week's housekeeping money in one of the small drawers of the writing desk. She took out five notes, and put them into an envelope. 'I shall write and tell you wherever I am,' she said, her hoarse voice giving an unusual impressiveness to what she said. 'But meantime, if you should want me for anything in a hurry, you could write to me at this address. The friend who lives there will know where I am and send it to me.' She wrote Cecil's name and address on a half-sheet, put it in the envelope and sealed it. Then she gave it to Tim. 'Do you think you can keep it safe?' The look he gave her showed pity for her inexperience. He had glided out of the room while she was shutting and locking the drawer.

Imogen remained sitting at the desk. She had a great deal to do, to plan; but she lost sight of it, thinking of Paul. The selfishness of her fondness for him which she always had admitted though

251

without compunction, now stabbed her through and through. His faithful, deep affection had seemed a precious possession enough, an asset to her existence, but the loss of it, even in so short a time, had made it seem something of an altogether different nature. Anything she had ever done for him had been done with the instinctive wish to heighten his admiration and his love. The very last vivid moments of their companionship, the expedition on the water, after which he had thanked and blessed her, she had made delightful to him from love of herself, not love of him. Her tears rose again, not with the wildness of the night, when she had exclaimed against him with such childish stupidity and ingratitude, but in a gentle manner that, strangely, gave relief. Though she knew she would never be capable of it, had no will even to attempt it, she would never deny now that the course Paul would have advised was in itself the right one.

'But I can't,' she said aloud. Her voice in the room emphasized the emptiness, the quiet, that forlorn as they were, had a lethean quality of freedom from pain. She remembered the horror of sounds: the sharp ring of a telephone, the crunch of wheels on gravel, the distant hum of a powerful car. She shuddered. Now that the fatal decision had been reached, she did not want ambiguities or delays. Everything that might have attached her to the house – the charm of its interior, the unusual loveliness of its surroundings, the memory of love with which they were inspired, now wore an altered face and appeared as so many sights from which to escape. She meant to go at once to London and put up at a hotel until she had made further plans, and to set about some work immediately. An untrained woman of her age would ordinarily be at a disadvantage in looking for employment, but she herself wanted to do the sort of work which is always available, and for which there are never enough candidates. Domestic work in hospitals or school canteens, or work in voluntary organizations at less than a living wage, she knew would be open to her.

All the practical details she left to Evelyn, to Evelyn and Blanche Silcox: from the great and complicated question of the divorce itself, and the immediate arrangements for Gavin's holidays, to the mere matters of the house. She would leave Miss Malpas in charge of everything there. The latter, so odd, enigmatic and acute, needed, she saw, no explanations; none, at least, from her. It was a relief to be spared such an ordeal at this point, to be able, merely, to say: 'I shall be going to town on such a day. Mr. Gresham will be down on Friday.'

As she was leaving the room, the telephone rang. She raised the receiver, cut off the call, and left the receiver off so that no one could ring again.

TWENTY

The marriage of Hunter and Cecil which was arranged for the middle of March gave Imogen such satisfaction, it was almost happiness. She agreed with Cecil to take over the latter's flat when the wedding should leave it vacant. Cecil asked her to come to it at once; it was roomy enough for two people of accommodating habits. This Imogen steadily refused. To be in the lovers' way would always have distressed her; now, when she knew she could add nothing of gaiety or pleasure, that her presence would be simply a charge on their good spirits, the idea was intolerable to her. Besides, she was altogether more at ease in the quiet hotel behind Manchester Square, where she could come and go without being answerable to anybody, and have her meals in a shady corner of the dining-room, where no one was likely to notice the condition of her face.

'She'll marry again,' said Hunter. They were spending the evening in his flat, so that Cecil could have the opportunity of suggesting any alterations, but she had none to suggest. She liked everything she saw and was ready to settle herself in surroundings altogether of Hunter's choosing.

'Perhaps she will,' she said, continuing their conversation as they reached the end wall of the flat and looked out of a passage window on to the courtyard of a mews. 'But I'm afraid this may have left her in such a state, she won't want to.'

'Men will want to marry her,' Hunter said. 'She'll end by marrying some chap who won't take no for an answer.'

'I have sometimes been astonished—'

'What at?'

'So many things, but I was thinking of the suddenness, the completeness of it. Considering how much her feelings were engaged and how – how dependent she was on Evelyn, it was strange that she accepted it all so quickly and never tried – or seemed even to hesitate – you might say it was she, really, who broke it up rather than he.'

'I agree. But that is according to my idea of her.'

'Tell me.' They moved away from the window, retracing their steps toward the drawing-room.

'Well, I think, in a gentle way, she is very vain and touchy, on that side. Not on any other, but in connection with anything of that sort.'

'But she is so very unassuming, and patient, I've always thought.'

'Yes, infinitely, long suffering as charity, in any other direction. But women who are attractive in that sort of way, it's their *thing*. They never think about anything else, practically. That's why they're such good value, up to a point. But an affront to that side of them, and they're beaten to the floor. It wouldn't occur to them to try to patch the thing up.' Cecil made no answer. Hunter, leading her to the drawing-room sofa, gave her a cigarette; he was about to bring the conversation back to their own affairs when she raised her head and said:

'You can be certain of *one* thing.'

'Not in racing.'

'We're not talking about racing, for once. Miss Silcox has seen nothing wrong in Evelyn's having a mistress while he was married to Imogen, but if he wants one after he's married to *her*—'

'I don't think he's at all likely to,' said Hunter with a slightly harried air. 'After all, he's not a rake.'

'No. But if he should want any sort of a romantic friendship, the second Mrs. Gresham's views on the sacredness of marriage will be quite—'

'Quite what?'

'Quite *awe-inspiring*. On the sacredness of being married to *her*, that is.'

'Well, no doubt. What about going out for some dinner? It'll be nice when we can dine at home, won't it?'

On an evening late in March Evelyn stood by the brightly burning fire in Blanche Silcox's drawing-room. He had been away from Chalk for a few days. He had paid a flying visit to Gavin at Brackley Hill, which he had purposely left until almost the end of term. The Headmaster and his wife had been regretful but most sympathetic when he explained his domestic situation. 'A parting of the ways' had been spoken of as always a painful thing but sometimes unavoidable. The probable effect on Gavin had been discussed with reasonable optimism; when Evelyn told them that he proposed Gavin should spend the holidays in Blanche Silcox's house, with himself, and probably Gavin's old school friend Tim Leeper, having regard to the dependable character of Miss Silcox, the Maudes themselves thought this was the best arrangement of which the circumstances admitted.

'I wouldn't have chosen it,' said Evelyn candidly, 'but my wife's sudden departure makes it so difficult to think of anything else. There are no grandparents on either side who could take him.' His conversation with Gavin was brief and he was glad when it was over.

'You can always see Mummy whenever you like, you know,' he

said; 'go and stay with her, too. You'll do that, of course anyhow. Only she won't be living at home with us.'

Gavin remained silent for a moment, then said: 'I don't see why she had to clear off like that. Tim will be pretty annoyed. Will you tell him about coming to the other house?'

'I will. Blanche says you can have him with you there just the same as at ours.'

'Good.' Gavin had no more to say. At the back of his eyes was an expression of boundless astonishment. He had often been irritated by his mother, to the point of hostility, but always because of some interference of hers, some tiresome solicitude or unreasonable restraint. He was accustomed to blame her to himself for doing or saying something he disliked, or even for being there when she had no need to be. The one thing he had never imagined she could do was to go away This was what she had done. He felt no pain, he could think, move, speak, see, hear, just as before, but the impact of surprise was like the subtle effect of a concussion. His father, looking at him narrowly, saw that it was so, and realized that they were not to escape scot-free. He congratulated himself fervently that in a few days' time Gavin would be coming to an atmosphere of such warmth, kindness and safety as that of Blanche's house.

On his way through London he had had one of his interviews with Imogen. He had found her smiling and unnaturally quiet. He noticed that her neck was very thin so that the line of jaw and chin were unusually distinct. She smiled and said: 'I'm glad,' when he told her that Gavin had received the news calmly, and repeated the words on hearing of the arrangements for the holidays, and that Blanche would be good to Tim. Evelyn added: 'I think the boys will settle down all right.' To this she could not bring herself to reply. He said gently that at some time they must consider the arrangements for divorce.

'Anything,' she said hurriedly, 'anything that seems best. I do not mind how it's done. Whatever you decide. We could say I'd deserted you. Only that would take too long?'

'Angelic,' he said under his breath. She looked alarmed at once. 'Oh no,' she said hastily. 'Mostly my vanity.'

He saw that if he showed any lively emotion for her, it would cause her agony. He obliged himself to be plain and brief.

His dinner and the prospect of a peaceful, radiant evening brought him back to himself. The room, warm and lit with soft brightness, looked the more luminous through his contented eye. Blanche Silcox sat with her feet up on the sofa, eating a *marron glacé* with a meditative air. No longer did she feel obliged to follow his every movement with agitated gaze. She looked in remarkably good ease, her forehead was pearly, her hands warm and white. On a table at her side were the two Sheffield plate dishes which she had brought from the other house. She would leave them with the Goldsmiths and Silversmiths' Company when she went up to town. When they had been re-silvered they would be very handsome. It would be nice for Evelyn to be able to get some pleasure out of them at last. He had obviously been rather upset by this interview he had had. The final stages of the parting could not be entirely painless, on his side at least. Of course Imogen had never understood him.

The ancient parlourmaid brought in coffee, with a face reflecting all the beaming complacence of an old retainer in the family's good fortune. When she had gone out again Evelyn sat down at the foot of the sofa, one leg crossed over the other, his arm thrown over the sofa-back. Peace, comfort, serenity steeped the room. The lamplight threw a silvery bloom over the drawn velvet curtains. Still as the night was, the river was too far off for its sound to reach them.

TWENTY-ONE

Cecil's flat was on the first floor of a house abutting on Caroline Place. The two rooms of which it was composed were lofty and one was spacious; the other had been diminished to make a small kitchen and a bathroom. Plane trees hung their leaves outside the sash windows. The interior was plain and graceful.

'Very,' Imogen repeated to herself, in nervous desperation. She had always loved and wanted rooms with just such elegance and simplicity. Now, when she looked round at the walls and the window-frames and the small fluted chimney-piece, they could not always allay the panic that threatened her. She had once loved to possess leisure for her own pastimes; now that it was all her own, time was a menace to be kept at bay. She used thoroughly to enjoy social engagements: now she found that these brief, lively encounters with acquaintances which multiplied themselves once she showed herself available: a lunch, a cinema, a drink before dinner, were anodynes which made her feverish and uneasy at the time, and increased the sense of blankness when they were over.

She relied on work to help her, and had put herself in touch with the branch of the W.V.S. to which she had been recommended by the branch in the country she had so abruptly left. The church also, across the neighbouring square, with its monuments of veiled figures leaning upon urns, and memorial tablets to men who fell at Plassey and nabobs of the East India Company, this centre of a London parish would find as much occupation for her as even her time could fill. Nothing stood in her way except that everything bearing on her future seemed hopeless and dead.

Cecil had left the essentials of furniture in the rooms and it would be the simplest matter for Imogen to choose and have sent from Chalk enough to make them comfortable and beautiful; so simple that the thing seemed scarcely worth doing; she put it off daily. Cecil had also left a stock of groceries of the non-perishable kind, thinking Imogen would at once order daily supplies. The latter had not done this. She would bring in a bottle of milk sometimes, apples, a loaf of brown bread. On a March afternoon when a light mist was gathering and everything gleamed with wet, she returned to Caroline Place, stopping at the small shop where she was accustomed to buy a loaf. She was too late for one, and the woman could offer her only flat, round tea-cakes. She had six of these left, so she put them all into a bag for Imogen, thinking that this customer might as well take them off her hands. It was almost dusk in Caroline Place. Imogen came up the stairs and put her key into the lock. As she did so, a figure rose from the steps above and as she went in, came silently across the landing and went in with her.

'Tim!' she exclaimed. No other words would come. She walked into the living-room and laid the paper bag on the table. She stood looking at him, still speechless. Tim stooped and lit the gas-fire. Then he took off his cap and coat. He moved about briskly, as delicate as a leprechaun. Imogen was for the moment wholly absorbed in an effort not to burst out crying.

'Shall I toast these?' Tim was saying. 'Is there a toasting fork?'

'No. I'm afraid there isn't.'

'Why, yes there is,' he said, taking it from an angle of the chimney-piece. 'Fancy your not knowing!'

She sat down on the sofa, watching his back and the soles of his shoes. Presently he went into the kitchen and came back.

'Is there any butter?' he asked.

'No, only jam I'm afraid.'

'There ought to be butter,' said Tim meditatively, 'but it's too late to get any now, I expect. We can manage all right for breakfast if there's marmalade.'

'Yes, there is some.'

'That's all right, then.' He went out again and she took off her hat, running her hands up the back of her head. When Tim came back he brought a tray with a pot of tea, a half-full bottle of milk, a jam-jar and cups and plates. He spread two halves of a toasted tea-cake with plum jam and gave her one. Then he poured her out a cup of tea.

'Thank you,' she said faintly. She roused herself. 'Are you – have you come to—'

'Yes,' he said. 'I've come to stay here.'

'But – how nice – I – you mean, just for—'

'No. I mean for all the time, except when I go to Gavin's. I'm not going home any more.'

'Tim! But, dearest boy, what will they think? Have you told them?' His head was so still, it looked like the marble head of a child; the delicacy, the youth were there, hard, immovable.

'It doesn't matter what they think. I'm not going back any more.' Then he moved and the lines melted into life. He raised a childish, anxious face. 'Won't it be all right for me to stay here? I can go to school free and I shouldn't eat very much.'

'It isn't that – I'm sure that could be managed – it's only—'

'When you marry the next person it might be different,' he said earnestly, leaning forward on his knees, 'but till you do, I should think you'd be quite glad to have somebody here.'

'I am! I love to have you here. It's only that I really don't see—' she paused.

261

'Aren't you going to drink up your tea?' Parted from her for so long, he could hardly take enough care of her. She drank, looking at him above the cup. He was stooping over the plates on the hearth, spreading another tea-cake. The suddenness, the preposterousness of his appearance, the mere nuisance even, of his presence, all went for nothing beside the fact that he was there. He raised his face, flushed and limpid-eyed.

'Did you tell them you were coming?' she asked.

'No.'

'We must let them know you're here.'

'Yes. But to-morrow will do.'

'Perhaps it will,' she agreed weakly, drinking. 'You make very good tea, Tim.'

'Yes. You need a lot of things out there. There seems to be hardly anything.'

'We'll get them to-morrow.' She and Tim were now at one on the essential point. Everything else, every consideration, every detail, could be arranged by others, by the Leepers, Evelyn, even by Blanche.

'You'll have to sleep on the sofa for the present,' she said.

'Yes, I know. It won't matter. We can soon get things settled.' He glanced about the room.

'I am afraid you won't find me very cheerful to live with. I cry rather a lot.'

'Never mind,' said Tim equably.

'Perhaps I won't mind presently. Not so much, anyway.' He was already in the kitchen. She heard the taps of the sink running. She looked, as he had looked, about the uncared-for room.

'I must improve,' she said half aloud. 'There is a very great deal to be done.'

AFTERWORD

The writer Rosamond Lehmann suggested to me that I read, and publish, *The Tortoise and the Hare*. She admired the work of Elizabeth Jenkins – both her biographies and novels. Since its first Virago publication in 1983, this novel has remained one of my favourite classics. Elegant and ironic, its continuing charm lies in its quirky and enigmatic love story which becomes more beguiling with each re-reading. Who is the Tortoise, who the Hare? Whichever choice we make, there is absolute certainty in another touch of genius in the novel – Elizabeth Jenkins' perfect and instinctive understanding of how it is to be a particular kind of woman, in this instance the woman Imogen, the heroine of this novel.

Since the first caveman thumped his chest many aeons ago, nature and humankind have raised women to please men by their beauty, and to value gentleness and submission as the way of continuing so to please. *The Tortoise and the Hare* turns this female behaviour entirely on its head. Imogen, agonizingly compliant and docile wife to her K.C. husband Evelyn, has all the physical qualities women long for: 'The charm of her looks, so far as it depended on purely visual effect, was that of shape and contour. Her head was poised very gracefully on her neck, her upper lip had the true outline of the cupid's bow, her bosom was round and her waist small . . . her ways and mannerisms had the enchanting quality of some favourite work of art.'

When the novel begins, Imogen is 37 and Evelyn 52. 'He was everything Imogen admired.' This includes those characteristics 'which made some people think him difficult or even disagreeable'. We quickly come to share 'some people's' view as Imogen's passive life is electrified by her gradual realization that her nearest neighbour, Blanche Silcox, a woman physically lumpen and conventionally unattractive, is on the rampage – on the rampage for Evelyn. Blanche 'was now fifty and made no attempt to appear younger' and 'the effect of her figure with its bloated waist, in contrast to which her small legs and her feet in pointed shoes, looked like the slender forelegs that unexpectedly support a bull', is ungainly and frumpish. She wears extraordinary hats, and though 'the Chinese do not make many ugly carpets', 'one of their very few had been unerringly chosen' by Blanche.

Yet Evelyn falls under her spell, just as if she was beautiful, as Imogen is. In addition to her looks, Imogen has every other attribute of the sheltered flower, she is a woman who can't do things: she can't drive, she can't control her son, she can't hunt, she knows nothing about country life, she is on no Boards or Committees, works for no Girl Guides or Women's Institutes. She exists as a lily of the field, whilst Blanche is a doer. She can drive a car, sort out problems, arrange lunches and dinners, hunt, fish, do voluntary work and generally make the world move, albeit tastelessly.

Deciding about Imogen and Blanche, allotting them the attributes of Tortoise or Hare, is one of those marvellous questions which divide the human race. For me, Imogen is the Tortoise. She loses what she has been reared to think of as her greatest possession – her husband – to the unattractive, older, active and competent Blanche Silcox. But in her defeat is her victory. Imogen is a perfect portrait of human, and specifically female, masochism: she is the kind of woman about whom judges, husbands, police-men *et al* have long been known to describe as 'asking for it'. She longs to obey, to have Evelyn think and act for her. This is what she has been reared to do. But, at the end of the novel, having lost her treasure, we leave her on the point of finding another, and a real life, in which different kinds of human love rise up to take the place of the love in her marriage, in which pain and suffering played so large a part.

For me then Imogen is the Tortoise because she struggles through a mire of misery but leaves it behind; Blanche is the Hare because though she has raced off with the trophy-husband, where love is betrayed once, so it may be again. Admittedly this reasoning depends upon a thorough dislike of their mutual husband Evelyn – whose authority and bombastic masculinity can still be found lurking in the courts of Law, the House of Commons, and other bastions of the Establishment. This is a dis-like not every reader will share. In that case, this fascinating novel can take on other intriguing interpretations. One of which may well be to ask questions about the sexual graph we are observing. There is much oddity and ambiguity in Elizabeth Jenkins' descriptions of the dominant Blanche 'who ought to have been a boy', the intensely feminine Imogen, the quintes-sentially manly Evelyn, with his bullying ways and his feminine name, 'with an inarticulateness that suggested a boy rather than an experienced man'. Evelyn's passionate attraction to the almost masculine Blanche invokes the emotions of the English public school and its equivocal sexual influence on certain English castes.

Though Elizabeth Jenkins sets her novel within the boundaries of a very specific – and to me pretty disagreeable – English class, class exerts no restriction on the interest of the novel. Imogen's predicament is universal and could take place anywhere. Nevertheless, set in the years immediately after the Second World War, Elizabeth Jenkins presents an incisive portrait of a certain kind of England, and of particular English ways. These people are more than comfortable. They come from the professional classes and work in the city or in medicine or in law; they hunt, they have large country houses, cooks and housekeepers and gardeners, Rolls-Royces and Bentleys that hum and purr. Food is delivered. For a wife like Imogen there is literally nothing to do to pass the time of day. And of course, because Imogen has nothing to do, she does even less. "'We shan't be late,' said Evelyn kindly. "In fact, if you like to give us tea at about five, we should be back for it.'" We shudder with fear that the cake will be stale, the milk sour, the tea five minutes late. Elizabeth Jenkins' intimate understanding of Imogen's emotions, as her self-confidence ebbs away, is blistering and accurate.

Imogen and Evelyn have friends of a similar kidney, but acquaintances and the people in the village confront them with a harsher world. This gives the author an excellent opportunity to portray the worst excesses of progressive parents, progressive education, undisciplined children and the taxes imposed by the Labour Government of the time. Everywhere there is the shift and rumble of England changing, as Imogen's idyllic daily life becomes increasingly painful. Elizabeth Jenkins' England mirrors the world of Graham Greene, who was of course writing at the same time, but who was more open in his loathing for his compatriots than anything Elizabeth Jenkins would think of. Despite that difference, her England has a harsh whiff of Greeneland.

The irritation of a threatened English class rises and falls as the story progresses, contributing to the almost unbearable tension of the novel. Of course we wonder what will happen – will the Tortoise or the Hare capture Evelyn? – but mostly we feel the tension through the heart and soul of Imogen, through our fervent anguish on her behalf. We want to stand up for her, fight, *do* something. At the time the novel was written – the early 1950s – this reaction might not have been so strong but today, in a culture in which Diana, Princess of Wales, exercised such influence, it is impossible to read *The Tortoise and the Hare* without mentally urging Imogen on to action, to self-defence.

These ideas and interpretations are irrelevant to Elizabeth Jenkins who feels that all she was doing when she wrote *The Tortoise and the Hare* was telling a story. I went to see her in September 1997. She is now 90, a little troubled with her hip, and her hearing, but with a mind perfectly in tune to whatever is going on. She told me immediately that the novel was autobiographical, 'not in fact, but in feeling'. This is her story:

When she was a young woman, she had a relationship with a married man. When his wife died, he married his neighbour, the Blanche Silcox of this novel. Elizabeth Jenkins then took the decision that they should stop seeing each other. In the aftermath she sat down and wrote *The Tortoise and the Hare*, very very quickly, with scarcely a pause. Then, suddenly, he came back, within a fortnight of the novel's being published, and asked could they go on as before? After agonizing as to what she should do, Elizabeth Jenkins did the right thing; she sent him a copy of the book. She never heard from him again.

But that is not the end of the story. Her friend – Elizabeth Jenkins does not wish to name him – collected nineteenth-century objects and, in particular, glass paintings of the life, death and funeral of Princess Charlotte. Two years after the events described, Elizabeth Jenkins found a glass painting of Princess Charlotte's funeral, which she knew he did not possess. She sent it to him with a kind note. It was returned, badly packaged, with the glass broken in places; but the handwriting on the package was that of his wife, whilst someone had lovingly replaced the old wire which was on the glass painting when Elizabeth Jenkins sent it, with a piece of new picture cord. He *had* received it, and hung it up.

She based her novel on the emotions she experienced during these events, and also drew, for Imogen, on the personality of a woman she knew who was cursed with fatal sexual attraction but who could not find happiness with a man. For Elizabeth Jenkins, with her great interest in character, this is enough, and when I said that I found Evelyn detestable she said, 'well of course you didn't know him'.

This is how it should be. The charm of this fine novel – and *The Tortoise and the Hare* is, and will remain, one of the finest of the last half-century – lies in what each reader makes of it. And in its characterization and beauty, beauty of language and of structure. Throughout there is a wonderful evocation of nature, green and languid, full of different lights, flowing through and around what is going on in Imogen's mind. Some of Elizabeth Jenkins' most sensuous writing lies in the descriptions of the house and countryside around it, where Imogen and Evelyn and their son Gavin, clone of Evelyn, live. Always it sighs and flutters, witness to Imogen's journey towards discovery. 'Presently the moon passed from the window, bearing away her emptiness and death, steeped in cold and brilliant light, and the warm, living earth settled to sleep in darkness'.

There are as many ways of loving and of being alive in *The Tortoise and the Hare*, as its compact structure allows. There are no *longueurs*, but with economy and feeling, Elizabeth Jenkins creates in the character of Tim, Imogen's saviour, in the personalities of her friends, Cecil and Paul, in her cook Miss Malpas, and others who flit through the pages, a solid ballast which makes Imogen's final port of call all the more happily accepted.

Elizabeth Jenkins has a wry and precise way of assessing and describing women, and the intelligence which illuminates this eloquent cry against betrayal in love is icy, dazzling. This is a novel about women and beauty, about husbands as protectors and demi-gods, about women and work, about different kinds of loving, about an England well gone, and about the centuries of instruction to women to be beautiful and submissive, reminding us, in the most enchanting way, what a waste of life and time such instructions always were.

Carmen Callil, London 1997